Praise for these other novels
from *New York Times* bestselling author
CHEYENNE McCRAY

DARK MAGIC

***Romantic Times* Magazine Reviewers Choice Award
for Best Paranormal Action-Adventure of the Year!**

"Action, romance, suspense, love, betrayal, sacrifice,
magic, and sex appeal to the nth degree! [McCray's]
heroines kick butt and run the gamut from feminine to
tomboy, and her heroes . . . well, they're all 200% grade-
A male. YUM!" —*Queue My Review*

"Vivid battles, deceit that digs deep into the coven, and a
love that can't be denied." —*Night Owl Romance*

"McCray has delivered another rip-roaring, passionate
adventure. [DARK MAGIC] will keep you on the edge of
your seat from first to last . . . a testament to Ms. McCray's
skill as a writer . . . Simply Magic!" —*Wild On Books*

SHADOW MAGIC

"I loved this book! . . . A solid story that is wonderfully
executed. Bravo!" —*Fresh Fiction*

"Cheyenne McCray takes her place as one of the A+ paranormal writers with this series." —*SingleTitles.com*

MORE...

"McCray has done a dazzling job developing an epic war with genuine danger and terrifying consequences. The author also doesn't skimp when it comes to imbuing her characters with touching emotions or delivering scorching sex."

—*Romantic Times BOOKreviews*
(4½ Stars)

"The great descriptions and powerful emotions pulled me immediately in the story. The action–adventure and smooth fight scenes are both entertaining and really kept the pace jumping."

—*Road to Romance*

WICKED MAGIC

"Blistering sex and riveting battles are plentiful as this series continues building toward its climax."

—*Romantic Times BOOKreviews* (4 stars)

"Has an even blend of action and romance… An exciting paranormal tale, don't miss it." —*Romance Reviews Today*

"Cheyenne McCray shows the best work between good and evil in *Wicked Magic*. The characters are molded perfectly…sure to delight and captivate with each turn of the page."

—*Night Owl Romance*

"A sinfully engaging read."

—*A Romance Review*

SEDUCED BY MAGIC

"Blistering passion and erotic sensuality are major McCray hallmarks, in addition to a deft and exciting storyline. This magical series continues to develop its increasing cast of characters and complex plotline."

—*Romantic Times BOOKreviews*
(4½ stars Top Pick)

"The slices of humor, the glimpses of the characters' world through fantastic descriptions, not to mention fascinating characters, landed this book on...[the] keeper shelf."

—*Romance Divas*

"Witches, drool-worthy warriors, and hot passion that will have readers reaching for a cool drink. Cheyenne McCray has created a fantastic and magical world where both the hero and heroine are strong and are willing to fight the darkness that threatens their worlds."

—*A Romance Review*

FORBIDDEN MAGIC

"Wildly erotic and dangerously sensual, this explosive paranormal thriller sizzles. McCray erupts on the scene with one of the sexiest stories of the year. Her darkly dramatic world is one readers won't mind visiting again... McCray knows how to make a reader sweat—either from spine-tingling suspense or soul-singeing sex..."

—*Romantic Times BOOKreviews*
(4½ stars Top Pick)

"A yummy hot-fudge sundae of a book!"

—MaryJanice Davidson, *New York Times*
bestselling author

"*Charmed* meets Kim Harrison's witch series, but with a heavy dose of erotica on top!" —Lynsay Sands,
New York Times bestselling author

"McCray's paranormal masterpiece is not for the faint-hearted. The battle between good and evil is brought to the reader in vivid and riveting detail to the point where the reader is drawn into the pages of this bewitching and seductive fantasy that delivers plenty of action-packed sequences and arousing love scenes." —*Rendezvous*

"*Forbidden Magic* is a spellbinding, sexy, superbly written dark fantasy. I couldn't put it down, and you won't want to either... [Cheyenne McCray has an] incredible skill at keeping readers engaged in every moment of the action. Longtime fans and newbies alike will be enchanted and swept away by this enduring tale of courage, love, passion, and magic." —*A Romance Review*

"If one were going to make a comparison to Cheyenne McCray with another writer of the supernatural/sensuality genre, it would have to be Laurell K. Hamilton... *Forbidden Magic* definitely puts McCray in the same league as Hamilton. The book is a very sexy work..." —*Shelf Life*

DEMONS
NOT
INCLUDED

A Night Tracker Novel

Cheyenne McCray

St. Martin's Paperbacks

This is a work of fiction. All of the characters, organizations and events portrayed in this novel are either products of the author's imagination or are used fictitiously.

DEMONS NOT INCLUDED

Copyright © 2009 by Cheyenne McCray.
Excerpt from *The Second Betrayal* copyright © 2009 by Cheyenne McCray.

For information address St. Martin's Press, 175 Fifth Avenue, New York, NY 10010.

ISBN: 0-312-94960-X
EAN: 978-0-312-94960-0

Printed in the United States of America

St. Martin's Paperbacks edition / June 2009

St. Martin's Paperbacks are published by St. Martin's Press, 175 Fifth Avenue, New York, NY 10010.

10 9 8 7 6 5 4 3 2 1

To my favorite Demon Editor, Monique Patterson, for everything, including making me work for it. Apparently *I am* a glutton for punishment.

ACKNOWLEDGMENTS

To Anna Windsor, always. And next time, if you're lucky, I won't hold back the last two chapters. Heh, heh, heh.

Jo Carol Jones, thanks for letting me crash your pad for my secluded writing retreat!

Texas Police Officer Jerry Patterson Jr., thank you!

Andrew V. Phillips, you kick ass as a copy-editor. Mostly my ass.

Tracey West, as always, you are my lifesaver and I'm so lucky to have you. *So* lucky. Phyllis Ingram, thanks for all you do—you are the best. Thank you, Karen Tanner, aka Mom, you rock for getting things into shape and keeping them there while I write. You are amazing.

To Alan Ashton, just for being you.

And to my agent, Nancy Yost, who makes a terrific chocolate-loving Pixie.

WELCOME TO NEW YORK CITY'S UNDERWORLD

Present Day

Here's a primer. Take notes.

Dark Elves/Drow: We'll get to that.

Doppler: A paranorm who can shift into one specific animal as well as their human form.

Fae: Do we really want to be here all night going through the list?

Gargoyles: Pretty damned ugly.

Light Elves: Pious pricks.

Metamorph: Slimy paranorms who can mirror any human. And not in a good way.

Shadow Shifter: A paranorm with the ability to shift from human form into shadows. Arrogant SOBs.

Shifter: Can transform into any animal of their choosing as well as their human form.

Vamp: Bloodsucker.

Werewolves: Can take wolf form almost any time; however, at the full moon they become dangerous creatures that resemble neither man nor wolf.

We'll get to Magi, Succubae, Incubae, Necromancers, and Zombies (shudder) some other time.

Demons: Not included.

"Whoever fights monsters should see to it that in the process he does not become a monster. And if you gaze long enough into an abyss, the abyss will gaze back into you."

—*Friedrich Nietzsche (1844-1900)*

CHAPTER 1

Just because you're not paranoid doesn't mean they're not out to get you.

A burn hit the back of my throat and I almost snorted my vanilla latte through my nose when I caught a glimpse of Olivia's T-shirt. Instead I choked and coughed as the PI firm's door slid shut behind my partner with a soft whoosh over the doormat.

"You okay?" Olivia's dark eyes looked more amused than concerned as she tugged off her blue New York Mets sweat jacket. She bypassed the two chairs in front of her desk and tossed her jacket next to her computer monitor. Her Sig Saucr was firmly in its shoulder holster.

The dark waves of her hair were swept up in a clip as usual, the style accentuating her high cheekbones and her beauty. A few strands had escaped due to a cool New York September breeze and she brushed them out of her eyes.

"You'd better be okay," she said. "I'd hate to lose my partner and go back to working for Captain Leiferman, the NYPD's finest jerkwad."

"You'd just miss being around the Vamps." I drummed my fingers on my polished desk, made from beautiful wood a Dryad would eventually make me pay dearly for. "I saw you with that bloodsucker, Seth, at the Pit Saturday night."

Worn blue jeans and the red T-shirt tightened against Olivia's full curves as she plopped in the black leather chair behind her desk. She put her feet up on the desk and crossed her legs at the ankles, her Keds red to match today's T-shirt.

Olivia leaned back in her chair and raised her arms, her skin like dark golden silk. She stretched her five-foot-two frame and tilted her head back before looking at me with eyes so dark brown they were almost black. With my enhanced Drow senses I caught her freesia perfume.

"Seth and I were only talking while we had a few drinks." Her expression was one of total innocence when she added, "We're not having sex until *next* Saturday night."

This time I almost spit out my latte, only it would have speckled my cream Dior blouse. "Olivia—"

"I'm kidding." She grinned as she settled herself in front of her wide-screen monitor and gel pad. "Sort of."

"Sort of, my ass."

Even though she was unassuming and down-to-earth, Olivia kept me guessing what she'd do next. She had a wit as sharp as a Drow blade and a bit of mischievousness that had gotten us both into trouble on a couple of occasions. Actually, mischievousness was too mild a word.

Olivia's mother was Kenyan, her father from Puerto Rico, and Olivia could speak several languages. Over the past year and a half, since she'd become my partner, she'd even picked up quite a bit of Drow, especially the curse words that I used when I exploded over one thing or another.

She refused to wear anything designer and prided herself on hitting the sales racks at just the right time. She was jeans and cotton from bargain stores, and the shirts usually had amusing sayings like the one she was wearing. Today's was perfect considering all of the paranormal dangers that existed without most norms having a clue.

The T-shirt that worried me was one she wore once to the Pit—

There's too much blood in my alcohol system.

Those damn Vamps.

Where Olivia was sales rack, I was Neiman Marcus and designer all the way from my Hermès silk scarf to my Fendi crepe jacket, and even my leather holster, specially crafted by the Dark Elves, that held my 9mm Kahr. A girl's got to spoil herself when she can. And I don't mind admitting it, being who I am, I was pretty spoiled already.

I brushed my fingers over the neckband that I wore as a concession to my father, so that any Drow male would know I'm a Princess. Which meant off-limits without the King's permission, or off with the warrior's head.

Like some kind of morbid fairy tale.

And it wasn't a bluff. One Drow male found that out the hard way. Not that he was around anymore to complain about it.

I drew my slim XPhone from my favorite Dolce &

Gabbana handbag, which matched today's outfit. "You're human and you should be with some great-looking norm," I said. "There are plenty of decent guys out there." I made a sweeping gesture with one arm as if encompassing all of Manhattan before I pointed my finger at her. "But if you're going to go for a paranorm, why not a nice Doppler? Preferably one without fangs and claws when he shifts. A Doppler beagle would be perfect."

"Ha." Olivia snorted. "Serving Purina Dog Chow for dinner isn't in this girl's future. Besides, Vamps are so *hot*," she said with a totally serious expression even though I knew she was working to get a rise out of me. She so liked to give me a hard time.

The XPhone screen felt like cool gel beneath my index finger as I touched the screen and it lit up. I wrinkled my nose when I looked back up at her. "Vamps are actually pasty, creepy bloodsuckers. You just can't see them hiding behind handsome glamours because you're a norm."

"We can't all have gorgeous Elvin bosses we can screw just because we feel like it." Olivia obviously enjoyed the sudden rush of red behind the heat in my cheeks. "So how is Rodán these days?"

"I'm not seeing him in that way anymore." I cleared my throat. "He's just my mentor and friend."

"Ah." Olivia nodded like she knew the exact reason. And of course she nailed it. "Detective Adam Boyd. You've had the hots for him since you met him. So why haven't you done anything about it?"

The warmth in my face blossomed to my chest.

"He's human. Not so sure he'd be crazy about me if he saw me after dark."

"Eh." Olivia waved me off with a dismissive gesture. "Purple and blue are cool colors. He'll be all over you once you give him a chance."

"Amethyst, not purple." I bit the inside of my cheek. If I let Adam see me change . . .

Somehow I knew he'd accept me for who I am, but there was still a part of me that couldn't get over the reaction of the norm in my first serious relationship.

My heart clenched for a moment. With Stan it hadn't been worth the chance at all. I should never have—

Should've, could've, would've. What difference did it make now?

The wheels of my office chair rattled over the ceramic tiled floor as I shifted so that I could set my XPhone on a clear space on my desk—which wasn't easy considering the stacks of files, sticky notes, and pens littering it. Sometimes—make that often—I was too lazy to put the notes into my XPhone until later, so I had to scrounge.

"Tell me, what were you doing with Rodán last night?" Olivia casually examined her fingernails. "If you weren't humping him."

The only way to get Olivia off a subject she was enjoying was to change it to something more important.

"Rodán, the other Trackers, and I have been working on finding ways to get rid of these underling

Demons before they kill any more paranorms," I
said.

"*Underling* Demons?" Olivia swung her feet onto
the floor, her expression intense. "You're telling me
there are worse Demons than the ones you've been
facing?"

I nodded. "Rodán has it directly from the Great
Guardian herself that this is only the beginning."

"Just great." Olivia scowled. "I imagine your all-
powerful Guardian isn't going to deign to help the
Trackers."

The way Olivia often spoke about the Great
Guardian, she was lucky the GG didn't bother with
humans.

I, on the other hand, should have been worried,
considering I was just as bad if not worse than Olivia
when it came to my frequent irreverent attitude toward the GG.

My partner settled herself and opened a file folder
on her equally loaded desk. "Developments?"

The ache in my jaws when I clenched my teeth
was great enough to shoot sharp pain to my forehead.
Strands of my long, straight black hair slid over my
silk blouse and against my check as I bent my head
to rub my temples with my thumb and forefinger.
"A group of Demons murdered—and ate—at least a
dozen paranorms in Manhattan last night."

"Oh, shit." All traces of amusement left Olivia's
voice.

"Those weren't the words I used." No, I'd sworn
in Drow, and if I hadn't fought to keep control I

would have created a maelstrom in Rodán's conference chamber by releasing every one of my elemental powers at once.

Olivia folded her arms on her desk. "This is getting worse every day."

"Yeah." I leaned back in my chair and stared at the Drow weapons and warrior breastplates I'd mounted on the walls, reminders of home. "All of the Trackers met with Rodán early this morning after the night patrol of our territories." I let my gaze drift from the weapons to meet Olivia's dark eyes as I continued. "Rodán asked me to contact all of the local human liaisons and let them know what's going on. And to see if they've had anything unusual pop up."

"Like human-looking flesh-eating Demons." Olivia touched the long gel keyboard in front of her that brought up files on her computer screen. "I'm sure the Demons have no problem fitting in with this big melting pot of a city."

"At least they only come out around midnight." Almost absently, I brushed my fingers again over the smooth lines of my choker, with its runes that were invisible to humans. The choker had been crafted when I was a child, made from an alloy the Dark Elves mined. The alloy was imbued with elemental magic and more precious than human platinum, and it had expanded to fit me as I grew.

Olivia continued frowning but had a distant look to her eyes. No doubt she was mulling over everything I had shared. Her sharp mind had helped us solve countless cases.

I let my thoughts drift to eliminating each Demon and focused again on the wall in front of my desk. Fine diamond-headed arrows in their quivers and bows fashioned from precious Dryad wood were braced on the wall. I could have used Drow arrows or a long sword like any of the ones on my wall, but I preferred my weapons of choice, which were better for close combat. The seventeen-inch-long, two-inch-wide Drow-made dragon-claw daggers that had been designed just for me were perfect.

I drew my stylus from the slot at the side of the XPhone, my fingers pale against the navy blue of the device. "The Demons seem to have a taste for paranorms instead of humans. Like they want to eradicate the lot of us."

Before I headed out, I'd use my stylus to scribble a few thoughts on my XPhone. It was easier for me to keep organized that way since I wrote in a Drow form of shorthand and had to translate. My friend Manny, the computer whiz, was working on a program to make that part of organizing my work easier by translating Drow into English.

"It's time I helped you on the Demon thing." Olivia's gaze was clear when I met her eyes again. "Stop shielding me."

"This case is too dangerous. We've never faced Demons before." I had not ever deliberately kept Olivia off a case before, but this one—I just couldn't let her out there. I looked up at the ornate crown molding on the ceiling before meeting her gaze again. "It's almost impossible to kill them."

"Almost. That's an important word." Olivia frowned

at me. "You keeping me out of this case is starting to piss me off, Nyx."

"I'm serious." I rubbed my temples again. "This is really bad. To get rid of a single Demon, a Tracker has to strike and pierce a small sac of blue fluid at the hollow of the Demon's neck."

I continued without giving her a chance to speak. "Even though they look human, it's impossible to behead or injure any part of a Demon's body. They're even fireproof." Which made my fire-element power useless against them. "Only piercing that one vulnerable spot can kill these Demons."

"You know I'm a perfect shot with my Sig." Olivia touched her shoulder holster, just above her weapon. "I can nail them right where it hurts."

"Guns aren't good for close combat," I said.

"I've got blades on me," she said, "which are perfect for close encounters of the third kind."

I wanted to yank my hair out in frustration. I didn't want Olivia hurt. "This is not something like tracking down a missing Sprite, a Metamorph taking over a human, a rogue Were, or a Vamp gone bad."

"Don't patronize me." Olivia's eyes flashed and I knew I had a battle on my hands.

I sighed. "You know I'm not. I just worry."

"Don't."

"I'll talk with Rodán." This was something I wasn't going to win, but I could stall for time if I was lucky. "He's the word on these things."

"You can get him to agree to anything." Her expression lightened a little. "Just fuck it out of him."

My cheeks went hot.

Since I'd started to get to know Adam, I had stayed away from sex with my lover and mentor, Rodán. He understood. He always understood me.

I avoided Olivia's eyes as I retrieved my XPhone. "For now I've got to get hold of the norm liaisons."

"I'm not giving in on this," she said.

"I know."

Her voice turned teasing in an instant. "Bet I know which human liaison you'll be calling first." The glint was back in Olivia's eyes when I looked up at her. "I'm sure Detective Boyd will be *very* happy to hear from you."

Memories flashed through my mind of Stan, the human male I'd cared about before he learned of my true nature. Months of a close relationship—during the day. Then all it took was one night, and he was gone.

I didn't know if I could put my heart through pain like that again.

CHAPTER 2

A couple of hours later I was about to say to hell with speculation and phone calls for now when I looked at Olivia. She had her head cocked and was staring at the window of our entrance. "I really think our business sign needs a little more jazz."

"Shhh." I leaned back in my office chair and looked around like there might be a spy. "Nancy will spell your mouth shut if she hears you say that. Although that might not be such a bad idea."

Olivia crumpled up a piece of paper on her desk and threw it at me. She would have nailed me in the forehead if I didn't have such fast Drow reflexes.

I caught it, threw it back at her, and hit her in the chest. "Ha."

A fellow Tracker, Nancy, had put a glamour on the entrance to the PI office and on our front window so humans wouldn't notice our business. Pixies can be bitchy but are excellent with glamours.

In iridescent amethyst and sapphire, the window read:

NYX CIAR
OLIVIA DESANTOS
Paranormal Crimes   Private Investigator
By appointment only

Ciar was in deference to my father, who I loved very much. Like Fae and Light Elves and just about any other being in Otherworld, Dark Elves don't have last names—only the usual "Zan, son of Barth" kind of thing.

"What's it been?" Olivia adjusted the bra strap that helped contain her melon-sized breasts. "Two years since you moved into this place and she put up the sign?"

"August, the day after my twenty-fifth birthday." When he'd recruited me, Rodán had helped purchase the office space and the apartment above for me. I hadn't had a clue what norms did for things like property, but my human mother had prepared me as much as she could before I left the Drow realm.

I got right to work when I was set up and ready to roll. Being the fast learner that I am, in no time I'd accumulated a lot of the knowledge and the tricks of the trade of being a PI.

I tried not to smile as I continued, "And after I was settled in, I had the misfortune of meeting you six months later."

Olivia snapped her bra straps in place. "This place was a mess before you had the *privilege* of me coming to work as your partner."

"Ha." I looked down at my breasts, which were small in comparison to Olivia's. I hadn't known they grew them as big as hers until I moved here from the Drow Realm. Elves and Fae—peaches in comparison. I looked back at her. "That Sprite would have had you singing Broadway show tunes if I hadn't arrived. Before he fed you to his buddy, the Were."

"I'll let you have your delusions." Olivia twisted a wisp of dark hair that had escaped her clip. "I would have had them if you hadn't *interfered*."

Considering Olivia had a black belt in karate, been on NYPD's SWAT team, and was kick-ass all the way, the Sprite hadn't had a chance with her. The Were, though—that would have been tough, but Olivia was also a dead-shot with her Sig.

My XPhone vibrated on the top of my desk and belted out "Walk this Way," an old classic tune by Aerosmith, my current ringtone.

"Unknown" came up on the caller screen. "Nyx," I answered.

"Are you going to be at the Pit tonight, chica?" Caprice, one of my closest friends, said. "I am so hungry for one of Hector's burgers."

"I could really go for a martini right now. Extra dry." I leaned back in my chair and imagined relaxing with my favorite drink. "Yeah, after the past twenty-four hours that's just what I need."

"Nadia's going, too." I could picture Caprice's pretty hazel eyes and warm smile as she spoke. "We'll meet up with you there."

I looked at Olivia, who nodded before I took my life in my own hands as I said to Caprice. "Olivia can't stay away, so I'm sure she'll be trying to pick up some paranorm." Olivia grabbed a rubber band off of her desktop, made a slingshot, loaded it with an eraser, and aimed it at me. With a grin, I held up my hand to ward off Olivia's revenge attack. "See you."

After I pushed the off button on my XPhone, Olivia set the eraser and rubber band on her desktop. She always had a weapon and ammunition on hand, no matter the circumstances.

"Did you get a hold of Boyd?" she asked instead of pinging an eraser off my forehead. Or trying to.

I shook my head. Too bad Adam hadn't answered his cell phone when I'd tried to reach him. "I left a message, but haven't heard back."

"I'm telling you, Nyx, the guy wants to jump your bones." Olivia took a pencil from her holder and jotted down something on a sticky note in front of her instead of putting it in her XPhone. "Stop wasting time."

"We'll see."

The door whooshed open and both Olivia and I looked up.

Detective Adam Boyd.

A combination of warmth and pleasure whirled in my belly. I smiled, trying not to let a silly grin cross my face. Adam was one of the few humans allowed to see Olivia's and my PI office. To almost all other humans our office was invisible.

"Hey." Adam shoved his hands in his well-worn brown bomber jacket and looked both glad to be here and kind of shy as his eyes met mine.

Damn, he was cute.

"Whoo-hoo," Olivia said waving her hand in an "earth to Adam" kind of motion. "I'm here, too."

I'm not sure, but I thought his cheeks might have flushed a little under his tan. "Hey, Olivia."

She had one of her evil-mischievous looks on her face.

Uh-oh.

"You got my message?" I rushed to say before Olivia could open her Big Fat Mouth.

"Yeah." There must have been a strong breeze outside that had tousled his sable hair adorably, and he ran his hand over the short strands. His eyes, the color of dark brown alder wood, focused on me as he moved forward and took one of the chairs in front of my desk. He was a model of masculine grace and strength. "What's up?" For a big guy, he had the cutest little smile when our eyes met, and he had a dimple in his left cheek.

Insert schoolgirl sigh.

Did I mention he was gorgeous? In a typical guy way of sitting, he slouched his six-two frame in the chair, knees wide, feet planted on the floor. He was just as delicious as he was gorgeous—like a football quarterback.

I'd developed a taste for human football and I especially liked the shape and form of quarterbacks. Not too muscular, but toned and fit, intelligent and with a power all their own. And great asses.

Adam sure had a nice ass.

"Nyx?" Olivia said in a dangerously evil tone.

"Um, yeah." I fidgeted with the stylus for my XPhone. "I wanted to know if you've seen anything strange."

He raised one eyebrow. "As in paranormal strange?"

Olivia sniggered.

Of course Adam would have contacted me if he had. What an idiot I was.

"I meant—" What did I mean? I glanced at Olivia, who, by the look on her face, must have been cooking up something devious in her mind. "*We* wanted to make sure you're aware of what's going on."

"Pretty bad, huh?" He still had his hands stuffed in his bomber jacket. I liked his hands. Long-fingered, a little callused, and strong.

I wet my lips. His gaze followed my tongue.

Dear Goddess.

What I'd like to do to Adam using my tongue . . .

Olivia interrupted my sudden fantasies and my face grew hot again. "Miss Tongue-tied here is trying to tell you about Demons that are killing paranorms."

"Christ," Adam said as his expression turned to cop-mode. "What are these Demons?"

She gave him the short version before she added, "We've had a hell of a day fielding calls from paranorms needing help finding family members. We've never had so many missing persons calls."

"It's not easy telling the families about the Demons," I said, "and the possibility that the person they're calling about might have encountered one. Or a few." But we had to, and we warned them to keep the rest of their families safe.

Adam shook his head. "I don't handle missing persons cases, but I'll check in the database at the precinct to see if they've had an increase and go from there."

"That would be a big help." I tried not to be distracted by the energy I felt between myself and Adam. "Olivia and I have taken down every paranorm's information and filed it electronically for now." I rubbed my temples "Goddess, there were so many calls to day."

"Have you been able to get the word out on a broader scale?" Adam asked. "Last I remember the paranorm communications system isn't exactly up to date."

"Considering most of the paranorm racial issues are even worse than norms," Olivia said, "it's a problem. Weres can't stand Vamps who can't stand Fae . . ." She looked at me. "Who don't like Dark—"

I cut her off as fast as I could. Adam didn't know what I was. "Rodán's doing his best," I hurried to say. "But some paranorms can't come out during the day, so it's asking a lot to tell them not to leave their homes at night, too."

I'm lucky because my human half allows me to be in the sunshine, unlike my Drow half. Dark Elves can't tolerate daylight. I have the best of both worlds.

My skin started to tingle. Speaking of my Drow half. Damn.

"I'm sorry, Adam. I've got to run." I scrambled to throw my XPhone into my purse and tug on my light Fendi jacket, to hide my holstered 9mm Kahr.

Olivia smirked. "Time for presto chango," she said, and I cut her a quick glare.

Adam was already standing but looked confused, and I wanted to kill Olivia.

The tingling grew stronger. Crap. "I'm sorry, Adam. I've got an appointment I forgot about and I'm so late." Really late.

I had to hold myself from a dead run as Adam hurried to catch up with me after he gave Olivia a quick "Bye."

Damn, damn, damn. Crap, crap, crap. I was going to change right in front of him. I could feel my hair prickling at the roots. Was my hair already turning blue? What about the color of my skin?

I charged out of the office and into the cool September evening, and the breeze lifted my hair from my shoulders. "I've got to run up to my apartment real quick before I go," I said to Adam. "Bye." I almost bolted for the stairs in my high-heeled Ferragamos.

His "See you later," sounded hesitant.

No blue hair. No blue hair. No blue hair. *Please.*

This was the closest I'd come to blowing everything and shifting into my Drow form in front of a human. A human I really, really liked and didn't want to scare off.

Although I knew Adam wasn't like that. He'd already seen his fair share of things that went bump in the night. Still, I didn't want him to ever look at me any differently, and if that meant not showing him my other side despite Olivia's encouragement that's what it would have to be for now.

I bolted past Mrs. Taylor on the stairs. She lived in the apartment below mine, along with her yappy Chihuahua, Terror. I didn't pause to say hi. What if *she* saw me with blue hair?

I barely had time to get inside, slam my door, and

strip before I started the transformation. My skin prickled even more as I took a deep breath and slowly exhaled, trying to relax and slow the pounding of my heart.

I'd made it. But I'd had to leave a confused Adam behind.

No, I couldn't worry about him for now. I had other things to attend to now that darkness was almost here.

Fully naked, I stretched up on my toes, extending to be taller than my five-eight height. Then I lowered myself and began to move like a cat in slow, sinuous movements. I loved the transformation of my body, my skin, and my hair into my Drow appearance.

My muscles grew tighter, stronger. My straight black hair shimmered into a luxurious cobalt blue that parted at my now pointed ears. The color of my now softer and more sensitive skin eased into a shade that was like pale amethyst marble.

I shook out my slender but strong and sculpted Drow arms. My short incisors lowered and I touched one of the sharp points and cut my finger. When I pulled back, the dark red fluid stood out against the pale amethyst of my skin.

Every time I make the change, whether from human to Drow or Drow to human, I feel complete, as if everything is as it's meant to be.

But it had been too much for Stan.

Me. The real me.

Air brushed my bare flesh as I moved into my bedroom and then my walk-in closet, where I slipped into a form-fitting pair of Drow-made leather pants. I grabbed one of my black leather corsets off of a shelf and tugged the supple material on.

Stan and I had gotten so close, and I'd cared for him so much that my heart still hurt to think about him. I clenched my fingers into a fist as I stared into the closet, not seeing anything but Stan in that moment. Blond, hazel eyes, a nice package all the way around, Stan had seemed like such a great guy.

I'd almost thought I was in love with him.

The black leather of my Night Tracker outfit was soft and sensual against my skin. I pulled some of my hair out of the corset's straps, then pushed all of my straight hair back, letting it fall past my shoulders.

I held several strands of my long, blue hair and stared at them. My eyes unfocused as I thought again about Stan. One night, after we'd been together for over six months, I'd finally decided he was ready for the truth. I'd told him and showed him. Showed him all of me.

That had been the beginning of the end. Stan had freaked out. Every word he'd said had been like a knife slicing my flesh.

Even now I flinched as the words cut into my thoughts.

"Lying bitch . . .

"Blue-haired freak . . .

"Purple whore . . ."

He'd said so many things that I'd tried for a long time to push out of my mind and never quite could.

Immediately I'd used my air powers to try to erase thoughts of me from his mind, but we'd become too close, been together too long. I'd had to use my Drow strength to pin him down and keep him in his apartment while I called Rodán on my XPhone. It had taken Rodán's powers to erase the human's—Stan's—mind so that he would forget everything about me.

Everything.

We couldn't have Stan running around New York raving about purple women. Not that anyone would have believed him. But still, for his sanity and mine, taking his memories of me away had been our only choice. Rodán had planted another woman who looked like me in Stan's mind, a woman who had just broken up with him and left. Then his other memories and emotions could remain intact.

When Rodán had finished erasing and replacing Stan's memories, Rodán had found me curled in a corner by the front entryway. I'd been shivering, wanting to let out sobs that would never come. But the pain was there. Pain so great I didn't know if I'd ever get past it.

But I had. Eventually. For the most part.

A very demanding growl came from the direction of the kitchen and I blinked. I was still staring at strands of my hair that I clenched in my fingers. Amethyst-skinned fingers.

An extremely annoying yowl this time.

"Coming, your highness," I said as I tugged on my feather-light black knee-high Elvin boots. "Can't make Kali wait, now can we?" I muttered to myself.

Because I'm Elvin, my boots didn't make a whisper of a sound as I walked over the hardwood floor through the immaculate white and cobalt-blue designer living room. I passed through the arched entryway into the spacious kitchen, complete with stainless-steel appliances, cherrywood cabinets, and brown marble countertops.

I'd hired an interior decorator who had made over every room in my apartment when I first came from the Drow Realm to work for Rodán. Since then I had a Shifter maid who kept my apartment spotless.

How could I afford all of this in New York City? I'm a Drow Princess, and Dark Elves mine precious gems. I was loaded.

My blue Persian was sitting next to her food bowl with an imperious look on her features. Kali had been a gift from Rodán when she was a kitten. I think he found it amusing, giving a blue-haired female a blue cat.

I used my best Italian mobster accent as I put my hand on my hip. "So I forgot to give you your Fancy Feast before I got dressed. Sue me."

Kali glared and I knew my underwear drawer was in serious danger.

She had no sense of humor.

I grabbed a can of Kali's favorite cat food out of the walk-in pantry and served it to her highness in her Waterford Crystal Lismore champagne saucer. "You might think you own me," I said to the cat, "but it's the other way around."

Sure it was.

Why did I ever name her after Shiva's fierce and destructive Hindu wife? I must have been out of my mind. Kali had no problem living up to her name.

It was still early, and there was no hurry to get to the Pit. I took a bottle of green tea out of the fridge and used my air element to create a glamour to disguise my appearance. I headed through a set of French doors and stepped out of my living room onto my corner terrace, one of my favorite places. I lived on 104th and Central Park West, and the views of the sunrises and sunsets from my terrace were spectacular. My place was in what had become a quirky, idiosyncratic neighborhood and artists' community.

The tea bottle chilled my palm as I stared out into the near darkness and the glittering lights of Manhattan. What would it be like to be a norm, with no fear of Demons or other paranorms that had to be kept in line?

"Dull." I tipped back the bottle of green tea and swallowed the rest of it. My fangs clinked on the glass as the cold tea hit my belly and my stomach growled. "Who'd want to be a full norm, anyway?"

Inside my apartment, I strapped on my weapons belt and sheathed my dragon-claw daggers—Lightning and Thunder—and fastened my double-bladed oval buckler, Storm, like a belt buckle at the front of my weapons belt. The buckler was like a razor-edged discus.

With my air element, I made sure the terrace doors and all of the windows in my apartment were locked and protected.

I almost forgot my XPhone, but remembered it when I took my 9mm out of its day holster. After I set my XPhone on vibrate, I put it in its clip on my weapons belt and holstered the Kahr close to the XPhone, near my daggers.

I left a treat for Kali in her dish in the kitchen, hoping to appease her. "Good-bye, your highness."

Kali, as usual, gave me "the look" that told me how much she didn't appreciate being left alone.

"Could you at least leave me a week's worth of bras and thongs?" I said as I grabbed the doorknob. "I really don't have time to go to Victoria's this week."

She responded by tilting her chin and looking away from me.

"I'm going to have to buy a safe just for my underwear," I said with a grumble. Although she might find a way—I wondered sometimes if Rodán had given me a cat with magic. It would be like him to do that and not tell me.

I plunged into the night that had the faintest lift to the darkness, a trace of twilight still in the sky.

A horrible sensation churned in my belly and acid rose in my throat, and at the same time my heart started pounding. I clenched one arm to my abdomen and tried to shake off the feeling until I finally pulled myself together.

In those seconds I knew. I knew with everything I had that something was going to happen tonight. Something bad.

CHAPTER 3

Wind blew my hair into my face and eyes as I drove my black Corvette with the top down. The power of the sensation I'd had as I left my apartment wouldn't leave me as I drove the few minutes to the Pit.

I've always been able to sense things happening in the moment, but I'd never had a precognition. Had I actually sensed the future, and that something really bad was going to happen tonight? Was there anything I could do about it?

Frustration encased me, as if I was one of the Demons and I was in their armorlike skin. The answer was easy. All I could do was be extra alert tonight. How could I warn the others when it was just a *feeling*, and I wasn't a Seer like the Magi?

I moved along with traffic until I neared the "haunted" Dakota Building on Seventy-second Street and Central Park West. The Pit's location was shielded with Rodán's magic, and New Yorkers and tourists never gave the entrance a second glance.

Like most supposedly haunted locations, the Dakota Building was just another place where centuries-old Brownies had their version of "fun" by scaring humans. The kids purported to haunt the building? Brownies at their best.

After I parked in the garage beneath the Pit, I smoothed my windblown hair. I pushed the loose strands over my shoulders before getting out of my car and locking it. The closer I walked toward the Pit, the more relaxed I felt. The nightclub was a "safe place" for paranorms to gather. Nothing could touch any being in the Pit—paranorms or the few norms allowed. Rodán had the place well guarded, inside and out. Between magic and muscle, it was covered.

If you pissed off Rodán, you'd never find the Pit again and you wouldn't remember what part of the city it was in. If someone made him angry enough it was possible that person wouldn't even remember his own name.

On the street level, I bypassed every being that was standing in line and made my way to the entrance. Hey, there were perks to being a Peacekeeper.

I reached the Doppler bouncer and smiled as Fred grinned at me. "Decide to take me up on dinner yet?"

No, I just couldn't. To me he'd always be that sweet golden retriever I'd first met and played Frisbee with in Central Park. But when he'd shifted into human form, whoo-ha. Almost seven feet of solid muscle and killer good looks.

"I'll call James and Derek, and we'll make a date for the Great Lawn in Central Park," I said. "I'll come with a basket of goodies and some Milk Bones," I added with a wink at him.

Fred laughed and waved me through the doorway. "Get your cute ass in there."

Neon signs glowed from the walls in the darkened nightclub, reflecting off beer and cocktail glasses on tables around the bar. Soft black leather couches and chairs were arranged in corners and other strategic places that weren't occupied by round high-tops or regular tables. Flashing colored lights on the dance floor were the only sources of illumination other than the neon signs.

Pipe smoke burned my eyes. The Pit, with all of its noise, the heat from so many bodies, and the myriad of smells, swallowed me. Music pounded through me like it was traveling from my toes to my scalp, but tension eased from my body.

The relaxed feeling may have been from all the pipe weed smoke I'd sucked in when I passed the couches in the corner closest to the entrance. Several muscular Shadow Shifter males were lounging there, passing a paranorm version of a bong.

Since it was early evening, Rodán's staff was serving up the works, and the shiny wood-bladed fans above guided smells of fries, steak, ale, and cherry-leaf tobacco around the room.

Along with sweat and bad breath. Too many Metamorphs and Vamps in here tonight.

Olivia had beaten me to the Pit and waved to me from across the room. She was on an elevated floor crowded with pool tables and video games, hanging out with some of the paranorms she knew. Thankfully this time she wasn't with some waxy-faced Vamp.

Goddess, Olivia cracked me up. She was in a bar full of paranorms and the green shirt she'd changed into read:

*Always remember you're unique
Just like everyone else.*

With a gesture of her hand, she indicated that I should join her. I mimed eating and drinking, and pointed to the bar. She nodded and turned back to the Petite Abatwa, a Zulu Spirit Faerie, next to her.

At the center of the Pit, patrons were packed even tighter together as they danced—if you could call barely-able-to-move-to-keep-from-suffocating-madness dancing.

I caught a glimpse of Caprice, and she was dancing with a blond guy I'd never seen before. A really hot-looking guy.

Oooh, score one for Caprice.

Fast and sudden, it felt like someone was trailing an ice cube down my back as I continued to look at the blond she was with. A feeling of panic, so deep that I could barely grasp it, much less understand it. For a moment I couldn't move as I stared at them on the dance floor. The man caught me looking at him and his smile was filled with sexual innuendo. I caught my breath as the man and Caprice disappeared into the dance crowd.

I rubbed my arms with both hands, trying to get off the imaginary feeling of ice crystallizing over my skin. What was he? Too many odors assaulted me from all the paranorms in the room to get a read on him from where I stood.

Maybe he was a Doppler or some other kind of Shifter. He could even be human, since Fred had apparently been cool with him and let the guy pass.

Yeah. He wouldn't be here if Fred didn't trust him, and Rodán's magic had let him in.

Finally I made it to the couches and tables farthest in the back corner, situated close to the end of the bar. Most of the Trackers hung out in this corner before hitting our territories.

"Hey, Nyx!" Nadia, my gorgeous redheaded friend, called out to me in her sexy Siren's voice and waved one of her slender arms. Because she was a Siren, she couldn't help but sound sexy.

"Here's a seat." A good friend, Lawan, pointed to the place on the couch next to her, the couch's backside close to the bar.

I plopped into the opening and caught Lawan's appealing scent. Tiger flowers. She was a gorgeous Siamese cat in her Doppler form.

The other Trackers gave good-natured hellos. Robert, Jon, Tracey, Phyllis, Carlos, Dave, and Ice were seven currently at the Pit, and Caprice and I made nine. We had a total of fifteen assigned Trackers and five roving Trackers.

Almost every Tracker who worked Manhattan was born, hatched, or blossomed right here. The only exceptions were Lawan from Thailand, Nadia from the Atlantic Ocean, and me, from Otherworld. It was easy to say we Trackers were the twenty toughest people in New York City—and that's saying a lot.

"The blue in your hair really shines tonight, chica," Caprice said from behind me. I glanced over my shoulder and looked at my hazel eyed, brown-haired friend as she stroked a lock over my shoulder. "New conditioner?"

I nodded and she let my hair slip through her fingers. "I went to that spa and salon on the penthouse floor at Bergdorf Goodman a couple of days ago." In my human form, of course. "Great view of Central Park while I was totally pampered."

Caprice ran her fingers through her own dark hair, tousling the curls. "We should have a girl's day out with Nadia and Olivia at the spa."

Spending a day with my three closest friends sounded really good to me. "Pick a date."

Maybe I was an oddity in two worlds, but as a Tracker I had friends. They didn't care that I had amethyst skin and blue hair. Or even that Nadia turned green when she sang her Siren's song. Almost all of the Trackers were my friends.

Although I did try to spend as little time as possible around Fere and Kelly, to avoid potential homicides and being taken away in handcuffs treated to contain any elemental magic.

"The Demons have been pretty consistent about showing up around midnight," Jon was saying as Caprice sat beside him, clutching a highball glass with her slender fingers.

"Gives us time to take care of the idiots who come out earlier." Caprice swirled ice in her glass and I could smell rum and Coke. "But it's still early, and we should concentrate on more important things."

"Eating," Nadia and I said at the same time, and we grinned at each other.

I glanced up at the Doppler barman, Hector, as he automatically brought me a dry vodka martini with three olives on a little sword. I loved Hector. "How's the jungle?" I asked.

"Wild tonight." When not in his human form, Hector usually shifted into a huge, tawny lion. Scary. "I'll start a tab, Streak, and get your steak as charburnt as possible," he said in his Hispanic accent. Hector had always called me Streak from the first time we'd met and he'd caught the black highlights in my blue hair.

By the time I finished my burnt steak, loaded baked potato, and two martinis, it was time to track.

I got up and bumped into Jon, who steadied me by my shoulders. I looked up at him and he smiled. He was a much too good-looking Shifter who patrolled the Upper East Side. So hot that a girl's heart should shout "Danger! Danger!" the moment she met him.

Caprice stood beside me and waved Jon off as he released my arms. "Get to work, pretty boy."

He ruffled her hair. "Sure thing, Cap."

"Hey." She smacked his hand.

I barely listened to Caprice and Jon's banter. Every muscle in my body suddenly burned as that bad feeling I'd had earlier overrode the smell of weed and the enjoyment of good company.

"*Chica.*" Caprice's emphasis of her nickname for me jerked my attention to her. "You okay?"

I realized I was holding my hand to my belly. I forced a smile and glanced around the room. "So where's that hunky blond?"

She laughed. "That describes a whole lot of the norms and paranorms in this place."

I rolled my eyes. "The guy you were dancing with."

Caprice was definitely holding back a big smile. "Chance had to leave to meet with a friend."

"Chance, huh?" I started walking toward the doorway with Caprice. Again the sense that something was horribly wrong caught me off guard. The mention of the guy's name filled my belly with a sick sensation.

"What do you know about him?" I said.

"Just met him tonight." Even beneath Caprice's olive complexion I detected a faint blush. "He said he'd be here tomorrow. I'm going to see him then."

"Where'd you meet him?" I asked as we stepped through the doorway into the night and away from the head-banging music.

"Here." Her bare arm brushed mine. "Tonight."

I liked seeing the happy look on her face. Caprice had lost her Doppler family a few years ago, so she was alone except for her friends.

"So is he a Shifter or a Doppler?" I asked.

She shook her head and frowned. "I couldn't tell what he was—I didn't recognize his scent. And it just didn't feel right to ask."

Usually paranorms had no qualms asking if they couldn't scent the other paranorm. Strange that Caprice had felt that way.

The closest lamppost's glow caused light and shadow to fall across her face as I watched her. "Maybe you can ask him tomorrow night."

She shrugged. "Does it matter?"

I thought for a moment. "No, it really doesn't."

Then I did give her a serious look. "As long as he's not a Metamorph."

"No way, chica." Caprice gave a visible shudder. "They're almost as bad as Demons."

"Not quite." I frowned as I looked into the darkness. "Speaking of Demons, it's time to hunt."

CHAPTER 4

My prey had mutilated and killed a Tracker in Manhattan.

Dear Goddess. A Tracker. One of us.

And I hadn't arrived fast enough.

Fury burned through me like liquid fire as I narrowed my eyes at the six Demons and drew one of my dragon-claw daggers from its sheath.

I raised my weapon. The two-inch-wide side of my dagger reflected the dangerous white light that flashed in my sapphire eyes.

"You're going down," I whispered to the Demons that would die from my blade. The Demons looked like they could be someone you'd bump into anywhere in Manhattan—if it wasn't for the fact that when they attacked, their teeth became long and jagged, and their fingers turned into claws. And if they weren't eating a being's flesh.

Acid burned my stomach and my throat. The desire to kill flamed higher inside me, combining with the urge to throw myself into the midst of the Demons. I wanted to start whacking the hell out of them and splattering their fluids all over the alleyway's walls. But it wasn't that easy. I had to find their one weakness, that one soft spot on each of the six Demons. And do it without getting myself killed.

I ground my teeth as I held myself back.

"Think clearly, Nyx. Remove emotion. No matter how difficult it is," I told myself in a low voice, as if chanting it would force me to calm down.

The lid of the stinking alleyway's Dumpster was rough and dirty beneath my fingertips as I crouched in the darkness. I had one hand braced on the Dumpster lid while the other hand wielded my seventeen-inch-long dagger, which would soon eliminate the six Demons.

How could the Demons have found, much less killed, a *Tracker* in New York City? It was one thing to kill a defenseless paranorm, but a Tracker? Countless paranorms had died in this same horrible way in the past three weeks, since the Demons escaped through the Ruhin Demon Gate. But not a Tracker.

This simply wasn't possible. All Trackers were too well trained, too powerful in their fighting abilities.

But it had happened. Right here where the northeast corner of Central Park touched the Upper East Side's territory. Close to Frawley Circle.

Jon or Randy. Dear Goddess, it could be either of them. Jon had the Upper East Side and Randy's territory was all of Central Park.

The dirty asphalt didn't give away a sound beneath my soft leather boots as I jumped from the Dumpster and landed in another crouch. Now, in addition to garbage, there was the increased odor of asphalt and oil.

Only a limited number of paranorms had Tracker

abilities and there was only one of us per territory. We'd had five rotating trackers over a fifteen-territory Manhattan spread. The operative word being *had*— now one of us had been murdered by Demons.

Shadows and my air powers absorbed the colors of my surroundings, allowing me to remain undetected while I surveyed the Demons and inched closer to them. Unfortunately I wouldn't be able to maintain the glamour once I started fighting.

"Hold, Nyx," I whispered. "One moment longer."

I'd only been a Tracker for two years, but Trackers throughout this world had worked for centuries as part of the Guardian's Peacekeepers. This new threat could destroy us if we didn't find a way to stop them.

Bones crunched between their jaws, a sickening sound, and the Demons laughed and made growling and grunting noises as they ate like animals with their vicious, sharp-pointed teeth. Their claws were tipped with poison once they morphed, the poison fatal to any being. Including Light and Dark Elves. Right now that meant me.

A heavy weight in my belly accompanied the flames of fury that continued to rise within me. If there had been any real fire around I would have drawn on my fire powers, no matter the cost to me. Then again, what good would that do? Fire didn't affect the Goddess-damned Demons.

"Which Tracker was it?" My question was inaudible but I had to ask it. Truly I was afraid to find out.

My stomach and heart lurched together as the knowledge came to me.

The slow drift of his lifeforce to Summerland, his essence leaving. I knew who he was.

Jon.

I swallowed, shaking in both grief and anger. I bowed my head briefly in his memory, seeing his grin in my thoughts from mere hours ago.

I paused only a second, so that I wouldn't lose my advantage over the Demons in avenging Jon's death.

Every Tracker was important to me, and Jon's murder hit me like I'd slammed into a wall.

At that exact moment, each of the Guardian's Peacekeepers—Soothsayers, Healers, Gatekeepers, Trackers, and our Proctor, Rodán—would have felt the change in the balance in Manhattan, and would have sensed Jon's essence departing.

I wanted to yell, to scream from the pain of his death. But I would get my revenge. Now.

My movements were silent, fluid, and smooth. I reached the Demon closest to me, one that looked like a teenage female in jeans and a half shirt. Along with long blond hair and flawless pale skin, she had tattoos and a belly piercing. Her flesh looked as vulnerable as that of any humanoid being.

She would have been considered beautiful—if not for the sickening claws and fierce teeth she now exposed, and Jon's blood smearing her face.

I gripped the hilt of my long, clawed dagger with both hands. Too low for the Demon to hear me, I said, "This is for you, Jon."

My glamour dropped just as I whirled from behind the Demon and rammed my dagger into its one soft spot. The hollow of the Demon's humanoid throat between the armorlike flesh of its neck and chest.

I felt the sensation of my blade slicing into flesh, then fluid. The spurt, then splatter, of the Demon's lifeblood in the alleyway, and the sudden stench of pus, was enough to make anyone shudder. It was also enough to capture the rest of the Demons' attention.

I jerked my dagger out of the throat of the first Demon at the same time I planted my boot on its belly and shoved the creature away from me. I spun and faced one of the five remaining Demons.

"Hello, bitch." My lips curved into a vicious grin and my dagger gleamed as I faced a dark-haired, dark-skinned, female-looking Demon. "Meet Lightning."

Before the Demons had the opportunity to react, the movement of my arms was smooth and quick, a blur to human or Demon sight.

When I buried my blade into the second Demon's vulnerable spot, it shrieked, stumbled back, and slid down the alley's grime-coated brick walls.

The bellows of the four other Demons bounced off the walls as they dove for me.

I double backflipped away from the Demons. At the same time, I sliced my dagger up the first lunging Demon's belly and ripped its shirt open from the waist to its neck. The sound my blade made against the deceptively fragile-looking skin was like metal against metal.

I landed lightly, about ten feet from the Demons and balanced on the balls of my boot-clad feet.

"You are so going to die." Anger and venom spilled

out in my steady words, and my slightly lowered canines brushed my lips as I stared at the Demons.

The four Demons charged at once. Their shrieks and growls were lost in the buzz and hum that was New York City, a city that truly never slept.

My hair rose from my shoulders as I whirled and tried to ram my dagger into a muscular, manlike Demon's throat. I missed and my blade pinged off its neck.

I barely avoided its claws when it swung at me and it slammed me against one of the alleyway walls. Pain reverberated from my back to my chest. For only a second stars sparked behind my eyes when my head hit the brick wall, and I felt blood well on my scalp.

I drew Thunder, my second dragon-clawed dagger, from its sheath at the same time I twisted and ducked under the man-Demon's claws as it lunged at me again.

A chill trailed up my spine and I dodged the Demon. The chill was almost familiar, deadly.

No time to think about anything but vengeance on these Demons.

I whirled and rammed one dagger into a third Demon's throat sac. Some of the goo splattered my pants and my bare belly, but I ignored it as the Demon, wearing a three-piece businessman's suit, collapsed.

I didn't pause to pay attention. Instead, I ducked and rolled between two of the three remaining Demons. Asphalt was beneath my feet in an instant as I rose behind the Demons.

"You sonsofbitches!" Their confusion at my move

gave me just enough time to rid myself of Demon number four, a large male, with another quick movement of my dagger.

Every kill brought home Jon's death. Instead of feeling any satisfaction in avenging him, only more hatred surged through me.

Splatters of blue fluid from the dead Demons reflected the light of the half-moon peeking through the clouds.

The last two Demons charged me, shrieking and screaming so loudly that the sound felt like it was piercing my eardrums. One of them would have looked like a frail elderly woman if it didn't have Demon claws and teeth. The other demon could have been anyone's mom.

The Demons were too close to fight easily.

Right before I performed a triple backflip, I felt a brush of air as one of the Demon's claws passed less than an inch from my face.

My pulse rocketed.

Damn, that was close.

I gripped Lightning and Thunder. Blue Demon goo covered one dagger's blade. The grips of my weapons felt worn and comfortable as I held one in each hand while crossing the blades in front of my chest.

The Demons charged again.

Careful to remain out of reach of their deadly claws, I spun. Again I knew I was a blur to their sight. I extended both of my arms while gripping my daggers and holding them straight out. The blades clinked against their armored-skinned bodies.

Then, to either side of me, I drove each dagger home at the same time.

The Demons' throat sacs spurted blue fluid and their faces twisted into images of excruciating pain. More blue fluid slapped my skin right before their humanoid bodies collapsed and plopped to the asphalt.

My muscles shook from adrenaline, tension, and anger as I came to a stop.

I closed my eyes for a moment and sucked in a deep breath. It was over. My revenge on these Demons was complete. But I would never be satisfied until every single Demon that had come through the Ruhin Demon Gate was destroyed.

My eyes remained closed. I couldn't look at Jon's destroyed body, but still the image was burned into my mind from seeing his remains earlier. Goddess, I wished I could cry, but Dark Elves don't have tear ducts.

After taking a deep breath, I fixed on the location of his remains with my senses, but in my mind kept a picture of him whole and handsome.

I paused a moment to catch another breath and let everything sink in. Dear Goddess.

Using my earth element, I drew deep from the soil beneath the asphalt. My muscles shook as I focused on my power to move earth and stone. Even though this would take a good portion of my elemental energies, this was worth it to give Jon's remains a proper ending.

The earth rumbled. The crack of asphalt bounced off the walls. In my mind's eye I could see what was left of Jon swallowed by the exposed earth when the asphalt opened to either side of him.

Then down. Down into the fissure I'd created. What was left of his body I took deep, deep into the earth. With a mental command the dirt and asphalt closed over him as if what I'd done had never happened. I elementally contained his remains in the earth to keep them safe until they could be retrieved by his family.

"Good-bye, Jon," I said, so quietly that even I barely heard my words.

A sensation swarmed my body like beetles crawling over my skin.

I jerked my head up and opened my eyes.

A different danger.

My grip tightened on Lightning and Thunder.

Adrenaline surged through me again in a hot, hard thrust.

An unknown danger.

My Drow senses radiated the energy I drew from the earth and air. The energy flowed in a radius wide enough to cover the alleyway as I crouched again. I'd weakened myself, but not too much.

Rosewood and musk rose over the pus smell of Demon fluid and the alley's filth.

I crossed my daggers over my chest.

Someone was watching me.

Or some *thing*.

CHAPTER 5

I turned my head toward the being watching me, still holding my daggers crossed over my chest.

My gaze met his—its—liquid silver eyes and I felt like I had been touched by a bolt of lightning. An electric current shot through me and I gripped my daggers even tighter. Had he just touched me with magic? I reached out with my senses but could feel no active magic coming from or near him. So what the hell had just happened?

Without fear, but with caution, I studied the alien presence.

It wasn't one of these underling Demons, somehow I knew that. Could it be another type of Demon?

That smelled like rosewood and musk?

I didn't think so.

It also wasn't a Metamorph, because they smelled like alyssum—newly mown hay.

The being in front of me had the appearance of a human male—

But he definitely wasn't human.

He had his shoulder hitched up against a blood-free wall while observing me. A dark, sensual, gorgeous hunk of a male.

Who was he?

What was he?

Why was he watching me, and how had he gotten past my senses so easily? Did I lose that much of my energies fighting the Demons?

And seeing a friend's butchered remains.

I swallowed. My choker seemed to tighten around my throat at the movement.

My Drow-enhanced vision made his features easy to see, but not easy to read. Those unusual silver eyes suggested perhaps a hint of amusement, yet the being didn't smile. He wore a long black trench coat. Being half Drow, I could sense and scent the odd alloy within the weapons he carried beneath the coat.

Strapped to his back was a pair of double-edged short swords of that same metal. Dark Elves were familiar with all metals, so why didn't I recognize his?

I gripped my daggers. My chest and back hurt, and pain shot through my head. But I slowly rose to my feet in a fluid movement, not letting him know I was injured in any way. One benefit of being Elvin is that I heal very quickly, and it wouldn't be long before all of my wounds no longer existed.

"Who are you?" My muscles relaxed as I reached my full height of five-eight. Because I sensed no immediate danger, I sheathed my daggers but never took my gaze from his. I put my right hand on my buckler at the front of my weapons belt. The buckler would separate this being's head from his shoulders with a flick of my wrist. He'd never see it coming. "*What* are you?"

"You move like a cat, Nyx." His voice rumbled my

name and a chill slid through me. How did he know who I was? "I've never seen such grace and power in any female. Or male." He studied me with his intent gray eyes. "Interesting."

"Is it?" I let the words roll from my tongue in a casual and sensual tone meant to disarm him. Because I'm half Drow, sensuality is something that comes to me as naturally as every breath I take.

Which at that moment felt like hell.

If he recognized the danger behind my words and my voice, the man didn't show it, not even by a twitch of an eyelid. "Very interesting." His arms remained crossed at his chest and I sensed no weapons in his hands.

I moved closer to him, my steps slow and sensuous, intending to keep him off guard. Good girl. I managed to walk without looking injured, or like my heart had been torn out, as I edged in on the fifteen feet between us.

"Dark Elves and Light Elves are known for stealth and absolute silence," I said.

He gave a slow and entirely sexual smile. "But not with such feline movements that you could be a panther."

"Flattery is a custom of your race?" Only ten feet separated us now. "How do you know my name?"

He gave a casual shrug accompanied by an arrogant look.

I kept my cool but made it clear in my voice that I would tolerate only so much. "What do you want, stranger?"

He glanced at my choker, with its almost invisible

runes signifying my heritage. "Princess, it's not what I want, but it is what it is."

"So you can read Drow runes." I cocked one eyebrow. "Impressive. Why are you really here?"

"The name's Torin." He smirked. "And Princess, I'm your new babysitter."

His words hit me like a small jolt. What was he talking about?

I kept my voice even and my fingers close to my buckler. "Maybe you should clarify that statement."

The being that called himself Torin pushed away from the wall and I saw him more clearly in the alleyway's single light. Beneath his open trench coat, he wore a black T-shirt and snug blue jeans. His almost black hair was tied into a long tail, pulling his hair from his face. He had a rugged Highlander look to him.

A scar zagged from the right side of his forehead through one eyebrow and to his cheek. A second scar ran along his left jaw. On his neck were odd scars, almost as if someone had tried to hang him.

Too bad they hadn't succeeded.

His rosewood-and-musk scent was even stronger now. The being was perhaps eight inches taller and towered over my five-eight. His height didn't intimidate me. Nor did the battle scars on his face and neck. I would have thought he was handsome if he hadn't pissed me off, and if I wasn't sick over Jon.

"*You* don't work alone anymore, Princess," he said.

Yeah, right. "Quit with the games."

He had a smug expression that immediately made me want to draw my blades, just out of sheer irritation. "Speak with Rodán," he said.

The Proctor's name coming from this being's mouth sent a combination of heat and a chill through me. "What do you know of Rodán?"

My fingers twitched closer to my buckler as the being took a step toward me. "He asked me to retrieve you."

The stranger's arrogance was definitely getting old, and my skin prickled. "You're to take me to Rodán like a lost puppy?"

His gaze became dark and intense. "More like a dangerous cat."

"He could have called me just as easily on my XPhone." I narrowed my eyes. "Who are you? And I ask again, *what* are you?"

He was only five feet from me now. "I'm the man who's going to back up your gorgeous little ass."

"This ass doesn't need backup, T." I couldn't have helped the dangerous glint that sparked from my eyes if I'd wanted to when he ignored the most important question. Blessed Anu. What was this male?

"You would have been dead if I had chosen to kill you instead of watch you." His tone and his expression bordered on condescending, and I thought his head might make a good trophy if I was into collecting them. "And the name is Torin."

"Whatever, T." I delighted in the irritation that crossed his features. "I don't have a doubt I would have been aware the instant you or your weapon came near me, and I would have deflected it. Then gutted you."

The arrogant male turned his gaze toward the carnage. "First we'll take care of this . . . mess."

I faced the six dead Demons. All of the elemental powers I had used tonight had nearly drained me to the point of exhaustion. We always had to have the remains removed before norms stumbled over them. This time I just didn't have the juice in me to do it myself. I'd need to call PTF, the Paranorm Task Force.

As I reached for my XPhone, T raised his hand. I stopped and narrowed my eyes as I watched him. The intense way he focused on the Demon carcasses was fascinating enough to give me pause.

A burst of black/orange fire shot from his palm straight at the Demons' remains.

I caught my breath, my hair rising from my scalp. I'd never seen anything like the magic in the flames. A dark, coal-black glitter winking in and out of a silent, cold fire.

The Demons erupted into flame and a new stench filtered down the alleyway. The charred pus smell was strong enough that I almost gagged.

What the hell? Fire had no effect on the Demons.

But this had been no normal fire. This one had been imbued with magic. Magic that I couldn't understand or explain.

Within moments all of the carcasses were gone and a few silver ashes swirled into a breeze and vanished. Before I had a chance to ask how he had rid us of the Demons, T started out of the alleyway and presented his back. It was in the confident way he moved that I knew he had no fear of an attack from me.

My Drow genes told me it wasn't too long until sunrise. Time for most baddies to go to ground, or wherever was dark or safe from sunlight.

"We're going to see Rodán," he said over his shoulder.

Oh, you bet. Time to find out what in the name of the Goddess was going on.

"Avanna." My skin tingled as I spoke the Elvin word that relieved all my body parts of filth and stenches from the Dumpster, the blue Demon blood, and any other unwanted substances.

I frowned at the broad-shouldered male ahead whose boot steps clumped against the concrete sidewalk. Why bother to try to catch up with him—it—whatever? I wasn't about to go trotting after him like a well-trained dog.

My XPhone was smooth in my hand as I withdrew it, then called Rodán.

He answered with, "You've met Torin?"

"I don't appreciate you sending someone to tag along with me while I track." I saw T's back stiffen at my words. Heh. "Especially without giving me a heads-up."

"You've had a busy night," Rodán said.

"Goddess bless it, Rodán." There were other things I wanted to scream, but Rodán was fluent in the Drow language. "Didn't you take your medication?"

I heard the frown in his voice when he replied, "What?"

"Your trollshit pill." My face burned as I spoke. "Because you need to flush it out of your system before I get there."

The XPhone made a rasping sound as I stuffed it in its clip on my belt.

Laughter came from the man-thing in front of me, and he looked over his shoulder. "Rodán is very tolerant of you."

T turned forward again. I rested both hands on the hilts of my daggers. After just seeing a Tracker, a friend, murdered, I was so not in the mood for this.

I stepped over a vagrant who had a newspaper over his head and his feet stuck out on the concrete. Of course he couldn't see me, even without the newspaper, because I was using my air power to form a glamour and I didn't want to be seen.

I couldn't help my thoughts turning back to Jon. As one of the Great Guardian's Trackers, I'd gone from outcast in the world of the Dark Elves to being accepted and embraced as one of a group that treated me like any other paranorm. I developed friendships for the first time in my life. It had taken a while to get used to it, but it felt good. Two years later and I couldn't imagine life any other way.

And now I'd lost one of my fellow Trackers. One of my friends.

My throat worked as I tried to swallow back the pain and concentrate on taking my time walking behind the being that called itself/himself Torin. Then the male stopped and waited for me.

I narrowed my brows. What did he want?

He fell into step beside me as the rumble and growl

of the city surrounded us. "Strange place," he muttered as he looked at the skyscrapers and flashing billboards.

An interesting tidbit. He didn't seem to be familiar with human cities. At least, not this one.

Cars and taxis arrowed past us in the fairly light predawn traffic. The humid late-September air weighted the night. I enjoy the change of seasons so I don't mind the humidity. In the Drow Realm, there's no such thing as seasons. Not even in the city of the Light Elves. In the city of the pious it's spring year-round.

The shriek of a Metro bus's brakes cut through the waning night. An hour and a half at most and it would be daylight—my Drow half sensed it as the feel of the oncoming day tickled through my being.

The bus's exhaust poured from its tailpipe when it pulled to a stop as we passed by. Early risers and late nighters boarded and debarked, sleepy-eyed and looking as if they sure didn't want to be where they were.

"Explain why Rodán would want to stick me with you," I said.

"Like I told you, Princess." His arrogant tone made me want to gut him. "It is what it is."

"Sure. Like I'll let it happen. I have no desire to train a new Tracker."

Irritation swiped his features before it vanished. "I'm not a Tracker."

My turn for more irritation, and my skin tightened. "Then what are you?"

He said nothing, and my dagger in his gut was

sounding better all the time. I wasn't in the mood for games.

I forced myself to think of other things than this huge idiot beside me. But then all that stayed in my mind was what had happened to Jon.

The smell of pizza made me feel like throwing up as we passed a small twenty-four hour restaurant. I felt like I would never be able to eat again.

Not after tonight.

CHAPTER 6

Everything that had happened tonight seemed surreal as T and I neared the Dakota Building and finally reached the Pit.

By the time we got to the nightclub my head and
back barely bothered me. It's really convenient being Drow.

At the entrance to the Pit, Fred winked at me, and
I forced a smile. "Hi, Fred," I managed, but couldn't
begin to come up with something like our usual back-
and-forth banter. He wouldn't know about Jon yet,
and I wasn't ready to talk about it. I'd let Rodán in-
form his staff and everyone else he needed to.

Just that thought alone made my heart and my gut
sink lower.

Fred's expression changed to one of puzzlement,
like he could tell something was wrong. He let my
unwanted companion follow me, but I heard Fred
give a low growl as T walked by him.

The odor of smoke and alcohol made me want to
gag this time, even though it was a lot lighter than it
had been earlier in the night. A lot of paranorms had
gone to ground or to bed—wherever they went when
the sun came up.

Bile tried to crawl up my throat but I forced it down. As much as I tried, I would never forget what had happened tonight. And what had been left of Jon.

I led the way, weaving in and out between the remaining patrons. Rock music pounded in the nightclub for those who were still up. The pain that had begun behind my temples started pounding just as hard as the beat of the music.

T and I came up to a group of my fellow Trackers, all of whom had probably just gotten in from work. I met gazes that were filled with sadness and regret for Jon.

Not seeing him there made my heart hurt.

Of course they all would have felt Jon's essence move on to Summerland.

"You found Jon?" Randy asked me as I paused by the table they were sitting around. It hadn't really been a question.

"Yeah." I met Randy's yellow eyes. "It was—it was bad." I looked away and tried to put aside the horrific images. Talking about Jon to the people we worked with made the pictures in my mind worse.

Everyone was staring at me when I looked back at them. "Six underling Demons." I swallowed. "I didn't sense the attack until it was too late."

Randy gave a frustrated huff. "I was all the way on the opposite end of Central Park by the time I felt Jon's life essence departing. I couldn't leave because I was battling four Demons at the same time as his death."

"The Demons finding Jon wasn't a coincidence,"

Kelly said quietly. "Catching him off guard like that would have been impossible."

"You're right," Carlos said. "No way in hell could those six Demons have downed him the way they did. Without some serious help."

"Why hadn't he transformed?" I said as the thought occurred to me. "He was a Shifter. He could have become a mouse. A cockroach even."

The other Trackers frowned and Nadia said, "What if something made it so that he *couldn't*?"

"It's possible . . ." Hades, who was a Shifter like Jon had been, leaned back in his seat as he gripped his beer bottle. "Shifters don't let on because we're not about to let it be used against us."

"What is it?" Nancy asked.

Hades gave her a pointed look. "You think I'm going to tell a Pixie?"

Nancy glared at him, crossed her arms, and raised her chin.

"No kidding." Meryl, one of the four Shifters on our team, looked at Hades. "You shouldn't have said anything at all."

I wanted to shake Meryl so hard her teeth rattled, and kick Hades's ass. How could they hold back information when our friend and fellow Tracker had just been murdered?

It was hard not to let Meryl or Hades have it with the sharpness of my tongue, but I said to Hades, "Does Rodán know about this Shifter weakness?"

"Rodán knows fucking everything." Ice spoke in a dry tone as he drew on a thinly rolled joint that smelled like the same pipe-weed the Shadow Shifters were smoking earlier. "At least he thinks he does."

"Does he know you're a weed head?" Nancy snapped at him. "Trackers are supposed to stay away from that kind of thing."

Ice shrugged. "I'm not kissing his Elvin ass."

I thought I heard the sound of everyone sucking in their breath. To insult Rodán was almost as bad as my irreverence for the GG.

Which also meant I didn't care about Ice's opinion of Rodán. I cared more about finding out how to keep any more Trackers from being murdered. And about why we non-Shifters hadn't been informed of the fact that something could keep Shifters from taking an animal form of their choice.

"I don't need this crap right now," I said in a barely even tone. "I need to talk with Rodán."

My back was to the other Trackers before any of them had a chance to respond.

T and I headed directly toward Rodán's "dungeon." The entrance was hidden behind a wall of gray fog that only the privileged few could see. Goody for me that I was one of those few.

Some of the other Trackers didn't like that I was the only Tracker who could enter Rodán's "inner sanctum." It had been explained that I was also a PI who had to report to him repeatedly. I knew that it was because he was not only my mentor, but a friend and, until recently, one of his many lovers.

T and I walked easily through the fog, which smelled of rain and moist earth. Anyone not welcome to Rodán's dungeon would slam into a solid wall. He had no need for guards. His magic was strong enough to obliterate anyone who tried to enter.

After passing through the fog, we walked down the long hallway. "How do you know Rodán?" I asked as T strode beside me down a passageway that was lit by torches in brackets mounted on the stone walls.

T looked down at me, and in the flickering light the scars on his face made him look almost menacing. "Through a mutual acquaintance," T said, his voice a deep rumble.

I almost asked who, but I had a gut feeling that what he'd said was all I was going to get out of him. For now.

We reached an arched black doorway that reminded me of a dungeon from medieval times. Rodán even had torches to either side of the doorway. He was all about appearances and making a splash. That was when he wasn't busy serving as Proctor. At those times he was all business.

T placed his palm against an oblong pad on the wall to the right of the door. Like a human mood ring, the pad sifted through various colors beneath T's palm. It stopped at a swirling gray that was the same shade as T's eyes.

He moved aside and the oval went black. Then I touched the spongy pad and my palm itched. Colors blended beneath my hand until the pad stilled at sapphire blue as it always did, matching my eyes. As usual it gave a brief burst of white light at the center— I'm sure Rodán's idea of amusement, to copy the danger that flashed in my eyes when I was angry.

I stepped back and rubbed my tingling palm on my leather pants as the pad went black again.

The door to Rodán's dungeon opened without the slightest sound. Immediately, scents of woodland and firethorn tickled my nose, and heated air flowed over me, causing perspiration to coat my skin. T and I stepped inside the candlelit room. Rodán was waiting for us.

Even though Rodán wore a loose forest-green tunic and breeches, it was obvious every muscle in his body was toned and sculpted. From his carved biceps to his well-defined abs, on down to his muscled thighs and calves, and everything in between, he was perfection. I knew that body *very* well.

Pointed ears peeked through his long white-blond hair, the shade contrasting against his golden skin as his hair fell straight over his broad shoulders. He moved toward us with the litheness of the Light Elves, and I met his crystal-green eyes.

"Nyx." He held out his arms and brought me into his embrace before giving me a soft kiss. Not a lover's kiss, but a caring friend's kiss.

I kissed him back before I turned my head and walked across the room to stare blankly at one of his displays. It contained items from Otherworld like Faerie cones, a crystal container of Pixie dust, and even a Siren's prized golden seashell.

Rodán's sigh was audible behind me before Torin said, "Your cat has sharp claws."

I whirled to face Torin, almost snarled, and nearly showed him what real claws were. The ones on my dagger would gut him nicely. I don't know why I was so angry with him—yes, yes, I did. He'd been an arrogant bastard from the moment I'd met him.

"Come." Rodán stepped between us and indicated that we should follow him through the expanse of his warm "entertaining chamber" to his office. Most of the time he would have any number of females and/or males in the huge expanse of his bed, which was made from finely carved Dryad wood.

My hip brushed a spanking bench. Rodán was into all kinds of sexual play, including bondage and domination, and he had a whole lot of the toys to prove it.

That was one kind of sex I'd refused to allow Rodán to indulge in with me. I wouldn't get into BDSM when I lived in the Drow Realm, and I wasn't about to start with Rodán.

Rodán took my hand and we walked toward a fog-shrouded wall that led toward his den. We stepped through and into the chilly air on the landing at the top of a flight of stairs. The perspiration on my skin dried, and I shivered as I dragged in a cool breath of air before we walked down stone steps to his den.

Behind us T's boot steps clunked hard on the stone as the stairs curved to the entrance to Rodán's den. Well, whatever T was, he certainly wasn't some distant relation to Fae or Elves. Not that I'd even considered that notion. His race was noisy as a troll pounding its club against a rock wall.

Rodán's den was much smaller than his entertaining chamber, and smelled of earth and wisteria. I took my hand from Rodán's and placed my fingers on a cool earthen wall, then touched one of the purple-leaved plants crawling over the earth along with patches of moss.

It was in the moments I was in this room that a bit of homesickness always clenched inside me. It reminded me of the underground realm of the Dark Elves, my home.

My other home.

Rodán's desk was huge and spotless. No sticky notes there. Maybe he had sticky notes in his brain. He forgot nothing. I slipped into one of the chairs in front of the desk, as did T. For a moment I lowered my head, thinking about Jon as he'd been earlier this same night, before he'd been slaughtered.

Seeing what the Demons had done to other paranorms had been beyond sickening. But a fellow Tracker seemed worse. It brought everything closer to home and made me realize how vulnerable we all were. We weren't invincible, as I'd let myself believe.

I raised my head and pushed my blue hair out of my eyes with both hands so that it fell straight past my shoulders again.

When he looked at me, Rodán's expression and tone were gentle. "We have a lot to discuss."

It was easier to stare Rodán down and be angry at T and his arrogance than to think about Jon. "Discuss? Like who in the Underworlds he is?" I said as I looked at T. "Or maybe what *it* is?"

T narrowed his brows and scowled.

"Well?" I said.

"Torin is here to help fight these Demons, Nyx," Rodán said, and I turned back to him.

"That doesn't answer my question."

Rodán leaned back in his chair. "Torin came highly recommended by the Proctor who serves Staten Island and the other nearby islands."

My brows narrowed. "Krishna sent this *thing* to help?"

He nodded.

I heard a low growl coming from T.

Okay, so I was being cranky. I think I had the right to be. "And she didn't tell you what *it* is?"

Another growl.

"Our problem is too serious for this topic." Rodán looked at T before his gaze rested on me. "The three of us have a lot to discuss."

I bit my tongue to keep from saying anything about this mystery man-thing next to me that even Rodán didn't seem to know a lot about.

"The pair of you will work together on this." Rodán studied me intently. Before I could interrupt, he continued, "As I informed you this morning, the Great Guardian believes beings other than these underling Demons entered when they murdered the Gatekeeper of the Ruhin Demon Gate.

"At the very least two or three major Demons." Rodán paused and let his words sink in. "And most likely a master Demon as well."

My skin chilled and I rubbed my hands on my bare arms. "This morning you did say these are underling Demons we've been fighting, but you didn't mention that major and master Demons made it through the gate, too."

"I needed to speak with the Guardian again."

Rodán tapped his index finger on his desk as he continued. "That's why these underling Demons were able to come through so fast, the moment the Gatekeeper, Mary, was killed, before Megan could replace her."

"That makes sense." The replacement should have been instantaneous, with no time for any being to cross the threshold of the Demon gate. "I suppose."

Rodán sighed. "At least one Demon with powerful magic had to have transported them through after orchestrating a plan to kill one of our most powerful Peacekeepers." He made a frustrated sound. "Whatever it is or they are, the Demons have proven to be extremely dangerous."

If I was in the mood to be sarcastic, I'd have said something like "duh." Of course it would have been stronger in the language of the Drow, despite the fact that Rodán would understand every word.

"That is one reason why Torin will be working your territory with you," Rodán said.

I gripped the armrests of my chair and bit down hard on the inside of my cheek to keep from arguing more. I knew it wouldn't do a Goddess-blessed thing if I did.

"We," Rodán continued, "meaning the Great Guardian and I, believe the Demons' lair is in your section of the city."

I frowned. "What makes you think that?"

"The majority of the Demon populace spreads from your territory to the others," Rodán said.

I churned that piece of information over in my

mind before I spoke. "That's why I usually see so much more action than any one other Tracker." The injuries that I thought had healed hurt my head and back as I tensed while Rodán's words sank in. "But that doesn't make total sense, because I should have been the first attacked instead of Jon."

"I think they sense what a danger you, in particular, are to them," he said.

"Me?" My brows narrowed and I knew the look on my face was one of disbelief. "Every single Tracker is equally powerful. We just have different skills."

"We believe it's *your* skills that will do the most harm to the Demons." Rodán gestured to T. "That's why you now have additional backup."

I clenched the arms of my chair. "Which skills?"

"Your power over the elements," Rodán said.

"That—that doesn't make sense." I gestured above us, like I was pointing to the other Trackers. "Their skills are equally effective."

"Yes, they have the ability to handle multiple beings," Rodán said. "Jon should have been able to kill six of the Demons. But he *didn't*. No one has faced as many as he did. And you were the one who survived."

"Jon probably wore them down," I said, although I hadn't seen any sign of a fight or other Demon remains.

"Face it, Princess," T said in a low, lazy drawl. "You're going to be graced with my presence for a while."

When I'm ticked I can be a real smartass, but

before I could make some kind of remark to T, Rodán said, "Your mission is to find the Demon lair. That's why I need Torin to work with you." By Rodán's expression and the very air of command that was around him, I knew I was stuck with this T guy. I was facing a battle I wouldn't win. For now.

"What do you think this Demon is trying to accomplish?" I said as I thought about the assignment.

Rodán's expression was hard to gauge. "We're not positive because we don't know what master Demon escaped through the gate."

"Aren't there records or something that each Gatekeeper holds onto?" I said. "Shouldn't we have copies of those records?"

"We should." Rodán gave a slow nod. "But we don't."

"Nothing?" I knew incredulity flashed in my gaze. "How is that possible?"

"Gatekeepers have been tending the Demon gates for centuries upon centuries," Rodán said. "In some cases, either records were not adequately kept or were lost before they were copied for our archives. This is one of those cases."

This Demon control was all going smooth as silk. Not. "What's the next step?"

Rodán's green eyes darkened. "We have a new 'problem' that may or may not be related."

The Dryad's wood was smooth beneath my hands as I grasped the armrests and leaned forward in my chair. "What's happened?"

"A human law enforcement officer's family has

been murdered by a Demon. The police officer is missing, and he was a liaison."

"A human liaison to the paranorm?" A chill went through me and I immediately thought of Adam Boyd. But Adam had no family so I breathed a sigh of relief. I felt a tremendous concern and ache for the missing liaison and his murdered family members. "How do we know the officer was taken, and not eaten or shredded?"

"We don't. That's what we have to find out," Rodán said. "Since the officer was one of our liaisons I need you and Olivia. You're the best we have."

That was the truth—we were the best. He wasn't just sweet-talking me. "Olivia and I will handle it."

"And Torin," Rodán said. "You'll make him part of your daytime firm, too."

"Goddess, please stop doing this to me, Rodán." I glanced at the stony-faced male next to me before looking at my mentor again. "Nighttime is bad enough. Olivia and I have a hundred percent record of solving cases. Without any other paranorm."

"A Soothsayer froze and put a glamour on the crime scene thirty minutes ago." Rodán obviously wasn't going to budge as he ignored my comment. Freezing and using a glamour with a crime scene was standard procedure when paranormal activity was involved. "Get there as soon as the sun rises, once you transform."

He gave me the address, which was close to 109th Street and Madison.

"That's near Frawley Circle, where I battled the

Demons last night." I felt my features tighten. "No way are these Demons going to get away with what they've been doing to paranorms." And what they did to Jon.

I ground my teeth as I added, "We'll do whatever it takes to destroy every last Demon."

CHAPTER 7

Olivia, T, and I arrived at almost the same time in the Upper East Side neighborhood where the NYPD officer's family had been murdered. We parked a distance from the home—couldn't get any closer due to the large number of emergency vehicles.

At least four police cruisers, three ambulances, a fire truck, and two unmarked vehicles had arrived at the scene. Standing outside the fringes of the crime scene tape and police barricades were neighbors, most still in their bathrobes.

Everyone and everything was motionless. Frozen.

Thanks to a Soothsayer's power to control air and the minute water particles in it, the moment an onlooker happened by, that person instantly "froze," too. The Soothsayer also would use an air spell to put a glamour over the entire block.

Of course, the spells excluded paranorms and a few norms like Olivia.

A strange scent came from the house and I grimaced as Olivia, T, and I walked toward the scene. Burned flesh and the additional sickly sweet scent of burned sugar.

I'd seen dead bodies before. Lots of them. But with

each step I took, my back and arms felt tighter. I had to bite my bottom lip to hold back a powerful retch.

There was more here than dead bodies. Something else. Something . . .

Evil?

I shivered as I walked. I tried to remind myself that there was no such division as good and evil. Only dark and light, and all the shades in between—but that was my Drow mind talking. The human part of me definitely wanted to scream and run away from this place.

Crime scene tape remained as motionless as the people. We made it to the front door of the home after dodging our way through motionless NYPD officers, an FDNY response unit, paramedics, and continued on past crime scene investigators, including a photographer and a sketch artist. Our Soothsayer would have to take care of them later, when she wiped their memories of the paranormal parts of the crimes.

The lurch of my heart was no less painful than the churning in the pit of my belly when I saw four body bags outside the home, two of the bags small.

The moment I entered the home, the stench hit me even harder—along with a sick, slithering feeling of something wrong, something unnatural and more terrible than I could put into words.

The smells and sensations were absurdly followed by the Soothsayer's gardenia scent, along with a hint of vanilla candles that must have been lit when the humans were attacked.

Olivia came up beside me. "Here comes Tinker-bell."

Great, the Soothsayer standing away from a chalk outline was Lulu, and she flexed her fingers at the sight of me and Olivia.

I was so not in the mood to be frozen. But I'm sure Lulu wasn't in the mood to be tracked down afterward and face my fist.

All Soothsayers were Doppler, and Lulu's form was a Manx cat with a bobbed tail. Funny as hell, but she still should have been a rat instead.

When Lulu saw T, her manner changed completely, and she turned her petite nose away from Olivia and me.

Olivia smirked when she met my gaze. "Oh, brother."

Lulu smiled and practically drifted over to T like the air carried her on a royal carpet. The beautiful beyond beautiful Soothsayer wore her hair in golden ringlets and had on a frilly, long, iridescent dress (give me a break) that made her look like a Disney fairy princess.

"I'm Lulu." She actually fluttered her eyelashes. "Who might you be?"

I tried not to roll my eyes. Honestly. But I couldn't help it.

Score one for T because he didn't fall all over herself to introduce himself. He gave a simple nod. "Torin."

Lulu raised her chin and immediately had a miffed expression. No doubt because T hadn't referred to her as "my lady" and bowed, or showed any other formalities to please her enormous ego.

I looked around what was apparently the living

room. Experts had been dusting for fingerprints while other police officers were obviously searching for clues.

And there was Adam, frozen in a crouch, his back to me, his muscles tight, radiating a bleak, gut-tearing energy I had never felt from him before.

Immediately my heart started pounding, from excitement at the sight of him, but right now more from worry. I left T and Olivia behind and went to Adam and crouched beside him.

He wouldn't know I was there until I touched him, but I could see in his deep brown eyes pain that made my chest ache.

His expression told me everything I needed to know.

These were his people, a cop's family. He was taking this as personally as I took the death of a fellow Tracker. Seeing these innocent people slaughtered was as bad for Adam as me watching Demons demolish what was left of Jon.

I braced one knee on the polished wood floor and touched the sleeve of Adam's worn leather bomber jacket, unfreezing him. "Adam," I whispered, overcome by his sadness.

"This blue looks like fresh paint—" Adam stopped and glanced at me. "Nyx."

He seemed both pleased to see me and angry at what had happened. I gave him a sad smile.

Adam moved his gaze to the man on the other side of him, who was still frozen. "Christ, I wish your Soothsayers wouldn't do this freezing sh—crap. It makes everything harder."

When he shifted his weight from one knee to the other, I caught his leather, coffee, and masculine scent, and wanted to wrap my arms around him. I leaned closer so that I could breathe more of him in, and hoped that he might take comfort from my presence.

He looked around and saw Lulu, who had her hands on her hips. Humans were the lowest of creatures as far as she was concerned.

"Oh, lighten up," Olivia said, moving away from T and intercepting Lulu before she could fire any smart remarks—or nasty spells—in Adam's direction. "Finding lipstick on your teeth is about the only thing worse than being sent on paranormal cases involving humans, isn't it, *Lu-lu*?"

Olivia emphasized the name as she pushed aside her Mets sweat jacket to rest her hand near her Sig.

The slogan on Olivia's navy blue T-shirt said it all:

> *People like you are the reason*
> *People like me need medication.*

Lulu's voice snapped like one of those firecrackers kids toss around during the norms' Fourth of July celebration. "Hurry and do *whatever* so that I might leave this Goddess-forsaken place."

She looked away, her nose in the air, and Adam and I glanced at each other, both of us trying to hide a laugh.

While Olivia started her part of the investigation, T came up and crouched on the other side of me. I worked to keep my attention fully on Adam to let him know I was there for him, that I understood how bad this kind of thing felt.

A few moments later, I felt T's awareness move to Adam, too, and Adam's turned to T.

"Boyd." Adam got to his feet and held out his hand to T.

"Torin." With a slight nod, T stood at the same time I did. He reached across me and shook hands with Adam.

"Definitely a paranormal crime," Adam said to me after he and T released their grips. "You won't believe some of the shit we found." He gestured toward what I knew wasn't paint, but blue blood. "This isn't the half of it. Think it could be those Demons you were telling me about?"

I took a good look around me. "I don't think that underling Demons could possibly do this."

"Why not?" Adam said.

"After fighting the underling Demons for a while, I just can't picture it." The total destruction of the home was almost overwhelming. "The power it would have taken to do this was as if a cyclone was contained within this house.

"Could be the major or master Demons Rodán told you about." I gripped my Dolce & Gabbana purse as I continued. "No one knows what they're capable of. Yet."

I made an absentminded sound of acknowledgment as I caught sight of more blue spots. They were on the carpet that lay over a portion of the wood floor. "The Demons do have blue blood, and there are more scattered droplets." I pointed. "Right there."

"Looks like paint," Adam said as we walked toward the spots of blue that hadn't fully dried.

"It's possible the major Demons or master Demon also have that same color of blood," T said.

"Did your Proctor tell you anything?" Adam cleared his throat. "Do you think Officer Crisman was, uh, eaten or something?"

"It *is* possible but we really don't know," I said. "Hopefully we'll find more clues than this blue stuff."

Somewhere in my purse was my XPhone, where I kept my notes on every case. I dug through my purse and came up with it. Adam watched me as I jotted down a few notes with the stylus.

I looked up at Adam. My human half didn't like to ask these kinds of questions. "Were the bodies mutilated?"

It was obvious to me that Adam was trying to keep his professional cop-cool. "Their faces are—hell, I don't know what you'd call it. Mutilated and burned off would be the closest thing I can come up with."

"Goddess." I glanced to T, who frowned. I moved my gaze back to Adam's. "That's definitely not underling Demon behavior."

T shook his head in a slight movement, his frown deepening. "Impossible."

"So you think we're probably dealing with another type of Demon or Demons," Adam said.

"Right now the only thing I know for sure is that

a Tracker and a human law enforcement officer were attacked the same night, in the same vicinity." I didn't want to ask, but I had to. "May I see one of the bodies?"

Adam studied me. "They're pretty bad."

"I need to get a look at them." I rubbed my fingers lightly over my Drow collar, which always gave me a burst of strength and confidence. "Olivia and I need to." I glanced at T. "Oh, and him, too."

T scowled.

Adam started toward the body bags. "I know you've seen some pretty crappy things, Nyx, but this—like I said, it's bad."

"Stop babying her," Olivia said as she came toward us with her XPhone and stylus gripped tight. "She needs toughening up."

As if.

Adam nodded and I walked beside him to the largest of the bags. "From the ID we found in the house, apparently this is the grandfather."

He inched down the zipper. A very much human gag reflex came over me as I breathed in the even stronger smell of burned sugar and flesh.

And saw the face—or what was left of the man's face.

It wasn't like the flesh had been seared. No part of the skull was exposed. Instead it was like something had taken a big stamp and flattened the flesh, so that it was as if the face was a wax blob and not human.

A shock went through my elemental energies, nearly stealing from me my ability to breathe. The haze in my mind was like I'd drained nearly all of my powers.

"Holy shit," Olivia said.

T grunted.

My Drow half was screaming for me to draw blades at the sight. I could hardly keep my own cool.

"Do you need to leave?" T said in an arrogant tone.

"Go fuck yourself," I said in a voice so harsh it didn't sound like my own. The words weren't even my own. They were deeper, more primal, as each sensation hit me.

"Nyx." Olivia's voice came through the haze in my mind. "What are you sensing?"

"I don't know." I swallowed down the desire to vomit, scream, and run like I've never run before.

"I think we'd better get you out of here." The concern in Adam's voice was unmistakable and protective. It was so different from T's asinine tone.

Even though I felt my energies draining, I forced myself to study the face. I had to be professional. But all I wanted to do was flee.

Calm down. *Calm down, Nyx.*

I scanned the horrific image. It took a moment, but then I made it out. A pattern had been "stamped" into the flesh.

"What the hell is that?" Olivia said, but like Adam maintained *her* professional cop-cool.

My gaze traced the strange lines and whorls. I couldn't speak.

T stood. "Let's see the others."

I looked at Adam and, even though all of my muscles felt weak, I managed to talk. "Believe me, it's the last thing I want to do."

He paused. Nodded. "Okay," he said quietly.

Olivia, T, and I checked the other bodies, and each time the human half of me wanted to throw up. Only my Drow half kept me from losing it.

Each face had the same symbol distorting the darkened flesh. A sort of cone or funnel. The symbol was like nothing I'd ever seen.

Pretending that the horrible images I was looking at were just on wax dummies and not on real people, I used my XPhone to photograph the faces.

Just in case the symbol wouldn't photograph well, like the Demon had put some kind of sick spell on the faces, I used the stylus on a blank screen to copy the pattern. My artistry isn't the best and I could barely keep my hand from shaking as I did it, but I managed a fair rendering.

I started to get up, but what T did next brought me to a complete halt. With slow purpose, he moved his hand over the face of the fourth victim. The nightmarish look of the face vanished and was replaced by the face of a sleeping child. The bad energy vanished around the child's body. She'd been dressed in pajamas. Hopefully she'd been asleep and hadn't woken when it all happened.

I held my hand to my mouth. As I looked at that small, angelic-looking girl I would have cried if I could. Whatever T had done made it all the more real.

"Maybe he'll be useful after all," Olivia said.

I watched as T did the same to the other three faces

so that they looked normal and human, and peaceful with their eyes closed.

Even the odor of charred flesh had vanished. Only the smell of burned sugar remained. I no longer felt a hint of the darkness remaining in the bodies, and my own energy started to flow back into me.

I stared at T for a moment when he was finished. "How did you do that?"

He studied the room. "We should start looking for clues."

Adam and I exchanged looks.

"Thank you," Adam said to T. "It would have been pretty damned bad for their extended families to see them that way."

I nodded. It was hard enough having the images burned into my own mind.

People were still frozen around us and we had to dodge police officers and others as we searched for any kind of clues. I walked slowly around the house, checking each room and looking around furniture.

Then I found it.

"Hey." I stared at the same image that had been on the faces, but it was much clearer on the wood floor of the dining room. It looked like it had been lasered into the wood, then painted with blood. Smelled like it, too. "Get over here."

They reached my side at almost the same time. Adam whistled through his teeth as T and Olivia crouched beside the symbol. I took a few pictures with my XPhone.

I lowered myself so that one of my knees was on the floor. I used my thigh to brace the pad so that

I could do my best to sketch the symbol again, this time a lot more clearly and with more detail—at least the best I could with my limited artistic talents.

The symbol started with a flat, bumpy surface. It spiraled down, like a cone, but was jagged and uneven in what looked like layers.

"What does this thing mean?" Adam crouched beside me so that all four of us were down, examining the strange symbol.

"Not sure." I shook my head. "I'll have to check with my Proctor to see if he has any idea. Derek, James's partner, is an occult expert. I'll scan and e-mail the image to Derek right away."

I could see Olivia's mind working overtime as she appraised the symbol. "We'll do an Internet search to see if we come up with a match."

"We can check a few symbol books, too," I said. "I have some, and Rodán has a good-sized library. Then there's always the public library."

"Sure." Olivia smirked. "Good ol' New York Public Library. I'm sure it's up to date on the latest Demons that escape through well-guarded Demon Gates."

T's voice came from my other side. "We have more on our hands than random acts by a rogue Demon."

A chill ran through me, even though I'd been thinking the same thing. All I could do was nod.

Adam's expression went from his usual calm to furious. "I'm going to get the fucking sonofabitch who did this to the kids, whatever it is."

The fire in his eyes and the fact that he'd forgotten to watch his language in front of me like he normally did gave me a pretty good idea of just how angry he was. And how angry he'd keep being until we shut down the creature or creatures who committed these atrocities.

"I think this Demon is taunting us with this clue," I said as I stuffed my XPhone into my purse.

T's strong features seemed strangely impassive. "It wants to let us know what it can do. And maybe that it can't be stopped."

With her brows narrowed and her lips twisted into a frown, Olivia got to her feet. "We'll find the sicko, whatever this Demon is, and it won't have time to wish it could go home to Mommy."

Adam had clear meaning in his eyes when he met my gaze. "I'm not letting the sonofabitch get away with this."

He had so much courage and determination to fight whatever paranormal creature was evil and involved humans. And he was a mere human himself.

He'd helped me solve paranormal crimes against humans, but I'd never given him the chance to eliminate the threats. With my Drow abilities, I always managed to slip away from him and take care of business myself, at night. Vampires, Brownies, a rogue Werepack, Metamorphs. Because all of the cases had been so easy for me and Olivia to eliminate, there had been no need for additional backup—human or paranorm.

Not to mention that I hadn't been ready for Adam

to see the other half of me. The dark half. The half that came out only when the sun slipped away and darkness took hold.

But soon. It was time to let him see all of me.

Each time I'd taken care of a paranormal crime myself, Adam had made it clear he wasn't happy about it. He believed that he should be with me, taking down whatever being had committed the crime. But he really had no idea what he was asking. He was a brave human and I didn't want him to get hurt.

This time I wasn't sure I could stop him from avenging these deaths. If I tried, he would probably never forgive me. But we were dealing with a Demon. What looked like a powerful Demon. A master Demon.

A gut feeling told me this Demon was playing with us, and that a timer had started to count down. *Tick. Tick. Tick.*

The Demon had given us a bizarre symbol that we had to decipher.

Before we ran out of time.

CHAPTER 8

Rodán was "entertaining" a couple of females when I stopped by the Pit to give the report. By their dainty sizes and the points of their ears, they were clearly from one of the many Fae races.

"Nymphs this time?" I said to Rodán as he finished tying his short, dark green robe and walked toward me.

"Nyx." Pleasure was in Rodán's voice. "Have you come to join us?" His lips had twisted in a smile. He knew my answer to that. I'd always insisted on sex with Rodán just being the two of us, despite his teasing that we should add spice one day. No thanks. "Would you like me to send them away and join me?"

By now I was used to seeing naked beings in his bed, so I didn't feel any embarrassment and no jealousy. I smiled, and it was genuine. "You're made to share your lovemaking talents with others, not with just one female or male."

He took my hands and kissed my knuckles. "If you weren't infatuated with that human, I would gladly spend as much time as possible in bed with you." I would have thought his expression was serious if I believed him when he said softly, "And out of bed, too."

Rodán's words, and his lips on my skin, always tingled throughout me. He wasn't serious, of course. I looked at the naked female Nymphs who squirmed in the large bed that took up quite a bit of the enormous room. The females ignored me as they moved sinuously on the bed. Soft but urgent moans came from the Nymphs.

"That'll be the day you'd settle for me alone," I said when I brought my gaze back to his. "You'd get bored."

"Never." Rodán gave a soft laugh and brushed my black hair from my cheeks. He kissed me softly on the lips like the friend and lover he was before taking me by the hand and leading me toward his office.

"At least the females aren't chained to the wall, or bent over a flogging bench while they beg to be spanked," I said in a dry tone. I'd reported to Rodán enough times to have seen him in just about every erotic act possible—at least I thought so.

"But you're Drow," he said, teasing me as always.

"Save the bondage for full female Dark Elves who get into it, and any Fae you can convince." I shook my head. "Not me, no thank you."

"Where's Torin?" he asked as he led me down the steps to his office.

"I ditched him." When we reached the earthen room, Rodán let go of my hand and I seated myself in a chair close to his. "Along with Lulu, T was going to each officer and paramedic, touching their thoughts and erasing memories when I slipped away." I wasn't sure if Lulu was happy to have help, or irritated that T was stepping in on her territory.

I was rather pleased with myself for getting rid of T for now. I felt bad about not saying good-bye to Adam, but putting some space between me and that arrogant male—T, not Adam—was more important.

Changing people's memories—in most cases only Soothsayers had that talent. I could do it with my air element, but it was draining, so I used the power infrequently, and to conscious beings only.

Rodán raised his brows. "So Torin has that talent as well."

"You didn't know?" I set my handbag by the chair and frowned. "What *do* you know about him?"

Rodán looked thoughtful. "I trust Krishna and her judgment."

"I'm not so sure I like that explanation."

He studied me, quiet for a moment. "It's the best I can give you right now."

"You, I trust." I definitely didn't like his answer, but he was Rodán. "So we'll leave it at that for now."

"What did you find out?"

As I thought of the horrors of what the Demon or Demons had done to that family, I tried to let the wisteria and earthy scents of the room calm me. I breathed deep and released a slow exhalation.

My stomach lurched, but I managed to keep a semblance of control as I talked about the murdered children, mother, and grandfather. The smells, the condition of the house, the blue splatters that could have been Demon blood.

When I finished, I turned the conversation to the strangeness with T. The way he had made the dead family look whole and normal again at the officer's house was just unfathomable. I wasn't even sure our Healers could do that.

Then I told Rodán about the black/orange fire that had burst from T's palm to incinerate the dead Demons that had killed Jon.

Rodán focused on me until I finished and then he said, "Interesting."

"What being could do all of these things without me knowing it exists?" I asked. "Were you aware before Krishna sent him to you?"

Rodán looked calm and beautiful as ever, his long white-blond hair shining in the soft office lighting, the tips of his pointed ears visible through the strands. Normally I would want to touch his golden skin. To feel him inside me.

But now, with Adam often occupying my thoughts, it didn't seem right to continue a sexual relationship with Rodán.

"No." Rodán sighed. "I don't know what he is."

The calm that had spread over me vanished. "Rodán—"

He held up his hand. "I've been trying to contact Krishna, but she's been busy with the Great Guardian."

"If only the GG would impart some of her 'wisdom' and wasn't such a—"

Before I could finish, Rodán said, "*Nyx*. You like your life in this world, don't you?"

"Yeah, you're right." The GG could zap me back to Otherworld before I could say, "Kiss my amethyst ass."

Rodán was good at guiding subjects away from dangerous territory.

"The human you're so fond of, Detective Boyd," he said with a truly concerned expression. "How is he?"

"Taking it pretty hard." I pictured how angry he'd been. "He's determined to get revenge, and not allow me to get in his way."

"Let him," Rodán said. "Be there with him, but don't shield him any longer."

"But he could get hurt." I clenched my hands in my lap. "Killed."

"You care a lot for him." Rodán smiled. "When will you take him to your bed?"

I ducked my head, my cheeks warm. We'd never talked about Adam in this way before. I looked at Rodán again. "I'm afraid of what he'll think when he finds out who and what I am."

Rodán shook his head slightly. "You don't give this detective enough credit."

"I know you're right. But—"

"You're still afraid."

I looked into Rodán's lovely green eyes. "Yes."

"This human won't hurt you."

"How do you know?"

"I have . . . abilities." Rodán was close enough that he could reach up and stroke my cheek with his knuckles. "I'm more concerned about you hurting him."

"What?" My eyes widened. "I wouldn't hurt Adam for anything."

"I could only sense it," Rodán said as he brushed my black hair over my shoulder. "I don't know how it might happen. But I want you to be aware."

"I won't hurt him," I whispered. "I'd never hurt him."

"Not intentionally, sweets." He let his fingers drift down the side of my neck. Not like a lover, but like a caring friend who wanted to soothe me. "Just take care."

My tongue was suddenly too thick to say anything at all. Hurt Adam? Never.

Rodán helped me find my words again when he said, "Tell me what else you have."

My fingers shook I drew my XPhone out of my purse.

Adam? Me, hurt Adam?

Never.

First thing, I tried to cue up one of the photos I'd taken.

"Bless it." I made a frustrated sound. "I wondered if the paranormal energy might keep the images from being photographed, and sure enough those came out blank."

I touched another tab on the gel screen. "Two positives, though. First of all, the energy didn't fry my XPhone. Secondly, here's my hand-sketched version, along with my notes." I handed the pad to Rodán. "It's not great, but hopefully it's close enough.

"The symbol burned into the wood was very detailed," I said. "Since I'm not an artist, I wasn't able to really capture every nuance of the symbol." I leaned forward. "I don't get it. A tornado? Or earth spiraling down in a cone?"

Rodán studied the drawing a little longer.

I gestured to the XPhone. "Do you have any idea what Demon made this mark, how powerful the Demon is, or even what the symbol says?"

"No to all of your questions." Rodán pushed his long hair behind his pointed ears as he frowned even more.

My heart dropped and I ran my fingers over my choker, feeling the lines of every hidden rune. "I need to borrow your books on symbols, and anything else that might be of use."

Rodán helped me gather five dusty tomes and I sneezed. A cloud of dust hit me straight in the face and I sneezed again. No, Dark Elves don't sneeze, but I'm half human. Nothing like a nose full of old dust.

I held the pile of heavy books as I stood by my chair. Rodán handed me my purse after he dropped my XPhone of it inside.

My grip tightened on my purse while I balanced the books in my arms. "I don't suppose the GG would deign to help by giving us more Trackers."

Rodán tipped his head toward me, giving an expression that said, "As if."

"Why not?" I couldn't help the bite in my words. "The Guardian's riddles and her refusal to give us any real help drives me out of my mind."

"You know she doesn't interfere." Rodán actually looked irritated himself, but the expression vanished. "She's given us what she can."

"You mean she gives us what she chooses to let us know." I tried to tone down the anger in my tone. "Yeah, yeah," I grumbled. "Not interfering in worlds and all that crap." I don't know why I'd even bothered to ask. I'd already known the answer.

Rodán spread his hands and looked up at the ceiling as if begging the GG to forgive me.

I knew he was teasing, but I still said, "Save it."

Rodán stopped me before I could go up the stairs. He cupped my face in his hands and put his forehead against mine, the books pressed between us. "Don't leave angry."

"I'm not mad at you." I tilted my face up when he raised his head. "I'm just frustrated. I don't understand why we can't know more. Why we can't get more Trackers. I'm sure we can find some really kick-ass paranorms. Like Shadow Shifters," I said. "Can you imagine what kind of Tracker they would make? Nothing could stop them once they're trained."

"They have their own weaknesses, like Shifters do," he said, and I raised my eyebrows. "But any Shifter weakness is not for me to say."

"Sometimes you're as bad as the GG," I said, but I smiled.

He kissed me lightly before letting me go.

CHAPTER 9

The moment I walked into my office, the scent of wisteria hit my senses.

Uh-oh.

"What took you so long?" Olivia looked up from a folder on the desk next to her computer screen. "A little midday recreation with Elves?"

"What's with the wisteria?" It was a scent that had a calming effect on Dark Elves—which was why Rodán kept it in his office, I'm sure. But when Olivia put it out . . . it usually meant something was up.

"Just thought you might be a little worked up over today."

Uh-huh.

Bet *someone* had another agenda.

Olivia kicked back, her feet on her desk. She wore a pair of yellow Keds that, as usual, matched her shirt, which was mostly hidden beneath her Mets jacket. The soles of her Keds were dirty from the city streets, the toes of the shoes had a few scuff marks, and the left heel was worn down more than the right.

She'd changed clothes after visiting the crime scene this morning, something she always did, like she was trying to get the stench and feel of death off of her body.

I set the stack of books Rodán had loaned me on the credenza next to my desk. Blue Persian hair was caught on the edge of a stack of file folders. Kali must be here somewhere. I had no idea how the cat traveled from my apartment to the office and back. Of course, even if she had the ability to tell me, she wouldn't have. The snot.

What Rodán had said to me about hurting Adam was something I couldn't get out of my mind. I'd never hurt Adam. Never. How could Rodán think I'd ever do that?

My head felt thick, as if it was packed with Kali's blue hair, as I slowly sat in my seat behind my desk. Hurt Adam? The mere idea made my stomach churn.

Olivia uncrossed her ankles and braced one foot on the edge of her desk. Good thing there was no way to damage, even scrape, Dryad wood furniture. "Does Rodán know what that symbol is?"

I blinked and let what she had said process in my mind before I shook my head. "No clue."

"Hell, if Rodán doesn't know what that symbol is," Olivia said, "I'm sure not getting any warm fuzzies."

"Mmmm-hmm." I reached into my Dolce & Gabbana and found my XPhone. I scanned my drawings of the symbol, then used the stylus to send the drawings to the computer's hard drive and to the printer. "Did you sketch the symbol?" I asked as I snatched my copies from my small desktop printer.

Her feet were back on the floor and she was looking at her XPhone. "Printing now." Olivia's printer silently spit out a piece of paper.

We each looked at our own renderings before reaching across the space between our desks and swapping.

"Yours is better." She pored over my two drawings. "Well, the one that doesn't suck."

"The sucky one is from the victims' faces." I couldn't help a shudder. "The other is from the symbol burned into the floor." I studied her version. "You're right, my drawings are better. And that's not saying a lot."

"Bitch," she said.

I grinned. You had to be good friends to call each other names and not take offense, because you know your friend meant it in the *kindest* way.

"I'll shoot my much better drawing to Derek to see what he has to say."

"Mighty convenient that James's husband is an occult expert," Olivia said. "Maybe *he's* a Demon."

"You never know." I prepared a quick note and attached a copy of the drawing to Derek's e-mail address. There. I pressed send and it was off. "Sometimes I think *you* are a Demon."

"That's because I am." She gave me her best wicked look and evil snarl.

"True." I tried not to laugh. "I've never had a doubt."

When I'd first seen Olivia, I'd been one with the shadows, as usual. But I'd watched and didn't interfere because she looked like she had a handle on a Sprite, and I was curious.

She'd just finished kicking the crap out of the Sprite using martial arts, while shouting several appropriate words (I thought) at the same time.

In that moment I knew I wanted to work with her. I'd been keeping an eye out for someone to ask to be a partner in my firm, and my instincts told me she was the one. Despite the fact that she was wearing a Mets sweat jacket over a T-shirt, I'd sensed Olivia was with the NYPD. Also that she was one hundred percent human.

But she was the right one. I *knew* it.

I just had to convince her.

Olivia had pinned the Sprite up against a brick wall, her Sig Sauer pressed to his temple, her hand around his throat. Sprites are ugly things. Big heads, hooked noses, lots of nose and ear hair along with protuberant, glassy blue eyes, and ears you could swing dinner plates from.

"Don't fuck with me, you Halloween reject," she'd said in a growl. "Tell me what happened to the girl you were just attacking."

The girl who'd escaped had been a Doppler. I'd watched her morph into a kitten that scampered away the instant she'd had the chance.

The Were came out of a shadowy corner behind the Dumpster and it was time for me to rock. I'd known he was hidden there, just waiting for the right time. As for me, I'd wanted to see how the cop handled the Sprite before I stepped in.

Werewolves in full-moon form stand upright, are at least seven feet tall, have muscles most men would kill for, but have extremely hairy faces and tails.

Yeah, tails. Dagger-sharp claws are on their feet as well as their hands.

If it hadn't been a full moon, the Were would simply be a wolf when not human.

"I don't think so," I said to the Were as I appeared from the darkness, my dragon-claw dagger ready to swing. "At least, not if you like the way your head and neck look on your shoulders."

The Were growled, a deep earth-moving sound.

Olivia had gone still, but she was a pro. The Sprite gurgled as she increased her hold on his neck. She cocked the Sig before she looked behind her and saw me with my dagger at the Were's throat.

She only spared me a glance before focusing completely on the Sprite. "Nice hair," she said.

"Don't let go of the Sprite." I kept my attention on Olivia, the Sprite, and the Were. "I mean, don't let go of the guy. He's an expert at escaping any kind of containment. Your handcuffs won't work. Keep your grip and your Sig on him until I take care of the Were—this ass."

"What the fuck?" she said. A cop through and through.

"Just listen to me," I said. "I've taken down piles of trollshit like these before."

"Uh, trollshit?" she said.

The Sprite tried to move and she slammed his head up against the wall. Hard.

I liked her.

"Just hold," I said to Olivia. The Were growled and clenched and unclenched his sharp-clawed fists at his sides. "Either you stand real still and wait for the PTF, or you won't be barking at the next full moon."

"You don't have the guts, female," he growled, and stepped back.

I moved with him and pressed the weapon's blade against the Were's Adam's apple until droplets of blood dripped onto the Drow steel.

"Trackers don't give a shit about scum like you." At the mention of the word "Tracker" he went still. "And I'm no exception."

"Fuck," he said in his reverberating growl, and looked totally pissed at being in a position he now knew he couldn't win.

"No thank you." I kept the blade steady as I moved one hand from the hilt to my belt, where I drew out my XPhone.

Without looking I pressed speed dial for the PTF. I didn't have to say anything to them. They had my position the moment I'd dialed in. After notifying the Paranorm Task Force, I put my XPhone back in its clip. The PTF would arrive in no time at all.

"Hey, Blue Hair," Olivia said to me. "Why don't you fill me in on what the hell is going on."

"I will as soon as the PTF takes care of these two." I never took my eyes or blade off the Were as I heard the sound of PTF sirens that could only be heard by paranorms.

"Bullshit," she said. "The NYPD will be on their asses as soon as I make the call."

"You won't have time," I said. "These two are about to be put into a cell that will hold them. Human jails won't work."

"*Human* jails?" She looked amused. "Sweetheart, we've got to talk. I'm off duty as soon as we finish up." Olivia scowled at the Sprite when he tried to wriggle, and she slammed his head against the wall again. "There's a coffee shop—"

I burst out laughing. "Me, with blue hair and amethyst skin going into a coffee shop at midnight?"

"This *is* New York City," she said.

"Have to give you that one."

After the PTF officers took the Sprite away in magically treated handcuffs, along with the Were at gunpoint—including a tranquilizer gun—it was just me and Olivia.

We faced one another.

"*Avanna*," I said, and the blood disappeared from my dagger before I sheathed my weapon. She narrowed her eyes. "Why don't we order in pizza at my office," I said, "and I'll fill you in."

She slowly holstered her Sig. "What kind of office?"

"I'm also a PI," I said.

She snorted. "A purple PI."

"Amethyst." I started out of the alleyway and she fell into step with me. "And during the day I look human."

"Uh-huh . . ."

Considering how hard-boiled she'd seemed, it surprised me that she agreed to go with me to my office.

Turned out we both had a thing for Hawaiian pizza—Canadian bacon, double mozzarella, with extra pineapple chunks on top. We were meant for each other.

She took off her sweat jacket and tossed it on the empty desk (soon to be hers if I did a good job of convincing her). She had her Sig in a shoulder holster and, for the first time, I saw her black T-shirt.

> *Come to the Dark Side.*
> *We have chocolate.*

I took that as a good sign.

After we stuffed ourselves with pizza I explained what I did as a PI and about the paranormal world, the best I could. She listened, then said, "You are so full of shit."

"Hellooo." I held out my arm. "An amethyst woman with blue hair is telling you this."

She reached out and scraped her short nails over my arm.

I snatched my arm back. "Ow."

"Not body makeup." She frowned and peered at the roots of my hair. "A good dye job or you've really got blue hair."

"At night," I said. "I'm half Drow."

She raised an eyebrow.

"Dark Elves."

"Uh-huhhhh."

"During the day I look normal, like you."

With an amused look she help up her arm, showing her dark, golden skin. "You're Kenyan and Puerto Rican?"

"Not exactly." I grinned. "Let me show you some of the stuff here."

In my office I had all kinds of unique paranorm artifacts that had magical properties. I even showed her a little of my elemental magic.

"You can buy a book to learn that crap," she said. "A *Magicians for Idiots Guide*."

"You are a tough one." I put my hands on my hips. "Okay. One more chance to make you a believer."

I took her to the Pit.

Weres, Doppler, Fae, and Shifters were all doing their thing. Shadow Shifters becoming nothing but shadows on the floor and vanishing, particularly freaked her out a little. And Olivia was pretty hard to freak out.

Unfortunately Olivia kept wanting to hang around the Vamps. Damn bloodsuckers.

The next day she gave her notice to her captain at the NYPD and she was mine.

Heh, heh, heh.

CHAPTER 10

Once I had sent the e-mail with the drawing to Derek, I looked at Olivia. "I'll get started on these door-stoppers from Rodán." I gestured to the stack of books on my credenza.

"Have fun." She turned to her monitor. "I'm going to see what I can find on the Internet. If anything, considering our only clues are this symbol and that it must have been a Demon."

"I'd sure like to make sense of this whole mess before searching tonight for that damned Demon that murdered the cop's family." I picked up one of Rodán's dusty tomes. "It would be nice to know exactly what we're looking for."

"Mmmm." Olivia was obviously already deep into her search. Every now and then paper would spit out of her printer, and I hoped she was finding good info.

The bells on the door jingled, and Olivia and I both looked up.

"Hiya, Olivia," Caprice said with one of her smiles that made a person automatically want to smile back. Her dark hair flowed around her shoulders and her eyes seemed even more hazel than usual. "Let me see today's shirt."

Olivia parted her Mets sweat jacket and the saying on the yellow T-shirt stretched across her melon-sized breasts.

> *A good friend will bail you out of jail.*
> *A best friend will be sitting next to you*
> *Saying, "Damn. We fucked up."*

Caprice's smile turned into a grin and she gave Olivia a high-five.

Olivia twirled her seat before getting up and heading away from her desk. She glanced over her shoulder when she reached the door. "Gotta run some errands. Be back in thirty."

We waved her off. When the office door had closed behind Olivia, Caprice sat on the corner of my partner's desk. "What's up, chica?"

I propped my elbow on one of the enormous books Rodán had loaned me and cupped my chin in my hand. "Right now, nothing good."

She cocked her head. "Tell me."

I told her about the crime scene, the murdered family, and the missing liaison.

Caprice shook her head when I finished. "I'm sure glad I don't have your job. Being a Tracker is enough as it is."

"No kidding." I sighed and braced both arms on top of the huge book. "I'm glad you stopped by." What the hell; I just dove into what I'd wanted to talk to her about since last night at the Pit. "About that guy you were with—"

Her smile blossomed with pleasure. "He's so freaking *hot*. I'm going to see him again tonight."

Jeez, this wasn't going to be easy. I tried to soften my words. "I know you think he's an all right guy," I said as I leaned forward, and I knew my expression was serious. "But last night at the club I had a really bad feeling about him. Really bad."

Caprice just looked at me a moment as her smile faded. Finally she said, "You're not a Seer, Nyx."

I looked away from her and picked up a pencil that sat between two cubes of hot pink sticky notes. "That's true." I clenched my fingers around the pencil as I met her gaze again. "But sometimes I get feelings. I sense things. Like last night when Jon was murdered. Before I left my apartment I had such a strong feeling that something horrible was going to happen. And it did."

Her face was tight and my belly hurt from taking away some of the happiness she'd felt at meeting that guy. "If you really had a premonition, maybe what you thought you sensed around Chance was just a remnant of that feeling you'd had earlier."

"Maybe." I tapped the pencil's eraser on the desk as I thought about the strength of the sensation I'd had about Chance. "But I don't think so." I took a deep breath before I said, "I don't think you should see him anymore."

"What?" Caprice slid off of Olivia's desk and stood, anger making her dark eyes impossibly darker. The bite to her words caused me to straighten, drawing back in my chair. "That's bullshit, Nyx. I can't believe you'd even go there."

"I'm just worried—"

"Save it." Caprice turned and headed to the front door. She opened and shut it behind her hard enough to make the bells jangle louder than normal.

Or maybe it just seemed like the bells were louder because the room was suddenly so empty without Caprice, and because I'd just upset one of my best friends.

Still, why did she get so angry so fast? That wasn't like Caprice. I sighed. Maybe I had overstepped my bounds and this Chance guy was okay. With all my heart, I hoped so.

I sighed again, then cracked open the first book, the one I'd been resting my forearms on. I started searching from the beginning, scanning each page with the speed of my race. Some of the pages were worn, brittle even. Halfway through the book my temples started aching.

Four and a half books to go.

My blue Persian landed lightly on my desk, appearing out of nowhere as usual, and began walking back and forth on the surface. She stepped on the big book I was currently searching through as she went from one end of the desk to the other.

"Cut it out, Kali." All that long blue Persian hair, and ending up with a cat's tail and rear end in my face, made for not being able to see what I was doing. Plus I was getting cat hair in my mouth with her so close to my face.

I gave Kali a gentle push to get her butt out of my face. "I'm working."

Kali finally gave an irritating yowl and, with her tail high in the air, she stalked off in the direction of our kitchenette/lounge. Probably to go shred some of my underwear once she traveled her secret route to my apartment. I hoped Kali left me *something* to wear for the morning.

At least at night I didn't need anything but my fighting outfit. And Kali had yet to find a way to destroy the Drow-worked leather.

Heh.

I brushed my fingers over my collar as I looked again at the page I'd last been scanning before Kali had shown up.

The door bells jangled again and I looked up, hoping it was Caprice. Instead it was Olivia, but she was carrying something that made my stomach growl.

"Doughnuts!" I held my hands out as I recognized the box from our favorite bakery and smelled the doughnuts. "Gimme, gimme."

"Figured you hadn't had anything to eat yet." She passed the pastry box to me as she stopped in front of my desk. "So I made sure to pick up something nutritious."

"Mmmm." I set the box down on a pile of file folders before opening the box and grabbing a Bavarian crème. My favorite. "I love you."

"I know." Olivia sat on the edge of my desk and looked at me, and I knew something was up.

The wisteria. Now doughnuts.

Oh, crap.

Still, I wasn't about to relinquish my Bavarian crème, no matter that she was buttering me up. "This is about going out with me tracking Demons, isn't it."

"Tonight." Olivia's gaze fixed on mine.

I almost squirted the crème from my doughnut onto my desk when I set my hand down. "I haven't talked to Rodán about it yet."

She pointed to the XPhone on my desk. "So call."

I looked at my Bavarian doughnut that was still making my mouth water. I hadn't even had a bite of it yet. I narrowed my eyes at her. "You don't play fair."

Olivia shrugged. "Stop wasting time."

I grabbed a napkin from the stack Olivia had set beside the doughnut box. I set my poor, lonely doughnut on the napkin before using another napkin to wipe the chocolate icing that had already gotten on my fingers.

With a glare at Olivia, I hit speed dial for Rodán. "Olivia wants to go Demon tracking with us tonight," I said the moment he answered.

Rodán paused. "I want a chance to speak with her before she ventures out with you. I'll meet with her tomorrow night in the Pit when she gets there."

Well, good. That put it off at least one more night. "I'll tell her."

Rodán said good-bye and I set down my XPhone and looked at Olivia. "He wants a face-to-face with you first, tomorrow night."

"Rodán is full of shit." She narrowed her eyes. "I've never met with him before we tackled any case. Hell, I've never even seen him."

I shrugged. "He's the boss." She slid from sitting on the edge of my desk to stand and reached for the doughnut box. I snatched it first. "Mine."

"Humph." Olivia went around to her desk and plopped in her seat. "One more night. That's it."

"Yeah, yeah," I said before I finally bit into my Bavarian crème, which was followed by an orgasmic sound of bliss. I savored the smell of the crème filling and chocolate icing.

Olivia focused on her monitor as she started typing on her gel pad. "I have some ideas for things to look at on the Net. Maybe we'll get lucky."

I leaned back and took another huge bite, and with my free hand thumped the book I'd been researching. "So far I haven't come across anything close."

"Let's see what we can do," she said, and I knew she was already lost in her research.

I made my way through the doughnuts, and Olivia and I searched most of the day for something related to the Demonic symbol and found zippo. An irregularly shaped cone . . . round and bumpy on top, with layers upon jagged layers as it went to a point. It looked like an earthy tornado.

Every time I looked at the symbol I wanted to shudder. It made me feel like the sky had darkened and life was draining away. It got to the point that chills ran up and down my arms and I didn't want to look at the symbol anymore.

Whatever it was meant evil. Pure, pure evil.

It wasn't easy, but I managed to shut out my more sensitive human half and continue searching.

None of Rodán's books on the occult and Demonology coughed up what I was looking for. Damn. Could I have missed something because I'd been scanning the pages so fast?

My XPhone rang and I looked at the ID that flashed on the screen. "It's Derek."

Olivia leaned back in her chair and gave a sigh of exhaustion as she put her feet up on the desk and leaned back. " 'Bout time."

"Hi, Tiger," I said when I answered, and Derek laughed.

"Hey, Blue," Derek said. I was so glad no one else had picked up on Derek's nickname for me. Made me feel like a Border collie.

Not that that's a bad thing. I knew a Doppler Border collie who was a great guy.

"Nothing yet," Derek said, and my heart dropped. I had so hoped that, as an occult expert, he'd find something. "So far my search has led to dead ends. Although the symbol does look somewhat familiar."

That gave my heart a lift. "Anything at all that will take us closer to finding this thing will be great."

"I'll get back to you." The sound of a door shutting in the background came over the line. "James just walked in and I haven't made dinner yet."

"Tell James hello."

"Will do."

Derek severed the connection and I set the XPhone on my desk.

A possible lead?

I could only hope.

CHAPTER 11

"I'm going to have a chat with Caprice's guy," I said to myself as I pushed my way through the packed nightclub, trying to block out the scents of all of the paranorms and norms so that I could focus fully on the man Caprice was with.

At first Caprice tilted her chin when she saw me, showing some of the anger from our earlier conversation. Then she visibly relaxed and smiled when I reached her. "Hi, chica." She turned to the guy. "Chance, this is one of my closest friends, Nyx Ciar. Nyx, this is Chance Cartwright."

"Great hair." He set his beer mug on a table, took my hand, and gave a light squeeze before releasing me. His grip was warm. But I felt uneasy. Unsteady as he touched me. Almost queasy.

"I've never met anyone like you," he was saying.

That's because there isn't anyone like me.

"Funny," I said. "I was thinking the same thing about you."

I tried to identify exactly what kind of being he was. Chance didn't smell human, unless all the weed smoke and odors of beer and bar food were getting to me.

"Chance and I are going out for lunch tomorrow," Caprice was saying as Chance and I held each other's gaze.

I nodded, barely hearing her. The guy definitely wasn't a Metamorph because he didn't smell like newly mown hay.

Oddly he smelled a bit like T, of rosewood and musk. Come to think of it, Chance even looked like a blond Highlander, where T was dark. Maybe they were related, or of the same race?

The thought sent a strange twisting sensation through my belly. If so, what were they doing here?

"Chance reserved number one," Caprice said, bringing my attention back to her as she gestured toward the pool tables. "Looks like they're about done. Chance said he enjoys a good game of pool." She gave me a grin. "I know you'll give him one."

Once Rodán taught me how to play pool, when I first came to New York City, I never lost a game. You could say I'm a fast learner—about a lot of things.

In a few minutes I was chalking my cue. After Chance took a drink and set his draft beer on a side table, he grabbed a cue from the wall rack, chalked it, and went to the table.

"Eight ball?" Chance asked as he racked up the balls, and I nodded. He made the break, sending the fifteen into the corner pocket.

"You've got solids," he said as he aimed his cue at a striped ball. "Ten in the corner." He sank the ball and called the next shot. "Nine in the side pocket." He banked the shot off the rail and missed. He smiled at me. "Your go, Nyx."

His smile wasn't right. Something just wasn't right.

I glanced at Caprice, who perched on one of the stools at a high-top table, close to Chance. *"Open your eyes,"* I wanted to say. *"He's not what he seems."*

After the pool game, I would tell her. In the meantime I wanted to see if I could find out more about this Chance Cartwright.

At the head of the table, I leaned in and aimed my cue. "Seven in the corner." With a smooth stroke I sunk the ball.

"Where are you from?" I asked Chance as I eased around the table for my next play.

"Where it's hot all the time." Chance's grin would have been disarming if I remotely trusted him. Caprice, on the other hand, was looking at the guy like he was a God.

"That covers a lot of territory." I propped my arm on the rail. "Four in the side." The ball dropped and I put the next two balls away in one move, then had to scoot around the table for a shot, close to Chance.

My stomach clenched and I shuddered from the slight contact when my body brushed his. I screwed up and took the shot too hard and the six bounced out of the pocket.

I was more concerned about the uneasy feeling that kept growing and growing inside me than I was about the bad play.

"You're good, Nyx." Chance studied the balls before he walked around the table. I watched him, and the way he moved reminded me of T. "I've got some catching up to do," Chance said.

Somehow Chance and T were related, whether by kin or race.

"What do you do?" I asked as he readied himself for the shot.

"Fourteen in the side." Chance took the shot, but the cue ball bounced and rode the cushion of the rail, and then fell back into play. "Not my night," he said, but didn't seem the least bit upset. He braced his cue stick on the floor and held it with both hands. "I manage a large team of engineers."

"Engineering what?" I put away the five and one in a single shot.

"Not going to give me a break, are you?" Chance said with a friendly grin as he chalked his cue again. He didn't answer my question and instead smiled at Caprice. "You were right, she's damned good."

The guy was totally messing with me. I don't know how, but I just knew it.

"Where do you live?" I asked as I leaned in to take my next shot.

Chance shrugged when I glanced up at him. "In the area."

Evasive. Every answer was a generality, and said in such a way that I would have sounded rude if I pressed him. Did I care if I sounded rude? I saw Caprice's smile and a war raged inside me. She looked so happy. Radiant, even.

A loud crack echoed in the room as I nailed the last ball and it dropped with smooth precision into the corner pocket. I eyed the table to choose the best position to put away the eight ball. "Eight in the side."

I dropped it into the pocket and the game was over. Like that. Not one bit of challenge. I didn't think he had really even tried.

Chance wrapped his arm around Caprice's shoulders and squeezed. The sight had my whole body stinging with tension and I wanted to yell at him to get away from her.

"Nyx slaughtered me," he said with a smile.

Slaughter. Interesting choice of words.

So he was from someplace hot, he was an engineer, and he lived in the area. If an ounce of truth had been in his words to begin with.

"Thanks for the game." I put up the cue. I wanted to shake Caprice. Something was *wrong*.

"Do you have a sec, Caprice?" I asked, and she seemed reluctant as she moved out of Chance's embrace before walking with me down the steps from the elevated gaming area. It was hard to be heard with the music so loud.

"I know you like the guy," I said as I tried to figure out how to say what I needed to. "But there's something wrong."

"Not this again." Caprice raised her hands and let them fall to her sides. "I can't live my life based on something you think you sense." She started to turn away. "Besides, I can take care of myself."

"Be careful," I called after her. "Please be careful." She didn't look back.

CHAPTER 12

Caprice was gone when I was close to setting out. That guy, Chance, had apparently left, too. My heart sank as I played with the olives on the little plastic sword in my martini. The sword was yellow. I hate yellow.

Everything was just white noise as I thought about Caprice and that guy. I barely heard any of the Trackers talking as my stomach knotted and a sick feeling washed over me.

I had to call Caprice and try again to get her to listen to me. I unlocked my phone ID so that she could see it was me calling, and then pressed the speed dial number I'd programmed in for her.

My call went straight to her voice mail. I heard her cheerful voice telling me to leave a message, followed by the beep. I attempted to keep the concern out of my tone as I told her to give me a call, and then pushed the off button before putting my XPhone back in its clip on my belt.

I tried to relax, but didn't have it in me to join in with the laughter and fun the other Trackers were having.

T didn't hang out with the Trackers at the Pit,

which was fine by me. Around nine he showed up and stood beside my chair, looking like a Highlander lost in time, stoic and not saying a word.

The other Trackers openly appraised him, but no one made an effort to introduce themselves and I didn't bother to introduce him. I was too distracted anyway, my thoughts on Caprice. They'd seen him, of course, when I'd come back to the Pit last night after Jon's death. Maybe Rodán already gave them the word that I was stuck with this guy.

Joy.

T and I left and walked into a crisp night that smelled of fall, with the eventual threat of winter on its fingertips.

"So how long have you and Rodán been getting it on?" T said when we weren't far from the Pit.

"What?" I snapped my attention to him and came to a full stop. "To begin with, if Rodán and I have a relationship, that's none of your business."

T shrugged. "Just trying to understand things around here. If something happens to his woman, is it going to be my ass he puts in a sling?"

I clenched and unclenched my fist, which was dangerously close to Lightning. "You really are as dumb as an underground Troll." I started walking again, trying to stay ahead of T, but he kept up with his long strides. "I'm no one's *woman*, and I don't have to explain my relationship with Rodán to you."

"All right, then tell me, Princess, why you're up here wading through Demon guts and not sitting on your throne having every need attended to?"

My fingers twitched and I ached to show him what

this Princess could do with her fists, not to mention the rest of her body. I rarely curse, but right then I was so close to telling the pile of trollshit to fuck off.

But noooo, he had to keep talking. "You're an enigma, Princess." When I glanced up at him, he looked genuinely interested in me. "Drow females are subservient to Drow males, and hell if I've ever heard of a Drow female like you."

I ground my teeth before I snapped my words. "Having a Drow King for a father and a human mother as Queen has its benefits." *As if* I would be a submissive female to a dominant male.

We reached Amsterdam, and I halted and propped my hands on my hips as I looked along the avenue. I didn't sense anything paranormal going down and definitely no Demons.

But I still had that sick, sick feeling in my gut about Caprice.

"So your mother doesn't have a taste for the bondage-and-domination lifestyle the Dark Elves get into," T went on, sounding like he was deep in thought. "And she apparently taught you to be like her."

T nailed that dead-on. Even though my father was King of the Dark Elves, he would do anything for my mother, who refused to live the submissive Drow female lifestyle, and he allowed me to be raised as my mother wished.

I glared at him. "You're really starting to piss me off."

"A female Drow warrior." T shook his head as if in wonder. "That's kind of hard to believe."

Why, oh, why was I stuck with this irritating male?

It was true that I was the only female ever allowed to train with the male warriors. My father, as King, could allow me to do anything, and he loved me so much he let me learn to fight to the point where I could beat just about any warrior. That sure hadn't made me popular with the males.

Not that I'd cared. Not really.

Well, maybe a little.

As for T . . .

"If you need me to make you a believer, then keep on talking," I said as my muscles flexed and tensed.

T gave a smile that somehow made his Highlander looks appear harsher. "I think I should know more about the female I'm stuck with for this assignment."

I narrowed my eyes at him. "If we're going to play this game, why don't we start with you? So tell me, T, what are you? Where did you come from? What are you doing here?"

His face seemed to grow darker, and instinct almost made me take a step back. "You don't want to know, Princess."

I wasn't about to let the jerk intimidate me. "Try me," I said, just before I caught the smell of fear from a human male and the newly mown hay smell of a Metamorph.

"Terrific," I said in a grumble as I started running to the first problem of the night. Other than T, that was.

The Great Guardian should send all Metamorphs to an Otherworld where only dinosaurs reigned. And send T there while she was at it.

With T beside me, I dodged pedestrians and crazy New York drivers, and in seconds I made it to a small side street near Amsterdam and Sixty-sixth Avenue.

When I arrived, I saw the Metamorph playing the part of a huge, muscle-bound mugger. His hair was long and stringy, and he reeked of sweat. He had a gun pressed to the human's temple while, at the same time, he clenched his other hand around the human's throat and had him shoved up against a wall. The only light was from what came through windows on either side of the street, and the slight illumination from a streetlight off of Sixty-sixth.

"I gave all my cash to my kids this morning," the human was saying, sounding like he was rushing to get the words out, his voice shaking. "Honest. I don't have anything on me but my credit cards."

Obviously the Metamorph didn't realize I was behind him because he hit the human male in the face with the butt of the handgun. The Metamorph split the human's lip and tore the skin on his cheek, causing the man to cry out. Blood splattered his tan suit.

The human was a realtor—I guessed that by the open briefcase with flyers for homes, apartments, and buildings for sale, with more flyers scattered all over the side street.

"Cough it up, man," the Metamorph said in a heavy Bronx accent. "I know you got more than five dollars on you."

"How about *you* cough it up?" I had my hands close to my daggers, and came *this* close to beheading the Metamorph just because I wasn't in the mood to mess with the creep.

"Oh—oh, fuck." When the Metamorph saw the white flash in my eyes, he dropped the gun and re-leased the man.

He ran.

I ran faster.

Before he got ten feet from the wall, I was in front of him. "Let's play Metamorph rugby," I said as I grabbed his shoulders and slammed my forehead against his.

I got my hard head from my father.

The Metamorph stumbled backward.

I hooked my ankle around his and yanked his foot out from under him.

He dropped flat on his back on a pile of the flyers. His shout echoed off the side street walls as his head hit concrete. I planted my boot on his chest.

The human started to inch his way out of the side street, then I saw T heading toward him.

I turned back to the asshole beneath my boot.

"If I deball you I might get called on a foul." I cocked my head as I looked down at his crotch, be-fore meeting his gaze. "But if I kick your head across the street, I score."

"Don't! Please!" The big, brawny Metamorph looked close to tears. Metamorphs are such wusses.

I shook my head. "Gotta go for the gold." I gave a nod toward the human. "He can play goalie."

The Metamorph started shaking—and shifting. In the next moment I was looking at a scrawny, scared-shitless teenager beneath my boot.

"Oh, for the Goddess's sake." I couldn't tell if this was a trick or his real form. But I wouldn't hurt a kid and I'm sure that was the whole idea. "Get to the sidelines." I pointed toward a corner of the building closest to us. "And don't move. I'm not in the mood for it. I'll change the game from rugby to hockey and use your head for a puck."

The Metamorph "kid" scrambled to his feet and did what I ordered him to. His arms were lanky, his legs thin beneath his jeans as he moved.

The human just stood beside T with his mouth hanging open.

"Your skin's purple," he said, as if it was the only thing that mattered in the whole freaking night.

"Amethyst. Now shut up." The only reason he could see me at all was because I'd had to drop my glamour to deal with the Metamorph. I brushed the mugged human's mind with my air power to make him forget the incident, and gave him a few instructions.

"You stumbled, and split your lip and cut your cheek when you fell." This part was always fun. "Go to the Broadway Dive Bar between 101st and 102nd Streets. Clean up, have a couple of shots of whiskey, then catch a cab home. Go take a ride on the carousel in Central Park with your family tomorrow. Have some fun. *During the day.*"

The man started to walk in the direction of the bar. "Get your briefcase and stuff, then get out of here," I said.

T just stood there, his arms across his chest, an amused expression on his face. Prick.

As the man obeyed me, I picked up the Metamorph's weapon. Nice. The .380-caliber Hi-Point pistol told me he might be into some arms trading, too. I turned my gaze on him as I slid the weapon into a sheath at the back of my belt, and the Metamorph tried to hide the smirk that had been on his face when my back was to him. "Kid, huh? Sure. Maybe I should have removed your head after all."

His face went as pale as a Vamp's.

Oh, brother. Like I said, Metamorphs are such wusses.

Mr. Realtor finished gathering his things and was off to get stoned without a look back.

"Might want to straighten that tie," I shouted to him.

I used my XPhone to call PTF, and then they were on their way to take the now elementally air-contained Metamorph.

That gut-deep feeling that something horrible, something unbelievably devastating, was going to happen hadn't gone away even when I'd been dealing with the Metamorph.

After T and I left the scene, the feeling got worse as the night progressed, and I had no doubt that it wasn't my imagination. I'd never felt anything so powerful before.

While we searched my territory for paranormal activity I kept my senses alert for Demons. They were here. They didn't take nights off.

We were near the Hudson when I stumbled back as if a boulder had been rammed against my chest.

Horrific images, sensations, sounds, and smells slammed into me.

Demons. Pain. Blood. Fear. Screams.

"Caprice!"

CHAPTER 13

"Caprice!" I screamed again as I pushed myself as fast as I could toward her territory.

I sensed and could see images of the Demons. The Demons had Caprice down and were crowding around her body.

"No!" My words were lost on the air as I bolted down several blocks in mere seconds. I rounded onto Avenue of the Americas. "I won't let them kill you, Caprice!"

My whole body felt like I was running through cracked ice. Sharp, jagged edges that kept me from going faster. Cold threatening to freeze my entire being.

Her screams reached my heightened senses and I could already smell the Demons. A sense of helplessness stabbed at me like razor-sharp icicles. I wasn't going to make it in time.

I pushed harder, even though I knew it wasn't going to do any good. Caprice's life force was already leaving her, and her essence was drifting away to Summerland.

When I reached West Fifty-fifth Street I came to a hard stop.

It was a wonder I didn't shatter.

The freezing cold I had felt when I was running was nothing like what I felt the moment I saw the Demons tearing apart what was left of Caprice.

For a moment I just stood there, wanting to scream, cry, tear into the Demons.

As the horror rose up in me like thick sludge, it felt as if the world was tilting upside down. An acrid taste filled my mouth as I fought back the rising bile and the ache in my tearless eyes.

Rage wrapped around the horror and anguish in my heart and soul like a boa constrictor crushing my ribs and lungs. My fingertips brushed my XPhone as I reached for my dagger. No time to call Rodán. I'd take out these bastards myself.

T appeared from out of the shadows, a grim look on his face as he unsheathed his pair of double-edged short swords.

He nodded to the Demons closest to him and I focused on the six of the eleven near me.

Eleven? Dear Goddess.

The earth wouldn't stop feeling as if it was sloping downhill.

A scream tried to claw its way up my throat at the horror of Caprice's death. Charging into the middle of the humanlike beings without thought would be virtual suicide.

I knew all too well that the Demons were fast, efficient, and deadly.

"Think. Think," I repeated again.

Breathe.

Breathe.

The cone of light from a nearby streetlight illuminated the Demons. They could have been any crowd that had gotten off a New York subway. A rapper, two businessmen, a group of teenage girls, a muscle-bound guy, and one that could have been a male gymnast.

The sound of snapping bones almost drove me to my knees. Dry heaves hit me as I fought to keep from puking.

I wanted to fling myself in their midst like a jagged boulder barreling at them from a catapult.

The hilts of my dragon-clawed daggers were smooth and hard in my hands as I slid them from their sheaths. My lower lip stung as my sharp canines grazed it just before I clenched my teeth.

Now. Now. Now.

My muscles coiled. I vaulted and somersaulted in the air, my knees close to my chest. I landed in another crouch, this time five feet behind the Demons.

The Demons couldn't possibly hear me. Dark Elves make no sounds when we move.

A Demon raised its head and cocked it as it looked vaguely in my direction.

My muscles went rigid as I stilled my body. It focused on the spot where I knelt on one knee and gripped my daggers. The Demon's eyes narrowed.

One heartbeat. Two. Three.

The Demon turned back to finishing Caprice's remains.

Acid burned my chest, and the churning in my stomach wouldn't go away.

Calm down. Calm. Down.

Fuck calm.

Like a runner from a starting gate, I shot up, both daggers gripped in my fists.

I gave a Drow warrior cry as I drove Lightning into one Demon's vulnerable spot at the same time I jabbed Thunder into the weak area of the Demon on the other side of me.

I never stopped moving. I jerked out my blood-covered daggers and the Demons dropped to the sidewalk. "Eat this," I shouted at the same time I took out another Demon.

A spray of blue splattered my face and clothing as the Demon's blood burst from its throat before it toppled over.

Killing the rest of the Demons wouldn't be as easy.

From the corner of my eye I saw T move in precise, controlled movements as he used his swords and dispatched two Demons to my three.

Six Demons to go.

My heart thundered like a storm raged inside my body. The remaining Demons screeched and came after me, their poison-tipped claws extended. I wanted to chop their arms off, chop them to pieces. If it wasn't for their armorlike skin, I would have torn them apart.

The Demon that looked like a petite gymnast flipped through the air as well as I could. My heart jerked as it landed behind me. I whirled to face it while being on guard for the other Demons closing in on me from behind. The gymnast Demon dodged my daggers at the same time it sliced the air with its claws, reaching for my skin.

Too close.

I dropped and rolled away from all of the Demons, spinning fast on the asphalt. Small, sharp rocks dug into my skin and a piece of glass sliced my arm. I lunged to my feet in time to face the muscle-bound Demon that looked like a bodybuilder, and was a good foot taller than me and three times as wide. The Demon roared and a gold tooth in its mouth glinted in the streetlights.

Caprice! echoed in my mind, loud and cavernous, then hollow because that's what I was without my friend.

More fury tore through me and my sight narrowed in on the Demon's vulnerable area, at its throat. The Demon charged toward me at the same time I ran to it. I dropped to my knees as it grabbed at empty air.

I surged upward and rammed my dagger home, rupturing the Demon sac. More sticky blue fluid splattered my skin and clothing.

The being toppled backward and slammed to the asphalt as I backflipped four times, stopping in the middle of the street.

It was then that I realized we had a couple of humans watching us, wide-eyed and openmouthed. One of the males was raising his cell phone, just about to dial 911. I sent a blast of my air power toward the cell and it shattered in the man's hand.

I focused fully on the Demons again, especially

the one closest to me that was holding up an enormous chunk of cement and asphalt as if it were a pebble. The Demon snarled, its sharp teeth at odds with its pretty-boy face.

Skin along my back tingled. Another Demon had managed to creep up behind me. The gymnast Demon. I turned just enough to see them both coming at me at the same time.

My heart raced as the two Demons closed in.

I swung one dagger upward and it clanged against the armor-skinned wrist of the Demon that had come from behind. I only managed to knock its hand away, keeping it from touching me with its claws. My heart spasmed when its poisonous claws swept past me by a hair's breadth.

At the same time I tried to dodge the concrete block that the pretty-boy Demon pitched at me.

The block hit me solidly in my right shoulder and I went down.

Screaming pain shot through my shoulder and arm, all the way to the hand that was holding Lightning.

It would cost me, but I needed to use my elemental powers or I wasn't going to survive.

My air power felt like a storm rushing through my body as I used it to propel myself from the ground. Instead of moving away from pretty-boy Demon, I went straight for it. It was obvious it didn't expect my move from the shocked look on its humanoid face.

My muscles tightened as I sliced my dagger upward. The blade skimmed the hard armor of its skin near its throat, but I thrust my dagger home and wasted the bastard.

As blood welled from my stinging shoulder wound, the red of it mingled with the blue of the Demon blood that coated me. I did everything I could not to look at what had been Caprice, the remains near me now. Again acid burned my throat. I didn't know what was going on with T. All I could hear were the shrieks and screams of the Demons he was battling.

Every vein in my body pounded with blood as I started to go after the gymnast Demon.

The Demon flipped over my head and landed next to scaffolding on a building.

Oh, my Goddess was all I had time to think as the scaffolding came down on me.

Several bars of the scaffolding slammed me to the ground.

My lungs burned as my breath left in a whoosh.

Air! Dear Goddess, the scaffolding's weight was too great to move, and I fought for my next breath.

Was my left leg broken? Pain was shooting through it, up to my hip.

My right arm ached from the pressure where it was pinned to the asphalt. The only part of me that was free was my left arm, but my dagger had slipped from my hand and lay inches from my fingers.

Laughter came from the Demon that had brought the scaffolding down on me.

A buzzing sound grew in my ears as I struggled for another breath. In a rush my mind sifted through the elements at my command, and which ones were available. No fire, but the others—*yes*.

The Demon came into view. It was smiling.

It reached for me with its hands, its poisoned claws coming for me.

"Not on your life, you slimy pile of trollshit." I managed to squeeze the words out as I prepared to use my power over the water element. Waste from sewer drains, as well as the water main running beneath the street, were at my bidding.

Just as the Demon's claws almost touched me, I made my mental command. Water exploded up beneath the Demon, in such a powerful geyser that it flung the Demon away from me and slammed it against the brick wall on the opposite side of the street. It landed on its back and started to roll over to get up.

But I'd already called to the sewage water, and it rammed through the asphalt straight at the Demon. Along with the sewage, I forced the water geyser at the Demon, too, and both drove into the Demon's face so hard they pinned the Demon against a building. Water and sewage filled the Demon's orifices, while at the same time they pounded the Demon's head against the wall.

I didn't know how long I could hold it there.

Still pinned beneath bars of the scaffolding, I stretched out my left hand, my fingers trying to grasp the hilt of my dagger. Its blade glinted in the light and I focused my air power to bring it to my hand.

Goddess, but it drained so much energy from my body when I used any elements to such extremes.

Yet I had to use more. Before the gymnast Demon broke free of the hold I had on it with my water powers, I had to get out from under the scaffolding that had flattened me.

I closed my eyes and a rush of power rose through me from the earth. My head swam. Focus. *Focus*.

The ground rumbled beneath my body. Dry, hard-packed earth tore through the asphalt to either side of me.

With my forced concentration, the power of the earth shoved the scaffolding off my body and pelted me with rocks, pebbles, and dirt.

Almost at once the rumbling stopped and the dirt that had been in the air dropped back down to the asphalt. The scaffolding was now tilted up enough to free me.

Was I crushed? No, thank the Goddess. Only parts of my body had been hit by the scaffolding, and my Drow half was too strong to break easily. Yet my lungs hurt as I drew in breath and got to my feet. My leg ached like a steel rod had been rammed through my foot all the way to my hip, but my leg wasn't broken.

The sharp pain in my shoulder caused me to wince as I clenched both daggers and headed for the Demon that was trying to escape my water trap. I pushed myself forward, limping as I walked toward the Demon.

It flailed as it worked to get itself free of the water pounding against it, pinning it to the wall. Just as I reached the Demon, it slipped from my trap.

The Demon was *mine*. With all of the force I had inside me I thrust my dagger so far into the Demon's sac that it touched the back of its armored skull.

I jerked my dagger out and the gymnast Demon dropped to the ground with a dull thud. I kicked it as hard as I could—then regretted it as pain shot through my foot from the impact against skin no blade could penetrate. I gritted my teeth.

Prickles skittered across my back. I whirled, every muscle in my body prepared for an assault, then came up short.

A little girl, maybe five years old and dressed all in pink, had a dazed and frightened look on her face. She had long blond curls, big blue eyes, and she was clutching a Barbie in her left hand and had her right thumb in her mouth.

What was she doing here among the wrecked street, the shooting sewage and water, and the Demons' bodies? My head was spinning from the elemental energies I'd used, and my body was weak from the battering it had taken. I couldn't connect any dots.

I blinked.

The little girl's frightened expression gave way to a sweet smile and she stepped closer. "I lost my mommy," she said in a voice that was neither childish nor any other age I could define.

The urge to pick her up and carry her out of this mess overwhelmed me. I reached out my arms—

Just as her hands turned into claws.

Her face morphed and she widened her jaws, her mouth now filled with spiked teeth.

I stumbled back. A Demon? Dear Goddess.

The child-Demon flung her Barbie aside and rushed toward me.

My mind couldn't compute. My hands wouldn't work to dispatch the child-Demon with one of my daggers.

A flash and someone jerked the child-Demon back by its neck a second before its claws would have dug into my skin. I snapped my head up and watched T hold the Demon under its chin and ram a knife up into its throat.

Horror at the sight of T thrusting a knife into a child's throat rushed through me even as blue fluid splattered the alleyway.

Not a child. A Demon.

T released its body and it slumped to the ground, looking like a murdered child.

More bile rose in my throat and I turned away.

I stumbled away, blocking the image of the child from my mind.

No. A Demon. Not a real child.

Dizziness from using additional elemental energy, as well as all my injuries, had me feeling like I'd just been well blended on high speed. I couldn't look at T as I did what I had to do next.

Despite the incredible drain on my body, I still managed to cut the water and sewage off by using air to repair the holes in the pipes by bending the pieces back into shape. A little static from the air gave me just enough power to meld the metal together as I did it. I was soaked with sewage and Demon blood. And I didn't give a Goddessdamn about it.

All was quiet except for the now familiar sound of T's boot steps as he came closer toward me.

We had destroyed the Demons.

I saw in my mind's eye the pretty little girl in pink, looking up at me with innocent eyes.

A Demon playing the part of a child. A Demon that would have killed me if it wasn't for T.

I closed my eyes and tried to center myself. Let my senses come back into focus.

Everything that went through my head in those moments was to help me fight the images still imprisoned in my mind. I didn't want to see Caprice's mutilated body, or hear the echoes of her screams that had met my ears even when I was far away.

My wet hair slid over my face as I bowed my head. I had failed my friend.

Caprice was gone.

CHAPTER 14

Everything that happened next was like being on a carousel that was spinning out of control, a total blur.

I remember draining myself of the last of my elemental energies as I sent Caprice's remains deep below the asphalt to await a fitting good-bye.

I remember T raising his hand and shooting black and orange fire at every Demon body and incinerating them.

I remember staring at the ashes of what had been the child-Demon and asking T why he couldn't have burned them to nothing before we killed them.

I remember his response, that the sac of blue fluid that kept them alive protected them from fire magic.

I remember T wiping the memories of the several humans who had gathered around us that I hadn't noticed before.

I remember sirens in the distance.

Then nothing. I remember nothing that happened after that, or how we made it to the Pit and Rodán's office.

My head swam as I found myself sitting in front of Rodán's desk. His mouth was moving. He was saying something, but I didn't understand his words. I couldn't make sense of anything.

I was numb. Everywhere.

Thoughts of Caprice's death sent blow after blow to my chest. My belly churned and the room's dim lights blurred. What would it be like, not having Caprice around to laugh with? To talk to?

Empty. Sad.

Anu, I thought to the Goddess, *please guide Caprice to her ancestors and their ancestors, and allow her to live in peace and joy.*

A whisper of a song flowed through me and, inside Rodán's office. Something like a breeze raised my hair from my shoulders. I shivered at the thought that it might be Anu herself answering me.

Caprice had so easily slipped into my life and had become a precious friend. When I first came to New York City I hadn't even known what it was like to have a friend, besides my mother, until Caprice and Nadia, and then, eventually, Olivia.

"Nyx," Rodán said quietly, his words penetrating the fog in my mind. "Caprice's death was faster than you think. She didn't suffer."

"Don't try that with me." My words came out harsh, angry, and I felt the flash of white fire in my eyes. "It's disrespectful to Caprice. She was eaten *alive.*"

"Caprice had a special gift," Rodán said, his tone still serious. "That gift was to block pain. It made her so strong it would have been impossible to torture her if she had been taken and interrogated."

"No." I stared at the earthen walls of his office,

my gaze trailing the purple leaves winding through the moss. "I *felt* her pain. I heard her screams."

"Only in her very last moment." Rodán's voice was soft, gentle. "For that fraction of time she no longer had control."

"Bullshit." I flung my words like a lash as I turned my head toward him, and my focus was finally clear. "It was more than a fraction."

Rodán looked at me for a long moment and I wanted to come out of my chair and kill something. More Demons. Every Demon.

It was then that I realized T was sitting in the chair next to mine. And I remembered the child-Demon.

I turned my attention to T, and my throat felt dry, scratchy as I spoke to him. "It almost killed me. That Demon that looked like a little girl."

He met my gaze, his eyes like gray flint. "You let yourself be caught off guard." His voice was coarse and harsh. "Never take anything at face value, especially in the middle of a battlefield."

His words and the tone of his voice were like a slap, and I jerked my head back. I wanted to scream at him. Better yet, decapitate him.

But he was right. And he had saved my life.

My throat worked as I swallowed down the urge to say anything and I looked away. I should have thanked him, but everything was too raw and I might have screamed at him instead.

"Would you like a hot cup of *nanath*?" Rodán said to me as I brought my attention to him. "The tea will soothe you."

At the suggestion my body tensed even more than

it already had been. "I don't want to be soothed." I brushed my hands up and down my arms, feeling a chill that didn't have anything to do with the cool temperature of the room. "Caprice is dead. Why should I allow myself to feel any release from pain after the pain she endured at the end?"

"Caprice has moved on to Summerland." Rodán's expression was unreadable. "She feels only peace and joy now that she's with her ancestors."

I bowed my head. It was true that Caprice would live on in another plane of existence. "But what she went through—"

Rodán stood and brought his chair closer to me, then sat, and his knees pressed against mine. He took my hands in his so that I was no longer rubbing my arms. His palms were warm, and somehow that warmth traveled through my body. Some kind of Elvin magic, I was certain.

He spoke to me in the formal language of the Elves. "Would you wish for those you care about to weight themselves with your death, if you should move on to Summerland?"

My blue hair slipped over my shoulders and covered my face as I bowed my head. "No," I whispered as he squeezed my hands.

He leaned forward and kissed the top of my head. "Then let us respect her memory by finding and destroying the master Demon that is responsible for all of this pain and suffering around us."

"You're right." I raised my chin. "I need to get out there and search for more of those monsters, find the one in charge, and destroy it."

"Not tonight." He gripped my hands and kept me from standing. "You've drained your elemental powers, you're injured, and you're exhausted." Rodán's clear green eyes held mine. "I've moved Nadia from Rover duty and she's now the Tracker for Caprice's territory. I also took Dave from Rover duty to cover your territory. For tonight only."

"No." I shook my head. "I can do it. I can go back out there," I said, even as I felt my body protest and my elemental energies were barely there. It would take twenty hours or so before I regained my full powers again, and before I healed.

Rodán just looked at me. I slumped in my chair. "I'll go home." But I wouldn't be able to sleep. I couldn't get the sight of Caprice's remains or that child-Demon's face out of my head. I didn't think I ever would.

T stood. "I have things to attend to."

I got to my feet, too, and started to leave. Rodán caught my hand. "I want to talk to you alone," he said as T passed me and started up the stairs, his boot steps echoing in the stairwell.

When it was completely silent, I looked into Rodán's crystal green eyes. "What do you want to talk about?"

He said nothing. He simply moved his mouth to mine and kissed me.

CHAPTER 15

Rodán's kisses were deep and sensual, and I felt them throughout my being, as if warm hands caressed my entire body.

I wanted to sink against him and let him hold me forever. And I wished I had the ability to cry. It wasn't fair that I hadn't inherited that part of my human half.

When I was with him, gradually I could think of nothing but him. Not another worry, not another trouble, not even another person. I felt alive and comforted with Rodán.

My injured body no longer felt pain. My injured mind was cleared. My injured heart was relieved of its agony.

For now.

I slid my fingers into his long white-blond hair, which felt light and thick at the same time, and I clasped my fingers behind his neck.

He never pushed me. No, he seduced my senses with his light touch, his pleasant taste, his scent of cedar and mountain laurel. But he couldn't have seduced me if I didn't want it. Or if I didn't need him.

Like I needed him now.

The sigh and moan that rose up in me was that of a woman giving herself to a man, a sound of need and want and desire. A woman who wanted to lose herself in the moment. To be soothed and cared for.

Yes, I needed this. I needed to be held and loved and to know that there were good things in this world. Special things. And Rodán was special to me.

A part of me felt I should be curled up alone at home, thinking about my friend.

The other part of me wanted the comfort of being in Rodán's arms and feeling loved. In our own way we did love one another. It was special, but it wasn't the same as finding your mate.

Rodán held me close to him and I felt like we'd fused together. My buckler pressed between us, but the ridge of his erection was big and comforting against me. Soon I'd have him inside me. I needed it like I'd never needed anything in my life.

Goddess, my head was spinning. I purred, and found myself climbing him and wrapping my thighs around his hips, hooking my ankles behind him.

When Rodán drew away he moved his lips to my ear and I purred louder. "Stay the rest of the night with me, my sweets." He bit my earlobe. "I want to hold you. Make love to you."

I tilted my head back and sighed as he kissed and nipped the column of my throat all the way to my collarbone. I clenched my fingers in his hair and slowly moved my hips so that my center rubbed against him. "Take me upstairs."

Rodán carried me as effortlessly and gently as he

might carry a bouquet of fire orchids to the Elvin Queen.

He must have used his magic to dim the room and light candles that flickered and danced in their crystal globes. No doubt that same magic was used to send a fresh burst of his room's familiar scents of woodlands and firethorn, and I think something to further calm the storm that was inside me. Even the sounds of the forest filled the room to make it pleasant, relaxing, and imbued with life.

Tomorrow was for storms. Tonight was for feeling alive with someone I cared for.

He set me on my feet and slipped his hands into my hair, and buried his face in the blue strands. "You smell so good, always. Exotic, like lotus blossoms."

To each male, my Drow pheromones gave off a different scent. The human I'd slept with thought I wore orange blossom perfume. Until my hair turned blue.

"Is it my pheromones that make you want me?" I said as I looked into those wonderful green eyes.

"You know better than that." He caressed the line of my jaw, his expression serious yet sensual. "I want you because you are who you are. Wild and free, intelligent and dedicated, caring and loving. The male who captures your heart will be a lucky man indeed."

I looped my arms around his neck and pulled him toward me. I smiled against his lips. "You promised to make love to me," I said before I kissed him.

Another long, sweet kiss as his hands roamed my body in slow, erotic movements. My leather corset and pants were almost like wearing nothing at all. As if he was touching my bare skin.

"Time to get rid of all of your weapons before you impale me," he said as he parted his mouth from mine.

I took one step back, moved my hands to my buckler, and unfastened my belt. Rodán took it from me and set the belt with all of my weapons carefully and silently on the nightstand beside his bed.

"You are so beautiful," he said as he helped me remove one of my Elvin boots and then the other, before he set the pair aside. Now I stood barefoot on the warm, polished wood of his bedroom floor. Shadows danced on the walls from the light of the many candles. He smiled. "I might keep you in my bed always."

I gripped the hem of his tunic and raised it, and he helped me pull it over his head. "You would never be satisfied with one woman," I said, which was true. Even one male wouldn't be enough for him. He entertained both women and men in his bed, and he enjoyed both far too much to settle for a single mate.

I ran my palms over his hairless chest and pinched his male nipples. He gave a deep rumble like a lion might. "I would be satisfied with only you."

This time I laughed. Softly, but it was a laugh. "Don't delude yourself. Or tease me."

He tipped my chin up, and the candlelight flickered in his eyes in the near darkness. "If any one woman could satisfy me it would be you."

I reached between us and untied his breeches.

"For tonight, as a part of our game, let's pretend that's true."

"Gladly." Rodán kissed me again and helped me remove his breeches. I paused to look at his tall, muscular perfection. His eyes focused on me as I skimmed my hands over his shoulders and pushed his long, white-blond hair away so that it hung down his back.

My light amethyst skin was so pale against his golden flesh. I used my fingers to trace his carved biceps, his smooth muscular chest, every bit of ripped abdomen—what humans considered an eight-pack.

Like other Elvin males, Rodán had no body or facial hair. I stroked the smooth area around his cock before running my fingers along the thick length of it and brushing my thumb over the slit at the top.

Rodán nipped my earlobe, then gave a low growl in my ear. "Not tonight, sweets. I think we both need joining more than anything else."

I started helping him take off my clothing. "More than I ever have."

He didn't hurry as he removed my clothes, caressing my breasts and stopping only to lightly bite my nipples. I moaned and stroked his silky hair. He trailed his tongue between my breasts and down the center of my flat belly to my hairless mound. I couldn't help the sound of frustration that burst from me as he only teased me with a flick of his tongue up the center of my slit.

He gave a soft laugh that I don't know if he really wanted me to hear. I had to clench my jaws together to keep from begging him for more as he finished taking off my leather pants before I stepped out of them. My folds were moist, my center wet, hot and aching to feel his thickness now.

Rodán caught me by surprise when he scooped me up in his strong, muscular arms and gently laid me on his magnificent bed. The forest-green sheets were like satin beneath me, so soft and sleek against my skin. The woodland scent was even stronger now. Clean, refreshing, relaxing. And the hint of cedar was intoxicating and sensual.

I watched him as he moved in slow, sensuous movements onto the bed. He pushed my thighs apart and I bent my knees before spreading myself wide for him.

"I want to taste your sweetness." He stroked my clit with one of his long, tapered fingers, and I hissed. My temples throbbed with the blood pounding through my system. "But I need to be inside you too much right now."

I smiled and held my arms out to him. "Come and let me feel your skin against mine."

He moved so that he was kneeling between my wide-open thighs. "You do know that I love you, Nyx."

"Yes." I caught some of his long hair in my fists as our eyes met and held. "In the same way that I love you."

His expression filled me with sunshine and warmth. He braced himself above me, then shifted so that his cock was ready to enter my core.

Rodán didn't thrust hard or fast. He slid inside me in a long, erotic movement until he was buried deep.

"Dear Goddess." I tilted my head and arched my back. "The time for talking is over. It's time for you to make love to me."

He gave a soft laugh when I lowered my gaze to look into his eyes. I loved the sound of his laugh. It was warm, deep. He drew his cock out, leaving me frustrated and wanting to take control.

I raised my hips to meet his when he slid inside me again. "I thought Kelly and Fere would be the first Peacekeepers I did away with. Lulu, too," I said as he kept up his slow, agonizing movements. "I might change my mind if you don't pick things up a bit."

"You're precious," he said before he kissed my forehead. "Bringing you here to this Otherworld was the best thing I have ever done."

I arched my hips higher, urging him on. He picked up his pace, started to thrust instead of moving so agonizingly slow. His movements were smooth and fluid. They became faster and harder as I squirmed beneath him. I think he got the point and realized how much I had to have this with him.

His long hair skimmed my face, my shoulders, my breasts, almost tickling me. I looked between us and saw his cock slide in and out of my core, and it sent more thrills through my belly just to see our bodies joined like this.

When I raised my eyes, I met Rodán's. "I love to watch you when I take you." He smiled and kept up a firm, rapid pace. "Your skin has a soft sheen to it, and your sapphire hair looks so beautiful against my pillow. You're equally beautiful when you're human."

I didn't have a chance to respond because he then thrust hard and started taking me in earnest.

Rodán was a sensual lover, but a powerful one when he chose to be. He sensed that I needed this, needed to feel him deep with his rapid, sure strokes.

My mind started to separate from my body. Seemed to float as if I wasn't a part of myself anymore. Instead I was an entity that only felt, didn't think. I was only aware of the feel of Rodán inside me, the feel of his cock sliding in and out.

But more than anything, I was losing myself to the feelings, the sensations. My whole body warmed with them, and even my separate consciousness felt the warmth, the buildup of the orgasm, the rush of the climax coming toward me at a speed I'd never be able to control. In truth I had no desire to control anything.

My conscious and my subconscious waited in anticipation, letting it build and build and build.

I tried to hold back, to wait as long as possible, but Rodán reached between us and rubbed my clit.

I was lost.

There was no thinking, only feeling, with the orgasm that took me away, like a leaf rushing down a stream that joins a raging river.

Vaguely I heard my throaty cries and felt my nails digging into Rodán's buttocks. They were tight and hard as I clenched them. Having him beneath my fingers seemed to ground me, bring me back to the moment.

My body continued to jerk and throb as Rodán thrust a few more times. He gave a sigh and a groan of pleasure and contentment as his cock pumped his semen inside me. I accepted all of him into my depths, welcoming him.

When his cock no longer throbbed and the spasms in my core had subsided, Rodán kissed me with fierce intensity. He withdrew, and then rolled me onto my side before spooning himself to my back and holding me tightly around my waist with one of his powerful arms.

"You won't leave me alone, will you?" I murmured as I started to drift into sleep. "You'll hold me, right?"

He gave me loving kisses from my shoulder up to my neck and stopped with a final kiss beneath my ear. "Sleep now, sweets. I won't leave until we wake together in the morning. I won't let go until it's time for us to face the day."

Face the day . . . There were so many things I had to face when the new day broke, but right now all I wanted to do was stay in my friend and lover's arms and feel the comfort of someone who cared for me.

CHAPTER 16

Rodán woke me before dawn. I'd slept maybe two hours. Sleep blurred my eyes as I tried to focus on him. I started to feel like ice picks were stabbing my head as I gained a sense of self and where I was.

"I'm sorry, Nyx." Rodán wore an oak-brown tunic and breeches, and was sitting on the edge of the bed. "Another liaison's home was attacked, and the liaison is missing. I need you and Olivia at the crime scene."

"Another?" I snapped fully awake.

Rodán took my hand and helped me climb off of his bed before he handed me my leather corset and pants. "You'll have just enough time to get home and change into your day clothing."

And day appearance.

I shimmied into my pants and pulled on my corset. "A Soothsayer's already on the job?"

"The scene is frozen, damage control handled," he said as I pulled on each boot.

My weapons belt seemed heavier as I buckled it. Damage control. Must have had a lot of attention already.

I gave Rodán a quick kiss before hurrying out of

his chambers, already pulling out my XPhone to call Olivia before the door closed behind me.

The sound of rain pounded on what was left of the roof of the police officer's home near Fifty-eighth Street and Fifth Avenue, not far from where Caprice had been murdered. Dripping noises echoed throughout the otherwise quiet house as I walked next to Adam and Olivia, and surveyed the scene that Lulu had frozen.

With Caprice's death so fresh in my mind and heart, I had to make the extra effort to put on my PI hat and concentrate on what I was here for.

The home had been destroyed, no bodies found. The house had the stench of burned sugar, like the liaison's home yesterday.

Adam had found another symbol scorched into the floor.

"It looks like Officer Jaworski might be missing," Adam said as we searched the house for other clues. "We don't really know that, but so far we haven't been able to find him in this wreck." He looked at Lulu. "Before the freezing thing was done."

My stomach twisted with a measure of guilt as I thought about spending last night in Rodán's bed, and here I was next to the man I wanted for far more than a friend.

Those thoughts just added to so many others bouncing around in my mind. I could almost hear the pinging sound of them hitting the inside of my skull.

I reached out with my weakened senses as I walked through a doorway with holes smashed into the wall to either side of it. Even mostly drained of my power from last night's battle, I knew the liaison had been here but was now gone. "The humans won't realize it until they've done every search they can," I said after a moment, "but I already know he's not here."

"Shit," Adam said as he walked beside me.

My gut clenched. "Yeah."

"I'm going to check out the dining room." Olivia paused, put her hand on my arm, and then spoke so only I could hear. "Are you okay?"

"Don't worry." I gave a halfhearted smile before I said, louder, "Just get your ass busy and do your half of the job."

She patted her rear. "You can kiss this ass, girl," she said, then left to do her own searching.

"B—" I had to stop myself from calling out "bitch" after her. Adam probably wouldn't get it. It's a girl thing.

I hadn't told Adam about Caprice yet. I just couldn't get the words out, like it would make it all that much more real. He'd met her in my office once, but I wasn't sure he'd remember her. Caprice was hard to forget, though.

"So where's that guy who came with you last time?" Adam brought my attention back to the moment. I looked at him, with his short brown hair and beautiful brown eyes, and I knew it was time to tell Adam the truth. I just had to get the guts to do it. "Torin—is that a last name?" he was saying.

I looked at the gaping holes in the beige living

room walls. "That's all I've heard him called by." I hefted my purse up higher over my shoulder and felt the weight of my dagger. I wondered why T hadn't shown up at the office this morning when I met up with Olivia. Rodán must not have been able to reach him. Come to think of it, I had no idea how to get a hold of T.

"We've got to hurry," Adam said. "Can't keep this thing frozen much longer."

Any early morning light the house had was muted by thick gray clouds. Rainwater dripped constantly through the partially destroyed roof and splattered drops on the floor.

Adam looked at the ceiling before bringing his gaze back to mine. "If we don't hurry, the water's going to wash away any more clues." A big drop landed on his head with a plop, and we both laughed as water ran down his cheeks.

"How do you do that?" Adam said as he glanced down before looking at me again. "Not make a single print?"

The nice thing about being one of the Elves was the ability to investigate a crime scene without disturbing anything. The plaster dust didn't show I'd been there as we picked our way through fallen beams, destroyed furniture, and walked around other law enforcement professionals who'd been frozen as they documented everything.

I pushed my straight black hair over my shoulders. "I promise to explain everything. Soon."

"How about over dinner?" Adam's smile was

almost shy, and it gave me one of those tummy tickles that felt good and warm. "I know a great little Thai restaurant in the Flatiron district."

I almost laughed at the thought of a blue-haired, amethyst-skinned me out to dinner at a public restaurant, but I managed to hold it in. He looked too serious.

"Lunch would work better." I paused. He was so handsome and genuine. "You know—the nighttime job I have."

"Yeah. That." Adam paused and studied me. "You'll fill me in on that other job, right? And whatever it is you've been holding back."

"I'm not sure you'll be crazy about what I need to explain. What I *want* to tell you." I felt a big sigh coming on and I looked away from him. "But I'm a little scared you'll run the other direction when you find out."

"Hey." Adam touched me intimately for the first time, and I felt a huge tingling in my belly as he cupped my chin and turned my head to face him. "As long as you're not the same big ugly Demon tearing up the city, I won't be running."

I laughed as he let his hand slip away. "That's one thing I'm most definitely *not*. A Demon."

For a big guy, Adam had such a cute, boyish grin. "Didn't think it for a minute."

"But I *am* different," I said as I watched him for signs of—of something.

He shrugged. "Aren't we all?"

"Just you wait."

I sobered when we again reached the image burned

into the floor. The second symbol from whatever Demon we were dealing with.

As I knelt on one knee beside the pattern, I gripped my XPhone and studied the symbol once more. I'd already drawn it on my pad. Also took some pictures, which no doubt was another futile exercise, like the image at the last scene.

"A warhorse with a human torso . . ." With a frown I muttered what we'd already figured out. "And a strange-looking tail . . . like a fishtail."

Adam gestured to the symbol. "How do you know that's a warhorse?"

"It's big, and it carries sheathed weapons for the human riding it. Or in this case the human who's a part of it." I narrowed my gaze. "But how would a horse get around with two legs and half of its body as a fish tail?"

"We're probably looking at it too literally." Adam crouched beside me. "Maybe we should think more about its symbolism."

He bent to touch the wood with his fingertips, but I pushed his hand away with mine.

For a moment we didn't move. My hand rested on his and the sensations traveling through me were new, strange, and welcome. I'd always been attracted to Adam, but in this one moment, some kind of connection happened between the two of us. Stronger than ever before.

Adam didn't stop staring into my eyes as I drew my hand away. "You smell like honeysuckle," he said. "Always so soft and sweet."

He looked a little embarrassed after he said it, but I

smiled. "Thank you." So that's what my pheromones smelled like to him.

Adam didn't say anything, just watched me.

I pointed to the image on the floor. "You shouldn't touch it because you don't know what kind of evil energies the Demon may have left in that symbol." I studied the design burned into the wood. "You're probably right about the symbolism. We just need to figure out what it means."

"Here's some of that blue crap," Adam said, gesturing toward an overturned chair.

"This time I'm going to see if James can analyze it." I moved toward the still-wet Demon blood, and used a little baggie and a small tool to scoop it into the bag.

"Let's hope your friend can," Adam said.

I turned to face him. "I think that's about all we've got—"

"Nyx, you better check this out," Olivia said from the dining room. I went to her and stood at her side as she pointed at a pile of furniture. "Something about that wierd-ass piece of whatever on the other side of that curio, doesn't feel right. Like it's giving off serious vibes."

The strange thing caught the light and gave me a chill at the same time.

"What is it?" Adam said.

It wasn't far from the dining table, past the upturned curio cabinet and under a chair. A—what? "Something copper-colored," I said.

"And it's not a penny for my thoughts." Olivia

braced her hands on her hips. "I'm going in after it." She looked at the tunnel of destroyed furniture that had to be passed to get to the thing.

I grasped her arm. "You know I can protect myself in—in a special way so that I won't get hurt if that whole thing crashes down."

Olivia gestured toward the mess. "Go for it, girl."

After handing her my purse, I got on my knees and crawled low under the curio cabinet, the top of the cabinet resting on a coffee table. Broken china was scattered everywhere, and bits of it pressed into my palms. The pieces didn't cut into my flesh, thanks to the air cocoon I wrapped myself in.

"Be careful." So much concern was in Adam's voice that it sent warmth through me.

When I reached the thing that had caught Olivia's attention, I wanted to recoil from the evil energy emanating from it. No doubt about it. This was from the Demon.

It was a slightly curved, copper-colored, and egg-sized piece of—what? Excitement warred with fear, a bizarre combination. It surged through me like a geyser, straight toward my scalp, making me heady.

This could be a clue that would help us figure out what this Demon was and how to destroy it.

I balanced on one hand as I slipped the other into the front pocket of my slacks for one of the plastic evidence bags, along with a pair of tweezers, that I always kept on me as a PI. I had to balance on my elbows, but I finally got the bag and the tweezers out.

With some maneuvering I managed to get the thing into the plastic bag. I shoved the evidence bag and tweezers into my front pocket.

"Coming out," I said as I backed up the way I entered.

I wrinkled my nose as I finally drew out from beneath the curio and rested on my haunches. The stench of burned sugar was strong.

"You okay, Nyx?" Adam knelt on one knee beside me.

I dug into my front pocket and brought out what I'd found. The scalelike thing was sharp at the edges, and almost tore through the bag and touched my fingers. Thank the Goddess it hadn't, because who knew if it was as poisonous as Demon claws? I pulled out another bag from my purse and double-bagged the copper-shaded thing.

"Looks like a shell or a shingle." Adam held the bag up to make the clue more visible in what light there was. "Never seen anything like it."

"I need to take this to—" I stopped.

Why I didn't want to say Rodán's name in front of Adam, I didn't understand. I'd never had a problem saying it to him before. Maybe it was the fact that I'd just slept with Rodán last night, when he'd comforted me, and now I was thinking of being with Adam.

I forced myself to continue anyway. "Rodán may know what kind of Demon this is from, or how it's related to the Demon," I said. "Also, my friend James can run it through some tests."

James might know in an instant. Maybe I should take it to him first. He had a good-sized lab in the back of his apartment. He loved to experiment and he loved a good challenge.

"Take it." Adam leaned close enough that his words tickled my ear, sending a swirl of excitement through me as his masculine scent of leather and coffee washed over me. "I'm off Friday. Meet at your office and I'll take you to lunch?"

I brushed my fingers over my collar. "I think I can fit it in my schedule," I said as he drew away, and our eyes held.

"Great." Adam got to his feet, still smiling at me, and clasped my hand as he helped me stand. His palm felt warm, hard, callused.

My smile faded as he swept the house with his gaze. "You need to let me go after these Demons with you," he said, his tone hard. "I've got every right."

The way he said it made my stomach hurt. "I know."

"Then tell me where to meet you when you go out tonight," he said, his expression determined.

"I'm not ready, Adam." I bit the inside of my lip. "You don't know the other part of me."

"Nyx." His tone was softer now. "Unless you're some purple, green-horned Demon with teeth like a piranha and claws like a lion, you've got nothing to worry about."

"Amethyst," I said automatically, even as my belly churned more.

"What?"

"Nothing." I took a deep breath. "Just give me until Friday when we have lunch. Then I'll explain everything to you. Okay?"

He gave a slow nod. "I'll wait until then. That's it."

"Uh, hello?" came Olivia's voice. She handed my purse to me. "I think we'd better let Tinkerbell unfreeze the scene before it gets much later in the day."

I looked away from Adam's intense gaze and glanced up at a hole in the ceiling that went through the roof. Rain drizzled down, splashing the floor. "At least it's not sunny," I said, more to change the subject than anything else. "It'll be less confusing for the crime scene investigators to come out of a mindswipe. It's easier for some reason."

"You'd better go." Adam grasped my hand and squeezed it before giving me one of his adorable smiles. Goddess, he had such inviting, warm, brown eyes. "Noon. Friday. Your office."

It felt so good having him look at me that way. "I'm really looking forward to it, Adam."

"Same here." He released my hand and we held each other's gazes for a long moment before I joined Olivia and the two of us headed out of what was left of the front door.

CHAPTER 17

When I returned from the crime scene, I headed up to my apartment to change my soaked clothing and dry my wet hair.

Mostly, though, I needed some time to myself to think about what had happened to Caprice. Spending the night with Rodán had been a distraction, and the events this morning had forced me to keep from dwelling on her murder. The pain inside me was hollow, as if a piece of the world was missing, like a face cut out of a photograph.

Blank. Empty.

My heels clunked when I kicked them off beside the door, and the carpet was soft beneath my bare feet as I went into my bedroom. By the time I sat on my bed I was numb. Not from the wet clothes sticking to my skin but from my thoughts of Caprice, Jon, the two missing liaisons, and the first liaison's murdered family.

But mostly I thought about Caprice.

My palms were damp when I lowered my face into my hands. Did the bed shake with the force of my shudders? The ache behind my eyes grew so much that my head hurt. As if the tears I wanted to shed were building and building, pressing against my temples.

Dear Goddess, why Caprice? I could see her smile so clearly, as if I could reach out and touch the warmth of her friendship.

My body shook even more. Would I fall apart? Maybe.

A rapping sound on the front door knifed through me, each knock sounding loud and harsh even though they weren't, really. I was so raw and vulnerable that even my damp hair felt scratchy against my neck, and I wanted to chop it off.

I forced myself to my feet, and when I made it to the front door I peered out the peephole.

Adam? What was he doing here?

A mixture of emotions I couldn't separate flowed through me with the pain. I felt off balance, as if he was catching me after my physical change. I looked down at my hands, and at the black hair hanging limply over my shoulders. Of course I didn't look Drow. It was the middle of the day.

The moment I opened the door, Adam stepped toward me and wrapped his arms around me. The act caught me so off guard that for a moment I stiffened, before I relaxed against his hard body and breathed in his comforting scent of coffee and leather.

"Why didn't you say anything about your friend?" Adam hugged me tight before raising his head and taking me by my shoulders. The intensity in his brown eyes showed his concern like nothing else could. "Olivia told me before she left the scene that one of your closest friends was murdered last night by Demons."

He moved us inside the apartment as he spoke, and closed the door behind us by leaning against it and bringing me closer to him.

My voice sounded strangled from the emotions raging inside me. "I wasn't ready to talk about it."

He cupped the side of my face and rubbed one thumb over my cheek. "I'm so sorry, Nyx."

I swallowed, feeling like an apple was lodged in my throat. "If only I had sensed it sooner—"

Adam stole my words when he brought his mouth to mine and kissed me.

This time I was even more startled, and I froze. He hesitated, but I didn't give him a chance to move away. I brought my mouth tight to his, and then he kissed me harder. I let myself fall into the warmth of his kiss and the wonderful way he tasted.

When he did draw back he brushed my damp hair away from my cheek with the back of his hand and I shivered. "That was for trying to blame yourself for what happened." He brought his mouth closer to mine again. "This is for you."

A soft sound of surprise, acceptance, and need slipped through my lips as he moved his mouth closer. He lightly brushed his lips over mine before slipping his tongue into my mouth. He slid his hands to my hips and held me as I wrapped my arms around his neck. This kiss was slow, our tongues meeting and tasting one another.

My belly tingled with the thrill of finally kissing Adam. The tingles radiated through my whole body, warming me, chasing away the numbness I had been feeling. He made a rumbling sound and I followed with a soft moan. I couldn't get enough of his scent and the hardness of his body fused with mine.

Suddenly the realization that I'd been with Rodán last night slapped me. I shouldn't be kissing Adam when I'd just been in Rodán's bed. It didn't matter that Rodán was my friend, mentor, and former lover, who had simply comforted me when I needed it so badly. I couldn't do this with Adam. Not yet.

I released him, put my hands on his chest, and stepped back. My lips felt moist, and tingled from his kiss. My entire body felt sensitized from too many emotions to define.

"Thank you," I said before I moved into his arms again. I pressed my cheek against the dry T-shirt beneath his open bomber jacket. He held me and stroked the tangles in my damp hair.

"Don't blame yourself, baby." The way he called me "baby" made pleasure flush throughout me. "You know you couldn't have done anything about it if you had been able to get there sooner."

I lightly picked at the soft cotton of his T-shirt with my fingers. "It sounds like Olivia told you everything."

"Not everything, but what she said sounded pretty devastating." He stroked the curve of my ear, and I shivered again. "I can't begin to imagine what you're going through."

I clenched his T-shirt with both hands and moved so that I bowed my head against his chest. "I don't know if I can talk about it. Everything—it's so . . . Goddess, no, I just can't. It's too soon." I shuddered, trying my best not to picture the horror from last night. "Caprice was one of my closest friends."

Adam moved his hand to the middle of my back and rubbed his fingers slowly over the damp silk of my blouse. "When you're ready, I'm here."

"Thank you," I said again, only this time in a whisper as I pressed my forehead tighter to his chest.

After a long, quiet moment, I stepped back so that he had to let his hands slide away from me. I took both of his hands in mine and squeezed as our eyes met and held. "It means a lot to me that you came." I wanted so badly for him to stay, and to kiss him forever, but it wasn't right. "Maybe I'll be ready to talk about it Friday."

"Day after tomorrow." He gave a little smile. "When you tell me everything else you've been holding back."

I managed a smile, just for him. "It's going to be a long lunch."

Adam gave me a quick kiss. "If you need me, call. Promise."

I withdrew my hands from his. "Promise."

His gaze was long and searching before he turned and opened the door. He paused to glance back at me. We said nothing, yet it was like we'd spoken a volume in that last look.

When he closed the door behind him, I leaned against the door and sighed. And felt a little healed inside.

I tossed my purse on my desk while Olivia hung her wet Mets sweat jacket on a hook by the door.

My lips still tingled from Adam's kiss, even though it was at least half an hour since he'd left.

But my mind still hurt from thinking about Caprice.

I picked up a file folder with pages sticking out and tapped each side of the folder on my desk to slide the loose papers completely inside. I had no idea what was in that folder. Didn't care, either. Just needed something for my hands to do.

Getting images of last night out of my mind was going to be impossible. And my heart ached so much I thought it would burst.

"If Rodán would have let me come last night—" Olivia started.

"It wouldn't have made any difference." I stared at the folder I had picked up. "Caprice was dead before we got to her."

"I'm sorry, Nyx," Olivia said quietly.

I took in a deep breath, and it seemed like every part of my body ached. "Let's focus on this damned master Demon. He's got to be the reason Jon and Caprice were taken so fast."

Olivia nodded. "On it."

"A beast with a man's head, warhorse body, and fish tail?" I set the folder down. "Along with a dirt-cyclone-looking thing and a scale or shingle." Kali hopped onto my desk and sat right on my handbag, next to the stack of Demonology research books. "What the hell kind of clues are those?"

Just great—Olivia opened a large bag of Lays barbeque chips, which she immediately dug into.

"Really"—*crunch, crunch*—"stupid clues." Olivia held out the bag, offering me some.

"You know better." The sound of my own crunching was enough to give me the shudders.

Olivia shrugged and dug into her chips again. *Crunch.*

I winced and searched for a bottle of Excedrin in the top drawer of my desk. Ow. So there were my scissors, next to a strip of staples. Sticky notes, pens, several pennies, markers, thumbtacks, Wite-Out, a ruler . . . Victory! Found the bottle of headache medicine.

Crunch.

Shudder.

Olivia set the bag of chips down. "Maybe I'll get lucky with a Google search on the Net." She grabbed another chip.

All of Olivia's continuous crunching and munching jacked up the headache that pushed at the back of my eyes. I took two Excedrin tablets without water, and nearly choked on them as they went down my dry throat. When my throat was clear, I said, "I need to get this sample to James."

She tilted her head and looked at me. Her tone was completely serious when she said, "I wonder if James and Derek get it on as gorillas."

I swear, if I had been drinking my Starbucks today it would have gone up my nose. Working with Olivia was dangerous to my latte habit.

Dark-haired, blue-eyed James was a Doppler whose animal form was a gorilla. A blue-eyed gorilla is a pretty interesting sight. His husband, blond, green-eyed Derek, was half human and half Shifter. He shifted into a gorilla when he was together with James as a couple, but Derek preferred a jungle cat at other times.

I tried to keep a straight face as I said, "I doubt they do it when Derek is a leopard."

"Would make for some interesting sex." Olivia looked thoughtful, as if she was serious. Maybe she was. She smiled and the spark of mischief was in her eyes again. "We'll just ask James how he and Derek have sex the next time we see him."

My brows narrowed. "Don't you dare."

Olivia grinned.

I nearly groaned again. She probably would anyway.

Focus on solving the puzzle, Nyx. "This Demon is playing some kind of game and it's really pissing me off."

"No shit." Olivia pulled a huge chip out of the bag. "We need to take down this fucker, and soon." *Crunch.*

"What do *you* think?" I asked Kali, as if she would meow an answer. Kali gave the equivalent of a shrug by delicately picking up her forepaw and starting to lick it.

"A whole lot of help you are." I gave her a nudge to get her off of my Dolce & Gabbana handbag. "This purse is worth more than you are. One of these days you could earn your Fancy Feast and give us a little assistance."

The look Kali gave could have skewered me on

one of my own blades. She stuck her pug nose in the air as she rose on all fours, turned, and gave me the tail-in-my-mouth, butt-in-my-face treatment.

I sputtered, shoving her furry behind away from me. "Ick."

With grace only a cat could have when she's mad, Kali leapt off my desk, stalked away, and disappeared near one of our packed file drawers. No doubt headed upstairs in her secret way to shred my laciest things.

"After I take whatever this thing is to James," I said to a bunch of crunching, "I'll hit Victoria's. Last I checked Kali only left me two pairs of lace thongs and a satin bra."

Olivia was moving her fingers over her gel pad, staring at the computer and not paying attention to me. She could care less about underwear that you couldn't buy at Wal-Mart.

Victoria's would be a worthwhile trip. Since I had lunch scheduled with Adam on Friday, I definitely needed something sexy to wear—just for the feel of it against my skin when I saw him.

He wouldn't run the moment I told him the whole truth, right? No, I wasn't going to go the negative route in my thinking.

With my elbow on the hard, smooth Dryad wood, I ignored Olivia's crunching, braced my chin in my palm, and looked out at the rain-drenched late morning. The scent of rain was still strong from the wind that had blown through the door when we walked in.

At least the handbag that I'd stuffed my weapons into had remained dry because I'd used a little air spell to cocoon it. The rest of me—didn't matter and

I hadn't wanted to waste the power. But my Dolce & Gabbana? I don't think so.

The Demon was what I should have been thinking about when Olivia and I started doing our research, but it was Adam who I couldn't get out of my mind. Maybe because it was a distraction from thoughts too painful to dwell on.

In a sort of daydream, I continued to watch the rain come down outside of the picture window. I wiggled my toes under my desk and slid off my Burberry heels. They joined the Morrisons, Pradas, and Tory Burch that I'd kicked off on other days and hadn't gotten around to retrieving yet.

Adam once said I was the only PI he knew who looked gorgeous, could navigate a crime scene in three-inch designer heels, and smelled good.

What a sweet-talker.

Okay, stop daydreaming, Nyx.

Even though I'd rather daydream about Adam, I forced my mind back to what I was supposed to be working on before I took the sample to James.

I reached into my handbag, which had blue Kali hair stuck to it now, and drew out my XPhone. I pressed the uplink option and began uploading the info, my notes, the photographs, and my drawing into my computer's database.

Of course, of course, the photos hadn't come out, and I hadn't done such a hot job drawing the man/horse/fish tail. That was the strangest-looking fish tail.

I stared at my computer screen that now showed my hand-drawn images and I arranged them side by side.

Swirly cone-shaped thing like a dirt tornado.

Man/horse/fish tail.

Scale.

Damn.

Yep, had to get this sample analyzed right away. I called James, who happened to be home for the afternoon, and he said to come on over.

Crumpling sounds and something hitting the metal waste can told me Olivia had finished her chips. Thank the Goddess. One of these days I was going to outlaw chip crunching in our office. That and bubblegum popping. Oh, and soup slurping.

"Hippocampus is the closest thing that comes up on the Internet." Olivia wiped her hands on a paper napkin she'd pulled out of her desk before tossing the napkin into the waste can. "In some references it's exactly what we're looking for—a man's head, horse's body, fish tail."

I rubbed my eyes with my thumb and forefinger. "No self-respecting Demon is going to present himself as a hippocampus."

Olivia gave me the look before she said, "You consider a Demon as being self-respecting?"

I managed to hold back a laugh but not a grin. "Um, no. What else have you got?"

She rolled her eyes, not at me but at the results of her search. I think. She moved her fingers over her gel pad. "Quite a number of sea monsters with some variation of a fish tail. But nothing else remotely close to the drawing."

I sighed.

With a grin she looked at me. "There's a cockfish."

The snort that rose up in me almost made me choke. "A cockfish?"

"That would be one interesting Demon." Olivia chucked a pencil eraser at me and caught me off guard. The eraser bounced from my forehead to the desk and she laughed. "Score one for me."

I flung the eraser back at her and it pinged off the end of her nose. "Heh. I think mine was worth at least two points."

"Speaking of cock." Olivia pushed the eraser across her desk to join her pile of ammunition. "Haven't had any of that in way too long. I need to get laid."

"As long as you don't fall for some Vamp." I swiveled in my chair and grabbed my purse before looking back at her. "Or a Metamorph."

Olivia gave me one of her wickedest grins. "We'll see."

I returned her grin with one of my best "Don't mess with me" glares. "I'll be watching you."

"Like I'm worried."

"I'm heading to James's to have him check out this scale thing." I patted my purse, where I'd stuffed the plastic bag with the whatever-it-was.

"See you at the Pit," Olivia said. "And after Rodán and I have our face-to-face I'm going out with you."

Oh, crap. Well, maybe Rodán wouldn't agree to let her hunt the Demons. I opened the door, and the bells tinkled as I walked through. "No Vamps," I yelled over my shoulder instead of acknowledging the possibility of another friend being in danger.

And murdered.

CHAPTER 18

The rain had finally let up, and the air smelled rain-washed and clean as I headed toward James's "pad with a lab." As he called it, not me.

James Gifford lived in Morningside Heights, near the border of Harlem. He was a professor in the School of Engineering and Applied Science at Columbia University by day. By evening he practically lived in the high-tech lab he'd built in his "pad," a first-floor apartment with absolutely no view.

When I arrived, James opened the door after I knocked twice. Instantly the scent of brownies and what smelled like stew hit me, and I realized I hadn't eaten since . . . I wasn't sure.

"Haven't been graced with your presence for quite a while, beautiful." James smiled as he stepped back to let me into a nice but small living room that totally masked what was behind those walls.

James adjusted his trendy wire-framed glasses after he shut the door, then gave me a quick hug. He put his hands on his trim hips. "What's up?"

"Can't remember." My stomach rumbled. "I think it's to eat whatever Derek is whipping up."

"Let me set your purse on the couch and we'll go

see if he'll let us sneak an early dinner." He took my handbag. "Oooh. Dolce & Gabbana." He looked at me over his rims. "This is so unfair. If I showed up at Columbia with something like this—"

"They'd kick your ass out." Derek was wiping his hands on a dish towel as he came from the kitchen. He grinned at me, teeth white against tanned skin and golden eyes flashing. After a quick hug, he ushered me to the kitchen, where the smells were even stronger. "So, fill us in on what's going on."

"Maybe we should eat first," I said as they seated me at the dining room table. Derek started serving up prime rib and steamed vegetables on fine porcelain that had sprigs of wildflowers around its rim.

James poured three glasses of merlot. "That bad?"

"That bad."

Derek was a half-human Shifter, but had been raised with his human father and human stepfamily. He'd met James at a gay nightclub a couple of years ago and they'd been together ever since.

We had normal chatter while Derek, a chef at one of the finer restaurants in the city, served up a chocolate mousse that was like dying and going to Summerland. I swear.

When we were finished eating and I was relaxed from a couple of glasses of wine, I told them everything that had happened. Including how Caprice had been murdered.

"Sweetheart." Derek came over from his side of the dining table and took my hand so that I was standing and he could give me a hug. It felt good to be held again, and to breathe in the hint of a male

Shifter's scent of amber. When he drew away there were tears in his eyes. "Caprice was such a doll." He wiped the corners of his eyes with his fingers. "I just can't believe it."

James hugged me next, and kissed my cheek. "Let me see what I can do to help so that you can stop the Demons from hurting anyone else."

Derek insisted on cleaning the dinner dishes himself and shooed us out of the dining room. James and I went alone into his amazing lab, filled with microscopes, test tubes, beakers, a centrifuge, and all that stuff he used to do whatever it was he did as a hobby.

James pulled on a pair of rubber gloves and a long-sleeved lab coat. He set his glasses on a long examination table, then put on safety eyewear. "Stand by the door in case this breaks and goes flying. Better yet, do your air cocoon thing."

I nodded and used a little air power between me and the shell. My elemental strength was still recharging and I hoped I'd have my full abilities back by the time I headed out to track Demons tonight.

James took the scale-thing out of the bag with a pair of tweezers, then held it up and stared at it under the incandescent lighting in his lab. He made a few "hmmm" sounds before he used a tool of some sort and broke off a small piece of the egg-sized shell. A loud crack came with the action, but nothing else happened. Thank the Goddess.

He put the piece under the microscope and took off the goggles to peer at the piece of whatever it was.

"What is it?" I asked, practically bouncing on the balls of my feet.

"Definitely an arthropod." James raised his head from the microscope and picked up his wire-rimmed glasses from beside it. "It's a piece of an exoskeleton."

"Huh?" So I wasn't up on arthropods or exo-skeletons—whatever they were. They didn't teach that in the Drow realm. "And this means?"

James cleaned the lenses of his eyeglasses with a soft cloth. "Best guess is that it's from a scorpion the size of a rhino."

"A scorpion?" A chill made me rub my arms with both hands. "How could it be so big?"

"Honey, I have no clue." He slipped his glasses back on as he frowned.

"What would a Demon have to do with a scor-pion?" I said out loud without meaning to as my thoughts drifted in that direction. I pulled my XPhone out and used the stylus to bring up the drawings. "This is a symbol we found today, near where I found that scorpion shell. A man's head, horse's body, fish tail."

James looked at it and shook his head. "That's a scorpion's tail."

A strange sensation crept over me, as if scorpions were actually climbing my skin. "Are you sure?"

James pointed to the drawing. "See the sections? Those aren't scales. Those are part of an exoskele-ton." He traced the tail with his fingertip. "And the way it curves? That's definitely a scorpion's tail."

"We've been looking for the wrong thing." I pulled up the picture of the tornado-like image. "Did you or

Derek come up with anything that will tell us what this is?"

James frowned. "No." He gestured toward the piece of shell. "But that definitely is another clue, and it will help me in my research."

"Thanks so much." I gave James a quick hug and a kiss on his cheek.

"No messing around with my man," came Derek's voice from behind me.

"I love you guys." I turned and hugged Derek again, and kissed his cheek, too. "I have to run. Now we've got something to go on."

CHAPTER 19

It was early evening as I stood on the corner terrace of my apartment and stared toward the foggy sunset, mostly obscured by rain clouds.

I had just returned home from James and Derek's place, and hadn't had a chance to tell Olivia the shell-thing was a piece of a scale from a monstrous scorpion. I didn't know what it meant, yet, but it had to be bad. It was late, and we could start working on it tomorrow.

The rain had halted for now and the cool dampness of the air felt good on my skin. I sifted out the various smells until only the scents of a rain-fresh evening and the abundance of nature in Central Park filled my senses. I drank in the perfume of flowers, scents of trees and bushes, and the smell of water from the lakes.

My bottle of green tea chilled my palm as I took a long drink. The liquid was cold and I felt it all the way to my empty stomach. My skin started to tingle as the sun lowered, and I took another drink of tea. I had a few moments yet.

It felt like my mind was twisting and bending, and I couldn't follow along. Like everything that had happened over the past forty-eight hours was too much and I barely held onto a thread of reality.

"Hi, Kali," I said as my Persian walked toward me on the terrace's balustrade, and she gave a "meow" in response.

She rubbed against my arm as I gripped the railing. I let go of the balustrade and began petting her, rubbing her favorite places at her neck and behind her ears.

Kali purred as I slid my palm over her soft blue hair while I took a final drink of my tea.

One thing I was sure of—I couldn't take Olivia tonight. I didn't even want T tagging along. I just needed to be by myself. Searching my territory and keeping it safe.

Alone.

With my thoughts.

My incisors dropped as the sun slipped away and darkness started setting in. I licked the tip of each incisor, feeling their sharpness against my tongue. My hair was almost blue when I walked through the French doors to my bedroom and shut them behind me.

I tossed the tea bottle into the wastebasket and, instead of enjoying the transformation by stretching or dancing, I looked at my hand and watched it change from white to amethyst.

Purple, green-horned Demon came into my mind as I remembered what Adam had said.

"Amethyst," I whispered.

No, I'm not a Demon, and I don't have horns.

But I'm amethyst. *Purple.*

Kali meowed, and I wished I knew what she was saying. Maybe Olivia could learn "cat" as well as Drow. She could pick up any language if she was around someone long enough who spoke it.

My skin turned more fully to its Drow shade. The push and pull of my muscles felt somehow alien as my body grew more powerful and dangerous.

An oddity.

That's what I am.

That's what I'll always be.

I sighed. I didn't know where the melancholy came from, but it shrouded me like the city's pollution on a particularly dense humid day.

I've always been proud of who I am and of the two halves of me. I don't know why it was affecting me then.

Maybe because of Adam and what he might think about me when he learned the truth.

Maybe because we were no closer to finding and getting rid of the Demons.

Maybe because I missed Caprice. Her death and my failure to save her. The fact that she'd left angry the last time I'd seen her added to the pain.

Everything contributed toward my melancholy feeling. All of what had been happening.

I stripped out of my clothing, which felt odd because I so rarely transformed in my street clothes.

As I stepped into my leather pants, my mind turned more fully to Caprice. The thought that I'd been too late still sat like lead in my belly, and somehow it hurt worse now, as if some of the numbness had worn off.

I could picture how Caprice was before we lost her. Dark hair, beautiful smile, intelligent hazel eyes, quick wit.

Now gone.

Just gone.

Like a chessboard where suddenly one of the knights disappeared. A blank spot on the board of life that could never truly be replaced because no two things were alike, no two beings alike.

I thought of one of Olivia's T-shirts that read,

> *You're unique . . .*
> *Just like everyone else.*

Yeah, we are all unique, but some people are more special to each of us than others.

My lips felt too stiff to smile and my throat too tight to swallow. I had to get my mind off of my friend.

After I slipped into my leather corset, I tugged on one boot and then the other like a wooden toy warrior. I needed to be alone. Going to the Pit and running into T or Olivia wasn't an option for me tonight, so I headed to the kitchen to fix myself something for dinner instead of eating at the Pit.

The Manhattan skyline always amazed me. Otherworld was simple, as if the world had been frozen during the Middle Ages, except that Otherworld was more beautiful and somewhat more civilized. Well, sort of.

First I made a quick sweep around the area of

Sixtieth and Columbus Circle in the rain. The Mandarin Oriental, a fabulous five-star hotel, was where we hid our most precious paranorms. The Magi. And we hid them in luxury.

Not too far from the Mandarin Hotel, I chose a block of four- to five-story brownstones. As easy and silent as a cat, I climbed up fire escapes and ledges and worked my way through the rain until I was on the rooftop.

I took a good look at my territory as I stepped around a chimney.

My leather clothing hugged my body, and the belt clinging to my hips carried my weapons, including my 9mm, in addition to my XPhone. I'd woven a little air spell to protect everything on my belt from the rain. I didn't want to use too much of my elemental strength by cocooning myself, so my hair was plastered to my head, and water rolled down my face and into my eyes.

As a Siren, Nadia would be having a ball right now, reveling in her element.

My gut twisted. Would a Tracker be attacked tonight, a third night in a row? Would it be Nadia?

"Anu, please watch over her." I tilted my face to the rain-filled sky. "Please watch over all Trackers."

I lowered my head and blinked away the rain.

We needed more Trackers. "This is bullshit," I said out loud to the Great Guardian, as if she was bothering to listen. I talked while I moved along the rooftop. "Can't you cut us a break?" I shouted.

Not that I expected an answer.

"If the GG doesn't start getting us help, I will," I grumbled. Although Rodán might have a say in it.

I leapt from one rooftop to another and worked my way toward the larger buildings. Spider-Man had nothing on me. The air power I used to stay airborne long enough to reach the next rooftop was simple, really, and it didn't drain me. All I did was ride the currents already there, and a little water power from the rain made traveling this way even easier.

Since all of my powers are derived from the four elements—earth, air, water, and fire—an element must be present for me to draw any magic from it. If I was to be captured and locked in a room with no bars, a floor too thick to reach the earth, walls and a ceiling too thick to grab enough air, and of course no water or fire, I would be, as humans say, "Up shit creek."

But no one knew about that weakness, and I sure wasn't sharing. That was *my* Kryptonite.

"I wonder what the Shifters' weakness is?" I frowned. Whatever it was might have kept Caprice from shifting and escaping, and could have been why she died. Or she was totally caught off guard and it came out of nowhere.

My face felt hot as I thought of Chance. He had been at the Pit the night Caprice died. Could he have somehow penetrated the Pit's defenses and "made" us Trackers?

I'd have to talk with Rodán about the possibility.

I worked my way from one rooftop to another, then landed on a rooftop in a crouch and listened. Air carried to me sounds, smells, and the kind of sensory input that would send prickles crawling up my back if something was wrong. But the rain did make it harder to reach out with my senses.

I kept moving through my territory, listening, smelling, reaching out with whatever the air would bring to me. Unlike other nights, like the night I was attacked, it was quiet.

Too quiet?

Maybe Demons didn't like rain.

As if we could be so lucky.

At the intersection of Broadway and Amsterdam Avenue, I climbed down a building to Verdi Square and walked through a puddle. I passed a couple of New Yorkers carrying big black umbrellas, but of course, because of my air glamour, the people didn't notice blue-haired, amethyst-skinned me.

I took a deep breath of rain-filled air, with rain-drops that sparkled as they passed through the glow of streetlights. Perhaps tonight the rain obscured any signs of Demons, so maybe the earth would help me find them. I went to the tallest and oldest tree.

Bark scraped my palms as I grabbed a sturdy branch of the tree and flipped up onto it. Wet branches and leaves slapped my face, but the canopy kept some of the pouring rain off of me. With my back to the tree trunk, I sat on one of the larger branches and easily balanced myself so that I was in a sitting position with my knees bent, feet on the branch, and my arms hugging my knees.

I already sensed that the tree's roots delved deep into the earth and spread out, far, far, far. I'd used tree roots a few times in the past, but not too often because it does use up some of my earth elemental power.

Using the tree roots was sort of like using antennae. My earth senses could shoot far, far beyond the roots.

"Relax," I said to myself. "Fall into it. Forget everything else."

I closed my eyes and let go of all the troubles of this world, and my own troubles, and sank my senses deep into the ground. In my mind I shot through the earth, below concrete and asphalt.

Yes, the tree's roots were strong and extended far beyond the immediate area. They were perfect for what I wanted to do.

Piece by piece, I searched each section of my territory. It was time to push. Push harder than I ever had before.

I felt the rough bark and the earth as I mentally grabbed onto a root and rode it. The root stretched out farther and farther and farther.

It was like I was flying underground. Mentally flying. It felt so free.

Then the root I'd been riding ended and I propelled myself farther, using the strength of those roots to go beyond.

Riverside Park rushed toward me and I came to a full stop.

Demons. Multiple Demons.

The jerk of my heart brought my senses swooping back inside me so hard I almost lost my balance on the tree branch.

How many Demons were there? I couldn't tell for

sure. Should I call Olivia for backup? Or should I stay hidden and follow the Demons to find their lair? Calling Olivia would be the smart thing to do.

Nobody said I was always smart.

CHAPTER 20

I ran hard and fast. With Caprice's death just last night, and Jon's the night before, my rage fueled me. My eyesight was sharp and keen, my breathing natural and even as I ran at top speed.

I needed to take down some Demons. I needed to stab the life out of every one of them. Screw following them to a lair. I *needed* the kills. It was like I was possessed.

Riverside Park and 108th Street were within my sight when I sensed a shift. Something I'd never felt before. Like the Demons had melted away and weren't in the park anymore.

Frowning, I came to a halt on the corner just across the street from the park. I reached out with every element I had.

Nothing.

What?

Had the Demons gone underground because their lair was here? Or perhaps they'd gone into the Hudson River that bordered the park?

The rain had stopped. I started moving and crossed the empty street. I kept going and went down to the lower level, until I reached the spot where I was sure the Demons had been.

To my right was Neville Colman Field, but I didn't see anything on the other side of the fence. A wire-mesh trash bin was a few feet away from me, filled with rain-soaked garbage that smelled of spoiled hot dogs and mustard.

Old-fashioned light posts lit the park intermittently down a stretch of sidewalk directly in front of me, park benches along the way. To my left was another field, lots of trees, and no Demons. Past the sidewalk, grass, and trees before me, I could see the glittering lights of the city reflecting on the Hudson River.

I pushed my wet hair out of my face with one hand, my other hand braced on my hip.

What was going on? Only a slight taint hung in the air, which didn't really feel or smell like Demons. Like anise seed, a smell like licorice. Strange, but not a Demon smell.

But they'd been here. I knew it.

"Godsdamnit!" I shouted. It wasn't nearly enough, and I wanted to shout more. To scream every obscenity in Drow that I could think of.

But more than that, I wanted to *kill*. I wanted to make the Demons pay for Caprice's death.

I didn't care about weakening myself. My anger and adrenaline would more than make up for any form of weakness in my body.

My jaws ached from clenching my teeth so hard. This time I called on the most difficult element to use—fire. It was even harder because there was no fire around, only static in the air.

Power rushed up my body and I felt like *I* was on fire as I shot my very essence into the air. I sailed the currents, feeling the heat and flames that I created from the static surrounding my body.

Fury rolled through me like hot iron rods. My anger was so great that I didn't feel the drain that I normally would have. I pushed and pushed and pushed until I had reached every corner of my territory.

Nothing. Not a godsdamn thing.

Something tickled at my consciousness.

Nyx, you idiot. You've left yourself vulnerable. You're going to pay for this.

I didn't care.

But the something that was pulling at me made me retreat, and I practically flew, riding the flames of static until I rushed into my body.

And fell to my knees. Air burned my lungs as if I'd been running.

Immediately I swept my gaze around me. Nothing.

Thank the Goddess.

What an idiot. I'd left myself vulnerable, and I'd used so much fire power that my belly clenched and ached. What was wrong with me that I'd take chances like this? My head felt so dizzy that I gagged. My stomach convulsed and the hamburger I'd made for dinner started to rush up my throat. Only by sheer will did I keep from vomiting.

"Stupid, stupid, stupid." I sat on my haunches as I clutched one arm against my belly.

I struggled to remain aware of everything around me. I knew better than this. I knew better than to make myself weak enough that I'd be unable to fight well if I was attacked. I'd barely recovered from last night.

My breathing was so harsh my ears seemed filled with it. Like I was in a tunnel and could only hear the echo of each breath.

Slowly, so slowly, my body began to recover. Strength came back into my muscles and the pain in my belly started to subside.

I'm Drow. I heal fast and easily. But this wasn't the same. It's much harder for me to recover from using such intense elemental powers.

A few more moments passed. I *should* call Olivia. I started to reach for my XPhone.

Then I felt, and even heard, a disturbance. Only this time it was a scream, and then the sounds of a human female sobbing. The laughter of two human males followed. Mean, cruel laughter.

"No way." I got to my feet, still holding my arm to my aching belly. I didn't give a crap that Trackers weren't supposed to interfere in human crimes. No way was I going to let men rape a woman. "Not in *my* territory."

I'd call Olivia as soon as I was done with these ass-holes. I dropped my arms to my sides. Took a deep breath and ran what would be about thirty blocks, until I was close to the lower end of the Cherry Walk, approximately Seventy-seventh Street and Riverside.

From my stopping point I could see two males and a female. One male had a dagger to the woman's throat so that she was only whimpering, her face flushed with tears.

Anger whirled through me like the firestorm I'd

just flown in, and I wished I could use that anger to incinerate those males.

My senses felt off-kilter again. Not right.

Something had to be going down. Where?

"I'm taking care of this first." I hissed the last word.

One of the males jerked his head up. Good. He looked afraid.

Too bad I wasn't allowed to kill humans unless absolutely necessary. Maybe I could consider this necessary.

No, damnit. But I could hurt them.

I avoided a lamppost, and crept through muted light and shadows before leaping onto a sycamore tree behind the men and woman. I balanced on a branch, then eased along it until I was in a crouch, directly over the males.

The men had started to strip off the whimpering female's jeans. One of them ripped open her shirt.

My whole body heated and I knew the dangerous flash was in my eyes.

No killing humans, Nyx.

Damn.

With the power of air I could bind the sonsof-bitches, or by taking magic from earth I could force them to the ground and let the earth hold them so that they wouldn't be able to budge. But I couldn't afford to drain myself more by using any elements when I had Demons to track. After the stunt I'd pulled with the fire element, I was low on reserves.

I could scare the shit out of the humans, though. A dragon-clawed dagger should do the trick.

One of the men nearly had the woman's jeans off

as I drew the weapon from its sheath and held it in one hand. The damp air carried an odd scent to me along with the sweaty smell of the men, but I couldn't place it.

And then I sensed Demons.

My heart raced and my skin went clammy.

Randy.

Dear Goddess, seven or eight of the Demons were closing in on the Tracker on the west side of Central Park, a short distance from me.

My skin crawled. I could feel the Demons. Almost smell their fetid breath.

And I sensed something else. Something so vague it was barely a brush against my mind.

I had to get to Randy. I couldn't let him down like I had Caprice.

The woman, whose face was wet with tears, whimpered as one man held the knife at her throat while the other stripped her. Her jeans were off now and she was only in her panties.

Randy. Randy. I had to get to him.

A split-second decision. I didn't have a choice in doing what I had to now, no matter how much trouble I'd be in.

With a firm grip on the dagger in one hand, I swung from the tree branch with the other hand. It would cost me five seconds in getting to Randy, but I had to do it.

I landed in a crouch behind the men.

In two quick moves I sliced their hamstrings.

At the same time I cut the man who was holding

the knife, I shoved him to the side so that his blade wouldn't touch the woman.

The males screamed, shouted, and dropped to the ground. They cried out as they tried to get to their feet, but were unable to stand and unable to comprehend what had just happened to them.

"Hurry!" I grabbed the woman's hand, jerking her up to haul her away from the men so they couldn't stab or hurt her in any way. "I can't stay, so you've got to take care of yourself," I said as I dragged the girl a few feet out of danger. The expression on her face would have puzzled me if I wasn't in such a hurry. Almost a smile.

Shock. She was in shock.

"You've got to got out of here. Fast!" I yelled as I yanked her a little farther.

Still holding her hand, I turned from her and prepared to run for the second time that night. I'd get her a few paces away, and then I'd go after Randy.

She came to a full halt behind me and wouldn't budge. It was suddenly like trying to pull a semi.

At the same time her hand *shifted* in mine.

Armored skin and claws against my palm.

Before I had a chance to react, the claws reversed the hold and had a grip on my hand.

Horror knifed my gut.

A Demon.

Without taking the time to assess or think about what I was doing, I twisted around and drove my dagger up toward the neck—

Of Chance. The man I'd seen Caprice with. Except

he now had sharp Demon teeth as well as claws for hands.

My dagger clanged off his neck as instant shock went through me. Somehow I knew this wasn't an underling Demon. It was a major Demon. At the same time I caught that odd scent from earlier. Anise seed, like black licorice. The smell I had ignored.

Adrenaline rushed through me and my heart pounded faster and faster.

Fury took over. "You sonofabitch. *You* killed Caprice," I shouted as I rammed my dagger toward its neck again.

The Chance-Demon laughed. "Easy prey," it said as it caught my wrist while I was going for the kill. "Just like you."

When the Demon yanked my arm, I lost my grip on my dagger and it thumped in the wet grass. "The other sack of meat—Jon, I believe Caprice called him—fell for the same stupid ploy that you did."

The Chance-Demon caught both of my wrists in a tight grip in front of me. "This was too easy, *Princess*," it said in the language of the Dark Elves, obviously trying to shock me.

It worked. For half a second.

My actions were automatic.

I gave a slight jump so that I was bent at the waist with my feet on the Demon's armored belly.

Then I jammed my boots against the Demon's face and I shoved as hard as I could, flipping my feet over my head.

He shouted as I whirled my body horizontally,

ripping my wrists from the Demon's claws. Blood dripped along my arms from the tears in my skin.

My feet were steady as I landed a few feet away in a crouch. My remaining dagger was already in my left hand by the time my feet touched the grass.

The torn flesh on my wrists burned so much I wanted to scream. My heart pounded even harder, but now it felt like it might explode.

I staggered to my feet. My vision started to go cloudy.

It hit me like a Troll's club slamming against my chest.

The Demon's claws were deadly. The poison fatal to all races, including Light and Dark Elves.

I was going to die.

The Chance-Demon had already won. Three times.

As I stumbled to the side, anger flooded me. It was like a rush of fire that blocked some of the pain and poison-induced confusion.

No! This fucking Demon wasn't going to win.

I might be dying, but I was so taking the Demon with me.

My muscles already fought me, trembling as I moved.

It took all of my concentration and focus to fling my dagger straight for the Demon's throat.

I managed to summon enough of the element of air to push the dagger faster toward the Demon.

This time I caught *it* by surprise. Its blue eyes widened.

Just before my dagger glanced off its neck and landed on the ground.

The Chance-Demon smiled at me.

Excruciating pain tried to drive me to my knees as it stormed through every limb, every nerve ending, every cell in my body.

I staggered again. Blinked to clear my sight.

No way.

This thing *would* die with me.

Your training. Use your training, Nyx.

I shoved back the pain.

As I charged the few feet between us the power of air brought my dagger to my hand. It took all my remaining strength.

I gripped the dagger tight for one last time and drove it straight for the Chance-Demon's vulnerable spot.

The blade slid cleanly into the sac of fluid that had given it life.

And now gave it death.

The power of my momentum smacked me into the Demon's armored body, and more pain shot through me. I didn't have the strength to push myself away.

I fell with the Demon as it dropped onto its back, and the ground shook from the impact. I could do nothing but lie on the Demon's chest.

The fire and blinding pain of the poison were taking me. Even as death rushed toward me, I had one last sight that pleased me.

The look of complete surprise in the Chance-Demon's wide-open, glazed eyes.

And one thought that I held onto. I had found my revenge. I had taken out Jon and Caprice's killer.

My killer, too.

CHAPTER 21

Darkness.

Complete and total darkness.

I blinked. Not a sliver of light. Even my normally enhanced vision could see nothing.

In the distance water was dripping and plopping into something. A pool, maybe. The scent of earth was strong. Smells filled my nostrils that I thought I recognized, but couldn't place because of the fog that was in my mind.

It almost smelled like—like home.

Pain. My wrists burned, and my head ached so badly I could hardly think.

I lay still, partly from the pain, and partly because of the images reeling through my mind about what had happened in the park. The Demon.

No confusion, no wondering what had happened. Just the fact that it had.

I was dead.

I was a Tracker. Often a killer. I'd always wondered if I would end up in Summerland or in Underworld.

Now I knew.

Total and complete blackness, the smell of earth,

and a sound like water dripping in a cave—where else could I be but Underworld?

Unless there was an underground version of Summerland for Dark Elves.

It didn't matter, though. I'd fallen for a trap and I hadn't been able to help Randy.

Or had that been part of the trap, too? Goddess, I hoped all of the other Trackers had made it through the night.

I hoped Rodán knew exactly what had happened to me so that he could warn the others. No one would have found my body because there would be no body to find. Drow always fade away in black sparkles, unlike other paranorms.

Unless my human half had been dominant this time?

Who knew? I sure didn't.

Did my mother and father know what had happened to me?

Thoughts of my parents made pain build up behind my eyes. I hadn't even had a chance to say good-bye.

The headache seared my brain and I couldn't think any longer. Maybe in this place not thinking was a good thing. At least for now.

It was completely void of light here in Underworld, but I still blacked out.

"Nyx."

It shouldn't have surprised me that Demons in Underworld knew my name. But the softness of the voice, the familiarity of the voice, did surprise me.

This time, even with my eyes closed, I could tell

there was light. It was dim, but it came through my eyelids. Unlike before, I smelled something bitter that made me want to wrinkle my nose.

But more importantly, I caught the sweet perfume of someone familiar. The warm, precious scent of someone I loved.

Now I had to be confused and dreaming.

"Nyx, honey." Mother's voice.

Oh, that was so cruel. Send me to Underworld and let me imagine my mother was with me. What God did I piss off that badly?

"Open your eyes." The voice that was supposed to be my mother's was calm, but sounded concerned. "You're okay." Now her voice trembled a little. "You have to be okay."

All right. I'd play the game. There would be a Demon hanging over me with my mother's voice, and then it would laugh at me.

I blinked and her face came into focus. "Mother?" I said, afraid this *was* a dream or a trick. That it really was a Demon instead of my mother. Because I was dead, right?

She smiled. Mother had the most brilliant smile, and I think that's one of the reasons why Father loves her so much.

And then I was in her arms, feeling the softness of her body and her warm tears on my neck. Nothing and no one smelled like my mother. Like flowers and sunshine and everything good and wonderful. No way could that incredible scent be duplicated by any creature.

Mother held me so tight it was hard to breathe.

But who needed to breathe? I held her just as tightly, not ever wanting to let go.

"Is this real?" My voice came out rough. "Are you real? I'm not dead?"

Mother gave a sniffle and drew away so that I was lying on my back again. "You are very much alive, thank God." Tears made her cheeks shine in the soft light. She held my hand in hers, mine amethyst against her pale skin.

It was night. Otherworld time was different than Earth's, and I guessed it was late afternoon there.

I got my sapphire-blue eyes from Mother, and I remember wishing sometimes, when I was a youngling, that I always looked human, like her. But then I'd see my father and realize I had the best of both worlds because half the day I looked like my mother and the other half like my father. The only difference between me and Mother was that she was blond, and I have black hair when I'm in human form.

I couldn't help smiling. After thinking I had died, so much happiness filled me at seeing my mother again that I didn't think I'd stop smiling. "So tell me why I'm either dreaming or in Underworld after all."

"You'd never go to Underworld." She gave me a frown. "Drow go to Summerland like anyone else, as long as they're not evil. You are a good and wonderful person, Nyx."

"Cool." I looked at the wrist of the hand she was holding—no sign it had ever been injured. I raised my other wrist to see it unmarked, too. "And I'm alive because . . ."

"Torin." Mother sounded a little choked up as my eyes widened. "If it wasn't for him, you would be dead."

"T?" I could feel my eyes widen so much that they hurt. "Him?"

"Torin—I don't know what type of being he is, but he has to be some kind of Healer." Mother raised her free hand before dropping it in her lap again. She wore blue jeans and a button-up blouse as she usually did, but the shirt was wrinkled, like she'd been sleeping in the chair beside my bed. "Torin found you and healed you. Somehow he sucked the poison out."

I couldn't think of a word to say. Not one.

"Whatever he did made him sick," Mother continued, "but he was all right after a few hours."

I pushed myself to a sitting position to find I was in the infirmary belowground in the Drow Realm. I recognized it since I'd been treated here a few times after sword and dagger fights with male warriors who had something to prove. I'd usually won anyway. "How long have I been here?"

Mother glanced to her right and I followed her gaze to see two of her guards, enormous, blue-skinned, black-haired Drow warriors. She gave a slight nod and one of them left. She looked back at me. "About twenty-four hours."

"A day?" That meant it was around noon in New York, evening here in Otherworld. "Was anyone else hurt? Trackers? Other paranorms?" I swallowed, thinking of Adam as I said, "Human liaisons?"

"One Tracker died the night you almost did. His

name was Randy." She pushed her long blond hair away from her cheek. "And, yes, a human liaison vanished."

It was the Drow half of me that kept me from crying, but I wanted to. I really wanted to. Jon. Caprice. Randy. Their deaths tore at me as if a dragon-claw dagger had disemboweled me.

For a long time I kept my head bowed—out of respect for my friends who had died, and with pain at the thought of what they'd gone through.

Another liaison? That meant more clues might have been found, and I needed to know what, if any, they were.

"Three days in a row . . ." I drifted off in thought as I frowned. "Three Trackers and three liaisons. Then one night of nothing . . .

"I've got to talk with Rodán." I met my mother's eyes again. "There's been a breach in security at the Pit and he needs to know as soon as possible." I rubbed my temples. "Too bad there's no cell phone service between here and the Earth Otherworld."

Mother looked concerned. "We'll send word to Rodán right away."

"I need to talk with him myself." I grabbed my mother's hand. "I have to get out there to help the other Trackers. Now."

"You are your father's daughter." Mother looked both sad and resigned. "I knew that's exactly what you'd insist on."

"I want to see my daughter," came a bellow from the hallway, and I could imagine everyone within a hundred-foot radius scattering. *"Now."*

A huge, handsome warrior stepped through the arched doorway. Broad-shouldered, muscular, and powerful, he had pure sapphire-blue hair past his shoulders and light blue skin. He wore leather breeches, boots, a jeweled breastplate, and a sword sheathed at his side.

I was already out of bed, and I threw myself into my father's embrace and wrapped my arms around his neck. I barely noticed the pain through my soft Elvin tunic when my body slammed against his breastplate.

"By all the Gods and Goddesses." His voice was so hoarse he sounded like he would cry, too, if he could. "We almost lost you."

"I'm here, Father." I had a hard time even talking, as choked up as I felt. "You can't get rid of me that easily."

"And that's why you're going to stay belowground, in our Realm," he said, every word hitting me like a rock. "I'm not about to lose you. Ever."

Twin emotions almost tore me in half. Happiness at seeing my father and anger at what he'd stated.

I came *this* close to causing a scene. As my father crushed me in his huge hug, I saw past his arm where my mother was shaking her head behind Father. Her eyes darted to the warrior guards.

Okay. No scene with the King in front of any other Drow. That would not help my case one bit. Nor would losing my head and not thinking this through clearly to solve it in a levelheaded manner.

You're an adult now, Nyx. Act like one.

Calm down.

Yeah, right.

As long as I could remember, once he made a decision, my father never backed down. His decisions were extremely well-thought out and intelligent.

This was not one of those decisions.

I pushed away from Father and glanced at the guards, who feigned incuriosity pretty well, but I saw the interest in their eyes.

My father had just made a decision in front of other Dark Elves. To change his mind for a female, even though she was his daughter, would undermine some of the confidence my father's people had in him. They were extremely loyal, and Father was well-loved and respected as King, but there were some things that wouldn't make him look good.

This was one of them. No way in all the Underworlds was he going to make me stay, and give up my life in New York City.

I looked into my father's determined gray eyes. He was a big, big male. I had to pull on his shoulders to get him to lean down enough that I could whisper in his ear.

"Father." Kudos to me for keeping my voice even. "Please take any nearby guards somewhere private and tell them that they are not to breathe one single word of this conversation to any being, Drow or Other. Or you will personally sever their heads."

My father rose and studied me, and I knew he saw the oncoming fight in my eyes. In turn I saw the determination and the "I've made my decision" in his gaze, but he was bound to know I wouldn't go down without a fight. I am my father's daughter, just like Mother had said.

Only this was one fight I was going to win.

He gave the slightest nod before saying, "If you are well enough you will join your mother and me for supper in our private chambers."

"I am looking forward to it." My words were in the formal tongue of the Dark Elves. "I am well."

"My Princess." Father hugged me again before he left the room and indicated to the guards that they were to accompany him.

In moments a fresh pair of guards joined Mother and me.

I sighed. The life of a royal.

At least the three of us made it through dinner without any arguing over what my father had stated. I was starving, and shoved food into my mouth like I'd never ever get another meal. Like tomorrow might never come.

There almost hadn't been a tomorrow.

The King and Queen always had the best of the best, and I was happy to eat as much of it as I could. I had a feeling I'd need the strength for my upcoming "conversation" with Father.

Goddess, how I'd missed the smell of freshly baked bread, the juicy taste of roasted fowl, and the flavor of crisp Otherworld vegetables. Dessert—nothing on Earth could compare to the puddings, which were more heavenly than the moistest human chocolate cake with whipped cream. It even beat Derek's incredible chocolate mousse. Both the cake and mousse happened to be my favorite desserts in the city.

Mother and Father had contacted Rodán via an Elvin messenger, and sent word that Rodán needed to tighten security and that I would explain as soon as possible. Of course Father had no doubt figured that meant Rodán meeting me here in Otherworld, aboveground at night, me with an escort.

The thought of my father's decision to make me stay here caused my ears to burn, and I lost interest in my dessert. It was all I could do to wait until they were finished eating, and not explode with anger.

After the servants had cleaned away the last of the dishes, utensils, and napkins, my skin started to tingle. Daylight was breaking aboveground.

"Excuse me, Mother, Father." I stood and gave a slight bow before going to the center of their enormous and very richly appointed chamber. The circular, patterned rug I stood on was Fae-made, and finer than any Persian rug one could find on Earth. I wore a blue tunic and breeches made of soft leather.

The transformation was more important to me now than ever. My father needed to see me as human.

I tipped my head back and felt my cobalt-blue hair flow into long black hair. I went through every stretch, every movement I always made when I transformed and, as usual, reveled in it. Whether it was from Drow to human, or human to Drow, I loved it.

As I moved, my amethyst skin faded to the same fair shade as my mother's. My small incisors retracted so that my white teeth were completely human, and the points of my ears rounded.

When I finished, my father's frown didn't bother me, and my mother's smile made me feel even better.

Father loved my human half, I had no doubt about that. I was also certain that right now he didn't want to be reminded that I'm half human. He was going to demand that I remain in the Drow Realm even though half of me belonged aboveground.

Actually, all of me did.

"I do not reverse my decisions," Father said in his most commanding Kingly Voice as he studied me. "You will live here and you will not leave again."

The way he *demanded*, and had already decided my fate, pissed me off. Heat flushed up my body and I was certain my fair skin had a slight pink tinge to it.

Mother's gaze encouraged me to speak my mind, and I knew she'd jump in on my side if my father became too difficult.

"I'm going to list several reasons why I will not remain here," I said as I met my father's gaze without blinking. "I would appreciate it if you would let me finish."

"You may have your say." Father crossed his large, muscular arms across his chest. "It will make no difference."

I wanted to stamp my foot and scream like I used to when I was a youngling. But I kept calm.

"First of all, I am twenty-seven, fully an adult in the eyes of the Elves for two years now." I held my hand up to quiet Father, because he tended to scoff at the fact that I was so young compared to everyone else around here, Dark Elves who were centuries and centuries old. With the exception of Mother, who was fifty-one—but she had stopped aging when she came to live in the Realm.

"Secondly," I continued, "I am half human, and the human half of me needs to be aboveground."

My father looked pointedly at my mother, who had given up life aboveground to live with my father. I gritted my teeth and continued.

"The third reason is that I have a career, if you will," I said. "It is my duty to help humans, as well as all of the Great Guardian's Peacekeepers."

Father scowled at the mention of the Guardian. He had his beef with her, one of which had been making me a Tracker in the Earth Otherworld.

"Number four is that I don't belong here, Father." I gestured toward the door. "I'm not some subservient Drow female who's going to let one of the warriors order me around and demand sex whenever he wants it."

My father's face tinged a darker blue when I mentioned the demanding-sex part. *Heh.* No father wants to think of his daughter as having sex with any male.

"I'll never be accepted here." This time I raised both hands. "The women won't talk to me because I'm a Princess and because the warriors don't approve of me, no matter how much they all respect you."

I was talking faster now as my anger ratcheted up. "And speaking of warriors, they can't stand me. Especially since I can kick their asses.

"Fifth reason." I put my hands on my hips and met

my father's glare head-on. "Only one male in this Realm can stop me from escaping, and that's you. Unless you keep me locked up in an elemental magic-treated cell, or tied from shoulders to feet with my powers stripped, no guard could keep me from leaving."

My father shook his head, his expression unrelenting. "No. I have made my decision."

Here we go.

This was going to be a long night.

Before my father could say anything else, my mother got to her feet and put her hands on her hips, a mirror of me. Her expression was furious.

Go, Mother!

She faced my father and spoke very clearly and sternly, but kept her voice even and at a normal volume. For a moment. "Every single one of Nyx's points is valid and you know it, Ciar."

Then she got wound up. If my mother's eyes could flare angry white like mine could, she'd be shooting real sparks and the table would be on fire. "Nyx is past being of age, and you have absolutely no right insisting—no, *demanding*—that she stay here."

"Kathryn—" he started, and I could tell he was trying to maintain a stern expression.

"Oh, don't you 'Kathryn' me." Mother bent closer to him. I'd never seen her so angry. Her cheeks were dark pink, her eyes narrowed, and her lips twisted into a furious expression. Her voice had ratcheted to an all-time high for her. "Nyx is my daughter, too, and in this, Ciar, you *will not* overrule me."

I don't think I've ever seen my father, King Ciar of the Dark Elves, speechless before.

Mother whirled and started toward the bedchamber's heavy oak door. "Nyx, come with me."

CHAPTER 22

It's true how the little things in life suddenly become so much more important when you've almost lost them.

Until you've almost lost life itself.

The afternoon sky was churning with clouds and the breeze was cool and rain-scented as I walked the short distance to my apartment from where my father had sent me through the transference. It was roughly thirty-six hours since I'd almost died.

I waved to Mrs. Taylor, who lived in the apartment below mine, as she drew out a cell phone from her apron pocket. She always wore an apron over a granny dress. Mrs. Taylor was a heavy chain-smoker with a face like a warped slab of wood—even though she was only about fifty. Today she looked beautiful to me as she walked Terror, her Chihuahua. The little thing *was* a terror, and Kali hated him.

It's also funny—not really *funny*, but more odd—how living in a world as sweet and pure as Otherworld didn't take away my enjoyment of the city. I breathed in the polluted air and smiled as I passed a Starbucks. Who cared about the pollution when there were so many unique humans and paranorms, restaurants, and Nordstrom's? Yeah, shopping. How I loved the shopping in this city. As a Princess, I'm very good at spending money.

I shifted the Drow leather rucksack on my shoulder as the wind picked up. The weight was nothing because of my Drow strength, even with the truckload of food Mother had the servants put together to stock my fridge. Yummy. In most cases it was always good to visit home.

This hadn't exactly been one of them. Just about dying and having your father decide you should virtually be made a prisoner "for your own good" kind of put a damper on things.

When Father had relented (backed down from Mother), they'd wanted me to stay longer to rest and to visit. No, I'd said. I had to get to work with the other Trackers.

Three Trackers were dead. Three liaisons were missing.

Letting my thoughts turn toward being a Tracker, my stomach twisted and I just about dropped the rucksack. I could almost feel the concrete beneath my knees as I felt like collapsing to the sidewalk because my legs didn't want to carry me any farther. It was too painful, thinking of everything that had happened. Three of my friends—dead. So many others in danger.

My resolve pushed away the pain. I'd take care of business here at home since it was still early enough, and I'd call Rodán and speak to him about the Chance-Demon that had managed to get into the Pit. I'd tell Rodán about the scorpion shell. We'd figure this out before anyone else was murdered by the Demons.

Cars honked, a siren wailed, and cool, almost rainy air brushed my skin as I forced myself on toward my apartment. A raindrop landed on my nose and I wiped it away with the back of my hand.

According to Mother, Olivia was pissed as hell that I'd gone out without waiting for her to finish talking to Rodán. T—didn't know how he felt. Flashes of the dead Trackers and other morbid thoughts kept repeating like an endless loop in my head, taking up most of my thoughts.

Stop thinking about it, Nyx. I did my best to shove everything Demon-related from my mind as I closed in on my apartment building. Tonight, in just hours, I'd be on the hunt, and Demons were going down.

The jeans my mother had given me were loose at my hips as I walked, and the button-up blouse felt light against my skin. Tears had sparkled in her pretty blue eyes when she hugged me good-bye and told me she loved me.

Then it was my father's turn, and like before, I think he would've had tears in his eyes if he could. After a ginormous hug that knocked the breath out of me, my gruff father had kissed the top of my head and told me in the language of the Dark Elves how much he loved me. Then he'd reluctantly used his greater earth and air powers to put me through the transference to get back to New York City. Who knew how long it would be before I'd have the power to do the transference on my own.

In some ways it sucked being as young as I was for Drow. Twenty-seven is practically considered an infant amongst the Dark Elves, most of whom are centuries-old beings. Because of my age, I didn't have as much elemental energy, or as much command over what powers I had.

Infant, my ass.

I started to jog to my apartment as a good drizzle started. Terror yipped his little head off at something. Probably me. The rucksack bounced against my back as I bounded up the stairs.

Once I was in my apartment, the first thing I headed for was the fridge. I unloaded my goodies, then set the rucksack with the rest of its items on the kitchen table.

I smiled. Home. Freedom.

It would have taken a while to escape the Drow Realm if Mother hadn't put Father in his place. I savored every moment of being aboveground again.

Kali was nowhere in sight, but then the blue Persian usually avoided me until she was certain I knew she was miffed that she'd been left alone too long. Mother said Olivia fed Kali while I was gone.

I reached into the rucksack and dug out my XPhone. When T had found me, all of my weapons and my XPhone were retrieved, cleansed, and put in the rucksack. I checked the XPhone—dead, but probably just the battery. I used a sizzle of static in the air and, sure enough, that charged it. When I had enough bars of power and signal, I hit speed dial for Rodán.

"Nyx." His voice was filled with relief when he answered. "Thank the Goddess Torin was able to save you. Are you well?"

"Very well." I smiled. "And ready to get back to work tonight."

"Are you certain?"

"Absolutely."

His voice sounded a little harder. "This time you will take Torin and Olivia with you."

I sighed. "I will."

"We found no breach in our security," he said. "Tell me why you think there was."

I explained to him about the Chance-Demon that had been in the Pit, his association with Caprice, and what he'd said when he almost killed me.

Rodán was silent for a moment before his words came out sharp, angry and in Drow, which is a coarse language compared to that of the Light Elves. "It is my guess that the Demon found some way to emulate one of the beings who frequent my establishment." He inserted a few Drow curse words I'd never heard him use before. "I'll take care of this. It will *never* happen again."

"The being was disguised from me, somewhat like T," I responded in the same tongue. "I could never place its scent, or get a feel for what type of being it was."

Rodán made a hissing sound, definitely Drow. "Only those who were regulars prior to the Demon escape from the Ruhin Gate will be allowed in. After a thorough check of each being by Fred and my other guards."

I told Rodán about the scorpion shell, and that the symbol we'd last come across had been part man and part horse, yes, but that it had a scorpion tail and not a fish tail.

Rodán went quiet again. "I would have liked to have known about this when you found out."

"I made a mistake." I pushed my hand through my hair. "I thought it could wait until the morning, when we could start researching it thoroughly."

"Anything else?" He spoke in English now and his tone had returned to normal.

"That's it," I said.

"Above all else I'm glad you're safe." His voice held so much caring that it warmed me inside. "We'll meet tonight at nine with Torin and Olivia, before you track. I'll brief you then on other developments."

We'd just gone through enough information for now, so I was fine with waiting until tonight. There wasn't a lot I could do at this moment, anyway, so we said good-bye, I pushed the off button, and I stared at the XPhone for a moment.

Okay. I needed to call Olivia and let her know I was back. No, wait. She was likely going to kill me for leaving her behind that night. One near-death experience was enough—I'd take my chances with her with a crowd around. Although that wouldn't stop her. This time she wouldn't be using rubber bands and erasers.

A knock at the door caught me off guard. The knock was loud, urgent. I hurried to the door and, through the peephole, saw Adam Boyd, his face drawn and his jaw tense.

What had happened?

I opened the door. "Adam—"

He grabbed me and kissed me fast and hard. I would have stumbled if he didn't have such a good hold on me. His kiss was as urgent as his knock at the door, and I could taste coffee and male when we kissed. I drank in his scent, cuddled against his hard body, and sank into his embrace.

Adam broke our kiss and cupped my face in his hands. His eyes were filled with emotion as he looked me over, as if making sure all of me was there.

"Are you okay, sweetheart?" He kissed me before I could answer. "I've been going out of my mind." He brushed hair away from my face, his fingers rough, not gentle, as they pushed my hair back, as if he was barely controlling some kind of power inside of him.

I smiled, partly to show him I was fine, and partly because of the way he was so concerned about me. A flutter blossomed in my chest at the depth of caring I heard in his voice. "I'm okay."

Without looking behind him he moved us both fully into the apartment so that he could close the door. His expression told me he didn't believe me. "When only Olivia and Torin showed up at the scene yesterday morning, I had a bad feeling in my gut." Adam's intensity made something more twist inside me. "Olivia told me what happened and I've been so goddamned worried ever since."

"Thank you, Adam." I reached up and kissed him, then lowered myself. "Really. I'm fine. How did you know I'm back?"

A bit of the harshness of his worry retreated, and I saw the ghost of a boyish smile. "Your neighbor with the yapper of a dog. I paid her to call me as soon as she saw you."

"Ah." That's why Mrs. Taylor had pulled a cell phone out of her apron pocket when I was walking toward her.

He held me around my waist. I placed my hands on his shoulders and leaned back as we held each other's gaze. He looked so good, his brown eyes so warm and inviting. "You missed our lunch today."

"Oh." I couldn't believe I'd forgotten all about it. "Are you hungry? I have a ton of food my mother sent home with me."

Adam shook his head. "I need to hold you to make sure you don't slip away from me again."

I tilted my head to the side. "And how long is that?"

"As long as it takes." He lowered his head to mine and kissed me. It was hard and urgent again. He kissed me in a way that told me how earnest he was about not wanting anything to happen to me.

It felt like Pixie dust tickled the inside of my belly as I kissed him back. I matched him stroke for stoke with my tongue and I gasped when he dragged his teeth over my lower lip.

The tickling inside my belly turned into a storm that shot straight to the place between my thighs. Adam pulled me tight to him. His Glock rubbed against my side, but pleasure swept through me to feel his erection pressed against my belly.

Goddess, I wanted to feel him inside of me. That's where he belonged, with his cock buried deep in my core, thrusting in and out until we both climaxed. I could visualize it clearly as he kissed me, and I wanted it so badly I could almost feel him taking me now.

My lips felt raw, swollen, as he drew his mouth from mine and placed kisses on my jawline before he moved his kisses to my neck. I clenched the shoulders of his leather bomber jacket as I tipped my head back, and I moaned when he kissed me all the way to the base of my throat.

"Honeysuckle," he murmured between kisses. "Sweet. I want to taste you every time I see you."

I wanted to tell him how good he made me feel, but all I could do was moan. Then I gasped as his mouth headed lower, to the V of my button-up shirt, where he flicked his tongue in tiny little circles over the skin between my breasts.

My nipples tingled and ached with his mouth so close to them. He nudged aside the opening of my blouse and kissed the rise of my breast as far as the material would allow him.

Frustration had me squirming in his arms. I couldn't take it. Too slow. I reached between us, grasped the front of my blouse with both hands, and the buttons popped off and scattered on the carpet when I ripped the opening apart.

Adam raised his head and his grin was devastating to my libido. "In a hurry?"

"Shut up," I said, but with a smile of my own as he helped me slip off my ruined blouse. "Back to what you were doing."

He gave a soft laugh. Then there was the matter

of my bra. I was ready to rip it off, too, but he saved it by pulling the bra beneath my breasts.

My nipples are so sensitive that, when his warm mouth captured my nipple, I almost climaxed. I squirmed and arched my back, pressing my breast against his face. I swore he laughed again, but then he sucked on my other nipple and my body continued to burst with sensation after sensation.

His jacket bothered me. I couldn't touch him the way I wanted to. I started shoving it over his shoulders so he'd get the point. He raised his head and studied me as he shrugged off his jacket, leaving him in a light blue T-shirt and jeans, his shoulder holster over his T-shirt.

I clasped my hands around his neck and held on as I drew myself up and wrapped my legs around his hips. My thigh pressed against his handgun.

His throat worked as he palmed my ass, supporting me. He sounded like he could barely speak when he said my name. "Nyx—"

I kissed him hard to show I wanted this, and then smiled as I nodded in the direction of my bedroom. "I have something I need you to investigate, Detective."

His expression was filled with hunger. Need. Desire. "Has a crime been committed?" he said in a teasing but strained voice.

"There will be," I said as he gripped my hips tighter. "If you don't get me in there now. It's called justifiable homicide."

CHAPTER 23

Adam's T-shirt rubbed my nipples, causing more delicious sensations to course through me as he carried me into my bedroom. I tilted my head back as I held onto him with my hands clasped behind his neck, and I moaned as he kissed the column of my throat.

My mind spun. I couldn't get enough of his scent, his taste, and the wonderful feeling of being in his arms. I don't think anything had ever felt so right in my life until that moment. As if I had been waiting for this without ever realizing it.

Adam laid me on my mattress and I brought him down with me. "I'm not about to let you leave," I said as he straddled me and braced his forearms on the bed.

His brown eyes held my gaze. "I'm not going anywhere." He lowered his head and blew air across my nipples. "I'd hate to be a homicide victim."

I gasped from the erotic sensation of his breath warming my nipples, and laughed at his words at the same time. "Good boy."

"Your nipples are so sensitive." He smiled as he licked one of them, then met my gaze as I squirmed beneath him.

"Right now I'm sensitive everywhere." I reached between us and felt the hard ridge of his thick erection through his jeans. I squeezed his cock. "How about you?"

Adam groaned. "Baby, keep touching me like that and you'll find out."

I caught him by surprise by twisting just right so that I could flip him onto his back, and I straddled him. He grabbed me by the waist and gave me a sexy grin. "You like to be the one in control?"

"Sometimes." I brushed my lips over his. "Especially because of what I'm going to do to you now."

He raised an eyebrow, and I smiled against his lips before I kissed him, then moved down his body until I was between his thighs. I wished I could take his T-shirt off, but the shoulder holster would have to be removed and I didn't want to mess with it right now. He probably had concealed backup weapons, so I would be limited in what I could do. For now.

"I have a feeling that stripping off your jeans isn't going to be an easy task." I breathed in his scent as I nuzzled his T-shirt and felt his taut abs against my face. "So I'll see what I can do." I looked up at him and gave him my naughtiest grin. "If not, your clothes will go the same way as my shirt."

Adam laughed as I started unfastening his belt, and he slipped his fingers into my hair. "I love the blue highlights when the sun hits your hair just right."

At the mention of the word *blue*, I stilled for a second, then brushed aside the thought of him one day seeing my hair when it was cobalt blue. It caused an uneasy flutter in my belly, but that was quickly replaced by the deeper rush of desire that traveled straight between my thighs as I unzipped his jeans. I saw his boxers and laughed.

"Sylvester and Tweety Bird?" I looked up at him to see his adorable grin.

"Next time I'll wear Taz."

"How about Marvin the Martian?"

"Maybe." He ran his fingers through my hair at the scalp and I shivered at the delicious sensation.

"A cop wearing Looney Tunes boxers." I tugged the boxers down. "Who'd have thought?"

"Nyx." Adam hissed through his teeth as I wrapped my fingers around his erection and lubricated it with the semen that had already escaped. "Damn."

"I hope that's a good 'damn,' " I murmured before I slipped my mouth over his cock.

"Jesus." Adam thrust his hips up as I took more of him into my mouth. One sexual talent I had apparently inherited from my Drow half was the ability to deep-throat, and take all of his incredible length and thickness in. "I never—*damn*."

I stroked the sac at the base of his cock with one hand while I worked the other at the base of his erection. I licked and sucked and scraped my teeth lightly over his cock as I moved my mouth up and down it. He tasted delicious, salty-sweet.

The scent of his semen aroused me even more and I knew my Drow pheromones were kicking into high gear. No matter how he tried, Adam wouldn't be able to hold back much longer.

His breathing sounded a little ragged as he said, "I'm going to come. I'll pull out if you don't want to swallow."

As if I'd let him. I made a purring sound and sucked harder.

I used a little of my fire element to direct static at his balls to intensify his orgasm. Adam's hips bucked like he'd been shocked with a bolt of electricity. His come spurted down my throat as I took him deep. He sounded like he was holding back a shout as he cupped the back of my head and rode out the length of his orgasm.

He groaned, and I knew that he was finished as tension escaped his body and his muscles slackened. "I don't know if it's possible to ever move again." He sounded sated and worn-out as I let his cock slip from my mouth.

I eased up so that I was straddling him again and kissed him. Would I ever get enough of his taste? Or the feel of his hands roaming up and down my body? Right then I didn't think I'd be totally satisfied. I'd want him again and again.

When I drew away from the kiss, my hair drifted over his cheeks like a curtain and I met his warm brown eyes. He stroked my hair again, and then I shivered as his fingers ran over the sensitive curve of my ear, as if he knew it was one of my erogenous zones.

"I think I just got my second wind," he said before catching me off guard and rolling me onto my back. Then he climbed off of me and off the bed, and I saw what he meant when he stood. His cock looked as hard as it had when I tasted him.

He watched me as he removed his Glock, then took off his shoulder holster and settled both on the nightstand, next to the miniature Tiffany lamp. His badge and a tactical pocketknife followed. He shoved up his jeans on his left leg and removed an ankle holster that held a smaller handgun.

I grew wetter and wetter between my thighs as he kicked off his running shoes, removed his socks, and shoved down his boxers and jeans. "Got any more weapons, Detective?" I murmured as I started to rub my palms across my nipples while I watched him.

Adam took off his T-shirt, his biceps flexing, his abs more defined as he shrugged out of the shirt before tossing it aside. And then I could see every inch of the masculine perfection of his naked body. His sculpted muscles shifted beneath smooth flesh that was a few shades darker than my pale skin.

My focus drifted to his erection, and my breathing grew more rapid as I imagined his thick cock sliding into my core while he sucked my nipples again.

"Will this do for a weapon?" he said in a husky voice as he stroked his cock and moved to the side of the bed.

"It's a lethal weapon all right." I licked my lips as I kicked off my tennis shoes while still lying on the bed, and then I reached for the button to my jeans.

He pushed my hands away and stripped off my jeans faster than I could. "Sweet," he murmured as he ran his finger along the inside band of my lace-and-satin panties. Thank the Goddess Mother had a drawer full of new sexy underwear that she'd purchased at Victoria's on one of her trips from Otherworld.

Adam glanced at my jeans that were now on the carpet and looked back at me. "I've never seen you in jeans before." He tugged on my panties and started sliding them down my legs. "You look so beautiful, no matter what you wear." The way he took off my socks even felt sexy.

Warmth infused my body at the feel of being almost completely naked and from the way he was looking at my body, his eyes hungry, filled with desire. I started to unfasten my bra, which was still beneath my breasts.

He shook his head. "Leave it."

I stretched out my arms for him. "Come here."

"Not yet." The bed dipped beneath his powerful body when he climbed onto the bed and pushed apart my thighs. More shivers of desire coursed through me. He caressed my hairless mound. "Brazilian wax?"

Not exactly. Elves and Dark Elves don't have body or facial hair, but I didn't want to get into that territory at this minute. Not when I needed him so badly. "Something like that," I said.

"I like it." He slid his finger along the slit and then into my wet folds, and I gasped when he slipped his finger inside my core. "I really like it," he murmured before he lowered himself and kissed my mound, flicking his tongue over the soft skin.

I sucked in my breath before letting it out in a gasp as he parted my folds and began licking my clit. The sheets were soft in my fists as I clenched handfuls of the material, as if to keep myself anchored to the bed.

"Dear Goddess," I said as I arched my back when he sucked my clit.

Blue. A brilliant shade of blue flashed through my mind as I climaxed. I'd never seen colors before when I had orgasms. It was like my mind short-circuited, and all I could see were waves of blue rushing in and out as my body rocked and shook.

Adam carried me to a second orgasm with his mouth and tongue, and the color in my mind shifted so that it was deep blue-green, as if I were falling into an endless sea.

My core still spasmed as I felt Adam move up my body. I opened my eyes and the blue faded as I looked into his deep brown gaze. I realized I was trembling.

"You okay?" He kissed the spot between my jaw and my ear, his muscular body pressed close.

"I will be when you're inside me," I said, and he rose up so that he was looking down at me.

He smiled, reached for his badge wallet on the nightstand, and pulled a condom package out of the wallet. As Drow I was fully protected from anything, and couldn't get pregnant unless I wanted to. But I wanted him to feel comfortable by practicing human safe sex. "I hope this is still good," he said. "It's been a while."

I raised my eyebrows. "You, the gorgeous Detective Boyd, celibate for any length of time?"

Another adorable grin as he tore the package open and tossed the wrapper aside, leaving him holding the condom. "Ever since I met you—I just haven't been interested in other women."

"Really?" I blinked as he rolled the condom down his erection. "Why—"

He kissed me. "It's taken this long to get close to you," he murmured against my lips. "You've been holding back for quite a while."

"To think what I've been missing." We smiled against each other's lips, and then he shifted and his cock was slightly inside my core. "Oh, Goddess, that feels good." My eyes nearly rolled back in my head as I arched my hips and took inches more of him.

And then he drove his cock all the way in. I whimpered, moaned, and cried out with each thrust. He took me harder than I expected, with even more passion than I'd imagined.

He sucked and licked my nipples, his hips spreading my thighs wide as he moved in and out. And then he was kissing me as I grew more and more frantic from my oncoming orgasm. I squirmed and raked my nails across his back.

Closer, closer, nearing that precipice.

Red. This time red flamed behind my closed eyes when I climaxed. Amazing. Goddess, it was amazing. My entire body was suffused with warm, sweet, stinging sensations. No place on my body was left untouched. My whole self was alive beyond my imagination.

Within moments of sliding down from that orgasm I had another. And then another. I was so sensitized by the last one that tears would have been in my eyes if it were possible.

Adam thrust even harder several times and then stopped, pressing his groin tight to mine. He gave a hoarse shout as his cocked throbbed inside me.

I opened my eyes and watched him. His brown hair was slightly messy, his brown eyes like melted dark chocolate, his strong jaw tense, his body taut. He was so beautiful in a masculine way as he rode out his climax.

When the orgasm faded, he slumped and his body pressed down on me. He adjusted himself so that his full weight wasn't on me. I found his muscular body weight warm and comforting, and I wanted to stay like that as long as we could.

Adam rolled onto his side, drawing me with him so that we were facing each other. We both smiled, and he stroked my hair away from my eyes.

He tucked me in close. "You're so beautiful, Nyx."

"So are you," I said as I snuggled close to him, and took a deep breath of the scent of sex the two of us had made together. Good. It smelled so good.

I'm not sure I'd ever felt so relaxed, so at peace. So much so that I tumbled into a deep sleep in his arms.

My whole body tingled, and I smiled as I drifted from sleep toward consciousness, loving being in Adam's embrace.

Oh, my Goddess. I jerked awake as I registered what the tingling meant.

My eyes immediately went to Adam's face. I couldn't let him see me change without explaining it first. I had to prepare him. Somehow I'd have to get him out of here. I'd hide in the bathroom.

Gutless wonder.

Then I realized it was too late and I went completely still on the bed as I watched Adam. He had braced one arm on the mattress so that he was partially up, and his other hand was holding a lock of my hair, which had already changed from black to cobalt blue.

The muscles in my slender arms and the rest of my body grew more sculpted, and my short incisors scraped my tongue as I lay beside him, afraid to move. His gaze met mine and his lips parted as he brought his fingers up and caressed the pale amethyst of my cool cheek, then traced the curves of my pointed ear.

"Is this the secret you've been keeping?" he said softly.

My throat hurt as I swallowed, as if I'd been screaming. "I'm half human and half Drow." At his confused expression, I added, "Drow are Dark Elves."

He continued to trail his fingers back from my ear and over my face to my mouth, and he touched one of my small incisors.

"No, Dark Elves are not related to Vampires," I said before he could ask.

"I didn't think you are." He ran his thumb along my lower lip before skimming his fingers down my throat, his gaze following the movements. He continued on between my breasts, where my areolae and nipples were now a deep shade of amethyst. He stopped when he reached my taut abs, settled his warm palm there for a moment, and met my gaze.

My heart wasn't beating anymore, I was sure of it, and I was holding my breath.

"I don't understand," he said as he moved his hand away from my abs. My heart started to sink as he cupped the side of my face with his palm. The intensity of his gaze and the emotions in his eyes were confusing. What was he thinking? "Why did you keep this from me for so long?" he said.

I let out my breath. "I was afraid of what you would think if you saw me like this."

"I'm not that shallow, Nyx." Adam's tone was almost a reprimand.

My eyes widened as more confusion set me on a shaky edge. "I never thought you were. I just—I had a bad experience with a man I cared for. He freaked out and it was pretty nasty. I've been afraid ever since."

He shook his head. What did that mean?

"The guy was a fucking idiot." Adam cupped the back of my head and met my gaze as I tried to register what he was saying. "Whoever it was sure as hell didn't deserve you."

He kissed me. Long and hard and sweet. All the fear rushed out of me as he took his time kissing me, as if making sure I knew he wasn't like the other guy.

When Adam drew away, I blinked a few times as I opened my eyes. He was smiling. "You are so damned beautiful, Nyx. Every inch of you. Half human, half Drow, whatever. You're incredible."

"Thank you." The words came out in a whisper. "I'm sorry I didn't tell you—show you—sooner."

"Just don't hold back anything else from me, okay?" He kissed my forehead as I nodded.

"I promise," I said.

"Good." He rolled me onto my back and a thrill went through me at the feel of his erection against my thigh. "Now I'm going to make love to the world's most beautiful purple woman."

"Amethyst," I said, and he smiled as he slid inside of me.

CHAPTER 24

In sort of a daydream, I walked to the rucksack where I'd left my XPhone after calling Rodán.

I smiled as I thought about Adam, the way he had made love to me, and how he had accepted the Drow half of me without question. Even the way he'd been almost angry with me for holding back from him, before I told him about Stan.

I missed Adam already, even thought it hadn't been that long since his cell phone rang and then he'd had to leave because something had come up on one of his cases.

Nadia or Olivia? I paused for a moment before deciding who I was going to call. Definitely Nadia. Because Olivia was going to kill me for not waiting for her to finish her conversation with Rodán night before last, when I almost ended up in Summerland.

I grabbed my XPhone and hit speed dial for Nadia. I tugged on my leather pants and corset at the same time the phone rang.

"Nyx!" Nadia was obviously reading her incoming caller screen. Her voice was filled with relief. "I can't tell you how happy I am to hear your voice."

"It's good to hear yours, too." I kept thinking about

Adam, even as I talked with her, and a giddy smile was on my face. "It's soooo great to be home."

"Come over and tell me all about what's making you sound so dreamy," Nadia said with a laugh. "I'm making dinner."

Seafood, no doubt. After all, she was a Siren.

"Yum." I looked at the entrance, remembering how wonderful Adam had looked when I opened the door. "See you in a bit."

Pounding rain echoed on the rooftop as I ended the call and finished adjusting my leather outfit. The leather felt good against my skin, and it only took me a few moments to hook my weapons belt around my hips.

I dug into the rucksack for my weapons. After I fastened my buckler at the front of my belt, I sheathed my daggers, holstered my 9mm Kahr, and made sure my XPhone was on vibrate before clipping it to my belt. Couldn't have it belting out AC/DC's "Back in Black," my latest ringtone, as I was stalking Demons.

It was September, and I couldn't believe all the rain we were getting. I could have used my air powers to keep myself dry once I went into the rain, but I had to admit I didn't feel totally at full speed, and I didn't want to waste any elemental energies.

By the time I reached Nadia's apartment two blocks away, I was completely soaked. I hadn't bothered with a glamour this time, also to save energy. After all, this was New York City, and in the near-darkness, a drowned rat of an amethyst-skinned, blue-haired woman barely got a glance. I did cloak and protect my weapons and XPhone, though.

Nadia opened her apartment door the moment my knuckles hit the wood. "Nyx!" She flung her arms around me, wet clothes and all, and kissed me on my cheek before drawing back. She always smelled of fresh, clean sea breezes. "Goddess, I was so worried. Even after Torin saved you, we were afraid you wouldn't make it."

I kissed her cheek in return. "I'm here, I'm fine, I'm better than ever." I looked down and saw I was dripping water all over her sea-blue carpet. "Sorry about that," I said when I looked back at her.

Nadia laughed. "You forget that water is my element." She held out her hands and all the water came rushing to her, even from my clothing and hair. Then I was totally dry and everything was spotless. I could have said *avanna* for myself, but it wouldn't have worked on the carpet.

She drew me into her apartment and closed the door behind us. Her long, red Siren's hair swung to one side as she tipped her head and smiled. "You got laid."

Sparkles of pleasure warmed my skin. "Did I *ever.*"

Being a Siren, the sensual smile on her lips was natural. "Obviously it wasn't Rodán."

A hint of guilt tried to pierce my happiness because I'd had sex with Rodán just a few days before tonight, with Adam. But I wasn't going to let it take anything away from what we'd shared. At least not now.

"It was the most amazing sex," I said.

"With who?"

"Adam Boyd."

"You got it on with Detective Boyd of the NYPD?" Delight sparkled in her sea-green gaze. "The cop you're always talking about?"

I sighed, and you could definitely call my sigh blissful. "Yeah."

"Finally." She reached up and caressed a lock of my now dry blue hair. "You've been holding back because of your Drow appearance. Did you let him see you?"

My cheeks warmed. "I fell asleep, and I woke just as the change was coming on." I held my hands to my belly, remembering how worried I'd been. "It was either that, or running and hiding in my bathroom while telling him to leave."

"That probably wouldn't be a good way to start a serious relationship." She let her fingers slide away from my hair. "Apparently he took it well."

"He was incredible."

Nadia and I walked across her sea-blue carpet and past living room wall murals that made me feel like I was in the ocean. Schools of fish and other sea life floated across the lifelike murals depicting her home in the Atlantic Ocean.

We reached her kitchen, which smelled like she was cooking an awesome dinner. Some kind of fish, definitely. "Go on," she said as she stopped in front of the fridge. "I want to hear everything."

"He just looked at me like I was the most beautiful

thing he'd ever seen." Dreamy smile firmly affixed. "And then he *said* I was beautiful."

"That's because you are," Nadia said. "That's what Olivia, Caprice, and I have been trying to tell you . . ."

She drifted off, apparently just realizing she'd mentioned Caprice as if she was still a part of our former quartet. "I miss her." Nadia's normally crystal-clear singing voice sounded husky.

I looked down at my slender fingers and thought again about saving her. But the Chance-Demon . . . The way he'd taken her in, she never would have seen it coming.

We ate salmon for dinner, spending time on girl chat. I told her about my afternoon and evening with Adam, and she pelted me with questions about what had happened during my battle with the Demon that almost killed me. I was going to have to tell Rodán and Olivia everything, too. Oh, and T.

Nadia's eyes suddenly reminded me of the ocean and she looked like she had drifted off to the waters of her home when Caprice's name was mentioned again. Nadia was a Siren from the Bermuda Triangle. Sirens are the reason why all those ships and planes have gone down and have never been seen again after they entered the Sirens' territory.

Rodán had recruited Nadia because the Guardian wanted Nadia's talents on the team of Trackers in the city.

Nadia picked up her pilsner and downed the beer. "I could use another," she said, and I handed her mine that I hadn't touched.

"I'll wait for a martini after work," I said. "You know I like the hard stuff."

Even after two years away from the Atlantic Ocean, Nadia still had a thing for seafood, hence the salmon dinner. Sirens are water Fae, and all Fae eat roots, berries, fish, and things like that. No meat. But Fae had developed a liking for this world's sweets, like Nancy and her chocolate. Nadia had expanded her palate to include hops—in other words, beer. Bud was her favorite.

"Do you want to go with me to see *La Bohème* at the Met a week from Friday?" Nadia absolutely loved the opera. Big surprise there, since Sirens have a thing for singing—only a Siren's song usually means some guy's death. "I just bought season tickets."

I smiled at her enthusiasm. "Sure. It'll be over before we have to get to work."

"Great!" Nadia's face positively lit up when she talked about going to any performance at the Metropolitan Opera House. I'd gone with her several times. "We could take in *L'elisir d'amore* the following week."

"The Elixir of Love." I thought about Adam. Would it ever go that far between us? Love?

Time to knock that idea out of my head. Jumping waaaay ahead of myself.

Nadia's long hair fell over her shoulders when she leaned forward. I swear she looked like Ariel from *The Little Mermaid* with all of her thick, vivid, red hair. "Maybe Adam Boyd is 'the one,'" she said, as if she'd read my thoughts.

"A step at a time," I said, not only to Nadia but to myself. A change in subject was in order. "We should get to work."

"It's hard tracking Midtown West. Everywhere I go I think of Caprice." A sad expression crept over her beautiful features again. "Now that I've been shifted off of roving duty and track her territory, she's constantly in my thoughts." Nadia's gaze looked a little distant. "I miss them. Caprice. Jon. Randy."

"It's hard not to think about what happened to them," I said quietly. "It hurts so much."

Nadia sighed. "We need more Trackers." She picked up my pilsner glass as she looked out the window, where droplets of rain rolled down the glass. She took a swallow of the beer, set the glass back on the table, and her gaze met mine again. "We're almost at bare bones."

I wiped my mouth with a napkin and set it by my plate. "That's what I've been saying."

She played with the pilsner, stroking her fingers up and down the glass. "I don't understand. Why isn't Rodán recruiting more?"

"If we had more Trackers, our friends might still be alive." Heat flashed through me. "I think this is a huge dose of the Great Guardian's stupid 'not interfering with Otherworlds' garbage."

If Nadia was Catholic I swear she would have made the sign of the cross. "*Nyx.* You can't say things like that about the Guardian." Her eyes were huge as she spoke.

"We need two Trackers per territory. It's been bad

enough having only one per territory, with just five rovers." The bite to my tone was strong. "I think the GG should get her ass in gear and send us more Trackers."

Nadia cleared her throat and started gathering dishes as she said in a loud voice, "The views and opinions expressed in this apartment are solely those of the commentator . . ."

CHAPTER 25

Save the whales! Trade them for valuable prizes!

I shook my head when I saw Olivia's black T-shirt. She was waiting for me near the entrance to the Pit, her hair loose around her shoulders, and her dark, exotic features seemed even more beautiful. How could anyone look so good in T-shirts, jeans, and tennis shoes all of the time?

"One of these days some zoologist or tree hugger is going to come after you," I said to Olivia as I gestured toward her T-shirt.

Olivia gave a mock serious look as she and Nadia bumped fists like rappers did. "It'll give the Beast something to do when he runs them over."

"That GTO needs to move on to Summerland," I said. "Or wherever it is that dead cars go."

Olivia tilted her chin and gave me a haughty look. "The Beast just needs a little tune-up."

"He needs to go to that junkyard in the sky," I said.

Olivia's expression went from teasing to serious. "I was afraid we'd lost you." She gave me a hug, and I hugged her back as she continued talking without stopping for a beat. "Because then I'd have to look for a new partner."

She drew away and I laughed. It was good to be back.

I'd called Olivia before I left Nadia's to let her know I was here and that I'd meet her outside the Pit. I wanted to tell Olivia about Adam, but I figured I'd wait until tomorrow, when it was just the two of us in the office.

Nadia crossed her arms over her chest and looked from Olivia to me. "So, did Olivia kill you for tracking without her night before last?"

I winced. *Gee, thanks, buddy.*

Olivia shot me a look that would have frozen the Hudson solid enough to skate on in September. "Not yet," she said in a slow, clear tone that cut through the throbbing music that poured out of the entrance to the Pit. "But you are so dead for leaving without me that night."

I tried to look as contrite as possible. "But if you kill me then you will have to find another partner."

She narrowed her dark eyes and put her hands on her hips. "It might be worth it after all."

Damn. Wasn't sure I *would* survive the Wrath of Olivia. "I'm sorry, okay?"

"No, it's not okay." Olivia stared at me for one long moment. "Do it again and I'll kick your skinny purple butt all over Manhattan. *Then* I'll kill you."

Groan.

T appeared out of the shadows, his expression dark, and I wanted to shrink from the stares all three of them were giving me now.

"Thank you, T." I wasn't about to hug him. I didn't

know what to do with my hands, so I put them on the hilts of my daggers. "I owe you. Twice now."

"Going out alone was idiotic." T scowled. "You should have waited for me."

My spine stiffened. "I've been tracking for two years on my own and I've handled everything just fine." *Until now.* The thought deflated me.

"You've never had to face Demons like this." Olivia kept her hands braced on her hips as she continued to glare at me. "It was a stupid thing to do."

I pushed my blue hair over my shoulders in frustration. "I get it."

"The three of us aren't about to let you out of our sight when it comes to tracking," Nadia said. I swung my gaze to her and she had a determined expression.

"So now it's three on one." I sighed and rubbed my temples. "Okay, okay. From this point on I don't go out without backup." I looked toward the Pit, dying to change the subject. "I need to meet with Rodán." I turned back to T and Olivia. "And both of you are supposed to be in on this, too."

I didn't give them a chance to answer before I headed for the entrance.

Fred gave me a hug so tight that I gasped and he told me how glad he was that I'd made it through what had happened. He seemed to be more approving of T than before. Guess the news of my near-death and T saving me had already made its way around.

The path through the club was thick with dancers, the smells of all the paranorms lumped together.

Tonight the odor was like taking different colors of clay and smooshing them all together so that a being couldn't tell one color from another. Just a gray blob.

My senses were on overdrive—or remnants of what had happened to me were affecting me—because at that moment the smells were almost overwhelming and I couldn't sift out individual scents.

Nadia left to join the remaining Trackers before they headed out. I waved across the room to my fellow Trackers, who waved at me and gave me thumbs-up signs, a way of telling me they were glad I was back. I couldn't help a smile in their direction. Here in New York City, they were my family, and I felt lucky to have them.

At the back of the club, Seth, the Vamp Olivia had been talking to a few days ago, jerked his thumb in the direction of one of the closed doors along the rear wall. "Rodán is waiting for you."

Olivia smiled at the Vamp, and I elbowed her. "Don't encourage them," I said under my breath.

"I'm having his baby," she said under hers, and I almost choked.

Of course Rodán wouldn't have us meet in his private chambers, because Olivia was with us. T, Olivia, and I went into one of the secluded rooms Rodán used for conferences, when he needed to meet with Trackers or other Peacekeepers.

T opened the door and held it until Olivia and I entered the large conference room. The door whispered closed behind us, but T's boots clunked against the wooden floor as we strode across the enormous chamber. It was a wonder he could sneak up on anything, as noisy as he was.

A woodsy smell passed over me as we walked, the scent from the polished Dryad wooden floor and table. A bouquet of wildflowers at the center of the conference table lent the room a sweet perfume.

The room easily accommodated all of the Manhattan Peacekeepers at one time when Rodán needed to make important announcements, standing room only. But that was rare. He usually spoke with the Soothsayers, Healers, and Gatekeepers in their special chambers.

In our conference room, the long oval conference table along one side of the room only had twenty-five chairs around it, for smaller meetings with the Trackers.

The moment Rodán saw me he strode across the polished wood floor, took me in his arms, and held me to him. "Sweets. Thank the Goddess."

He drew away and gripped me by my upper arms, and for a long moment stared into my eyes. The depth of caring and concern that I saw shocked me. He looked at me, not just as someone who would have been devastated at the loss of a friend, but also as though he would have been lost without me had I died. A deep and personal feeling beyond being a friend, mentor, and casual lover.

He kissed each of my cheeks before breaking that brief contact and my strange thoughts.

"Torin and Olivia briefed me on the third liaison's

disappearance," Rodán said to me. "Have they had a chance to discuss it with you?"

I shook my head. "And I haven't given my news to them, either."

Well, I could have told them about the scorpion shell that night if I hadn't felt the need to avoid them and go out on my own. Maybe it seemed stupid, but I'd been tracking my territory alone for two years— other than the times Olivia accompanied me on specific cases. I'd been able to handle anything and everything that came my way. Until now. Goddess-damn.

I rolled my shoulders, trying to ease away the desire to defend myself and my actions. I didn't need to go on the defensive.

Rodán made his way to the oval conference table. Today he wore a sleeveless blood-red tunic, and his silvery-blond hair hung to the middle of his back. The muscles in his bare arms flexed as he moved with power and grace to his chair at the head of the table. Olivia and I took seats to Rodán's right, T on his left.

I started first, explaining to T and Olivia about the scorpion shell, that the tail from the drawing was actually a scorpion tail. Then I told them about the Chance-Demon. T's scowl grew darker and Olivia narrowed her eyes, but neither gave me a difficult time for not telling them sooner about the shell or the scorpion tail. I figured that was because they'd already ridden me hard enough.

"The third liaison," Rodán started as leaned back in the reclining chair, "was taken not far from where you were attacked and the location where the Demons murdered Randy."

Prickles stung my skin. "Randy was killed near me?"

"He sensed the attack on you and left Central Park to go to your aid." The prickles turned into a cold chill that flushed over me as he continued. "He ran up against a horde of Demons while Torin was attending to you. Randy was gutted before Torin could help him, so there was no saving him."

My vision blurred and I put my head in my hands, my elbows on the polished wood surface of the conference table. Dear Goddess. I was responsible for his death. If I hadn't been so foolish and tried to save what I thought was a human woman, I wouldn't have been down and out because of the Chance-Demon.

"You mentioned you were heading toward Central Park for Randy after trying to save the woman," Rodán said.

My thoughts clouded. That was true. Why did I sense that he was in trouble before I'd been attacked?

"We believe the Demons managed to call to you and Randy both," Rodán said.

"For insurance—to make sure they had at least one Tracker death," Olivia said. "Somehow it ties in with the missing liaisons. They need a Tracker to die when they take a liaison."

I raised my head from my hands and frowned. "Some kind of ritual?"

"Possibly." The chair creaked as he adjusted his position. "The left-behind signs could be part of that ritual and not clues meant to taunt us."

"But why take the liaisons instead of killing them, too?" I ran my fingers along my choker as I thought out loud, before putting my hand back on the table.

"Why paranormal liaisons at all?" Olivia said. "We do need to consider the fact that we don't know if they were taken alive or eaten. We're guessing."

"Based on paranorm intuition." Rodán swiveled slightly in his chair. "And what information the Great Guardian has chosen to give me."

"Oh, brother." Olivia rolled her eyes.

"The Guardian gives us bits and pieces, but won't give us what we need, including Trackers." I pushed my hand through my hair in a harsh movement. "Maybe the GG is going senile." I was so going to be sent to Underworld for that comment.

Rodán snapped his attention to me. "Nyx," he said in Drow. "Enough."

Under the intensity of his gaze I felt chastised enough that I would have slid down in my chair if I were still a youngling.

I cleared my throat. "You haven't told me about that third liaison attack, and whether or not you found any clues."

"The liaison lived a couple of blocks from your location," Olivia said. "Seventy-ninth and Riverside. It was like a friggin' train wreck had happened inside the house."

What was going on? "They're obviously tied together." I tapped my fingers on the top of the conference table. "But how? Why?" I looked from Olivia to Torin and back again. "Did you find any more clues at the site?"

"Detective Boyd found splatters of blue blood," Olivia said, and delicious sensations twirled in my belly at the mention of Adam's name. What I would give to be back in bed with him. Olivia continued, knocking me back to reality. "And I found the image of a locust that looked like it had been lasered into the kitchen's tile floor."

I furrowed my brow. "A locust? Is this the most bizarre Demon or what?"

"We're more concerned with how powerful this Demon is," Rodán said. "And exactly what its plans are."

"No other developments?" I asked.

Rodán shook his head. "What I need you three to do now is find the Demon lair, so that we can go after them before the Demons can complete what is most likely a devastating ritual."

I saluted him as we all stood. "Aye, aye, Captain."

He smiled, but then his smile was replaced by a more serious expression. "I want you three to be careful tonight. I have a feeling this is all leading to something big, something beyond disastrous."

CHAPTER 26

"Holy crap." Olivia flopped her hair out of her eyes and rubbed her face on the outside of her sweat jacket as T did his incinerating thing with the dead Demons. Smelled like hell. "That last motherfucker was a tough one."

"Good shot at that Demon sac." I looked at my partner. It was after midnight and Olivia had exceeded my expectations. I should never have held back. She could kick major Demon ass.

Olivia pushed more hair out of her face. Her hair was completely soaked blue with the last Demon's blood, and her face was splattered with it, too. The demon sac had ruptured on impact from her dead-center shot with the Sig Sauer.

Olivia held up a chunk of her blue-soaked hair. "Now I look like you. All I need is purple skin."

"Amethyst." I brushed blue blood off my cheek with the back of my hand. "And watch it, or I won't include you in the cleansing spell."

Olivia held up her Sig, the barrel pointed up. The handgun was also coated in blue. "Pretty please."

"Avanna," I said, and blood and filth vanished from our bodies, hair, and weapons.

"I really need to take you home." Olivia examined her hands. "You'd come in handy in the mornings, so I wouldn't have to take showers."

"No way." I sheathed my daggers. "Your snores are like the sound of a metro bus when you fall asleep in the office."

She narrowed her eyes. "I do not snore."

"All I have to do is record you."

Olivia casually looked at her Sig. "You wouldn't dare."

"You don't scare me," I said.

"You should be afraid . . ." She gave me a wicked look. "Very afraid."

"As if," I said.

T came toward us, passing under a streetlight as he strode closer with his slow yet powerful gait.

"We've covered almost my entire territory," I said.

"And still no idea where the damned Demon lair is." Olivia's now clean dark hair swung around her cheeks as she scanned the Manhattan skyline.

I frowned as I looked at the location where we'd just taken out nine Demons. Earlier, seven Demons had come after us. "Things sure are busy tonight." My thoughts tried to wrap around this whole, giant mess. "I've never seen so many Demons out in one night."

Olivia frowned, too. "Maybe it's to serve as a distraction?"

"From what?" I thought out loud.

T and Olivia had as much of an answer as I did—which meant they had nothing.

Olivia shoved a new magazine into her Sig with a solid click. "What now?"

"Why don't we go to Fort Tryon?" I stepped away from the two of them and headed for the 'Vette.

We took my car tonight, since Olivia didn't have the ability to run as fast as me, or to get to point B from point A as fast as T could—however he did what he did. He always managed to arrive ahead of me, but I never saw him running.

All night, after giving her the location when we had sensed a disturbance, T and I left Olivia to follow in the 'Vette. I can race faster across town than a car—unless the car had wings. Something I'd yet to see.

Because T and I didn't sense any disturbances right now, I rode in the 'Vette with Olivia while T did his thing to get to the park. He couldn't be running like I can. T had to have a similar ability to my father's—able to move from one location to another by some kind of transference.

It would be a few years yet before I'd have the Drow version of that ability. Father said I'd grow into that power when I was a century old. I'm impatient, tenacious, and driven. I wasn't planning on waiting that long. I'd figure it out and I'd be doing it by the time I was twenty-eight, next year. That was my goal.

"Sucks that we haven't been able to turn up anything with that symbol," Olivia said as she drove us to Fort Tryon. "At least no other Tracker was murdered last night. Or any liaisons."

The pain of Caprice and my other friends' deaths slammed into my chest and I had to take a deep breath. In the same moment my insides were twisting for them, I felt additional pain for the liaisons' families, and for whatever had happened to the liaisons.

"Get your butt going," Olivia said, and I looked up to see we'd reached Fort Tryon. "Where were you?" she added before we climbed out. "What's churning in that little brain of yours?"

I shrugged. "Just trying to figure out this puzzle."

Olivia and I made our way to the highest point in Manhattan, an incredible lookout over the city.

"This view never ceases to amaze me." Olivia put her hands in the pockets of her sweat jacket. "I need to come here more often."

She was right. It was amazing. From this vantage point we could see the glittering lights along the Hudson River, as well as the George Washington Bridge and the Harlem River.

An eerie vibration stirred in the air. T came up to stand beside Olivia. I moved away from them, toward the center of the lookout point, trying to figure out where the bizarre vibes were coming from. Something was wrong. Very wrong.

A raking sensation clawed at my back. My spine started to ache so much my eyes would have watered if I had tear ducts.

Olivia's voice sounded off, almost far away. ". . . like something's crawling all over my back."

The sensation grabbed me harder. Fiercer.

Olivia cried out. I wanted to turn and go to her, but I was immobilized with pain. It spread throughout my body, and my skull felt as if it would split.

What was happening to me? I couldn't have shouted to T and Olivia if I tried. I couldn't use my elements to reach out to see what was doing this to me.

The pain vanished. I dropped to my hands and knees, and pebbles dug into my palms. Sweat coated my face and my head swam as if I'd spent a week of nonstop fighting.

A powerful presence.

An evil presence.

Behind me.

An agonizing shudder arrowed along my back like ice picks driving into my spine. Vibrations renewed and grew stronger around me.

I tried to grasp my elements, and drew one of my dragon-claw daggers. At the same time, I scrambled to my feet and turned.

"Oh, shit" were the first words that came to mind.

A massive Demon. A male, at least seven feet tall and five times my size. Its clawed hands and sharp teeth glinted in the moonlight like steel blades.

I needed bigger daggers.

My heart pounded like Drow ritual drums. The sensation of ice picks attacking my body increased and I fought to keep from stumbling.

The Demon opened its mouth wide and roared.

My heart dropped.

The ground trembled. Birds screeched and flew out of their resting places in the trees. The Demon's roar drowned out the sounds of traffic, sirens, and every other city noise.

Pain stabbed me again and I almost cried out.

I blinked hard as I judged the distance between

me and the Demon, and focused on the location of its sac of blue fluid.

It started toward me. The ground shook with every step.

I swallowed. Bring it on.

Yeah, right.

Where was T? Olivia?

The Demon lunged. Automatically I performed a double backflip, despite pain that was becoming excruciating. I barely avoided its claws as it reached for me.

What was causing that vibration? Everything vibrated, from the air to the ground.

A more powerful sensation of ice picks plunging into my flesh caused me to cry out.

Pain exploded down my spine.

I lost hold of my dagger.

Dear Goddess. My spine was going to snap.

It couldn't possibly hold me up much longer.

The Demon rushed me.

All of my senses screamed with pain as I whirled away from the Demon. I jumped and twisted sideways in midair, just above its outstretched arms.

When my feet hit a rock outcropping I fell to the side. Pain burst through my elbow when I landed on the rock, hard.

The vibrations—I swore it felt like ice picks really were driving through me, about to pin me to the ground.

Through my dimmed vision I saw the Demon's massive body facing me.

More vibrations.

More screaming pain.

The Demon roared.

I tried to get to my feet. Fell.

The vibrations. The pain. Somehow connected.

Block the pain. Block the pain.

Remember your warrior training, Nyx.

Vibrations. Pain.

As I looked up at the Demon, I gritted my teeth. I unsheathed the second dagger and focused on my air power. I used so much of the element that I staggered as it exploded around me and formed an air pocket between me and the Demon.

The Demon—it was more monster than humanoid in appearance. It roared as it tried to grab me, but its claws rebounded off of my air pocket.

Vibrations started shaking my body, but the air power I'd built up shielded me enough that I could tolerate the pain. Now to use more of my element. I was pushing it, but I didn't have a choice.

Around and around, my air element began circling the demon. Twisting around it like a spider cocooning her prey.

I used my magic to yank the thread of air binding the Demon. It stumbled backward and shrieked.

I raised my dagger and dropped my air shield. With all my strength, I flung the blade at the Demon's life sac.

The demon vanished. My dagger landed on the ground and skidded several feet away.

It had vanished. Before my dagger could touch it.

The vibrations and pain stopped.

My heart beat like crazy. I'd been so close. I would

have nailed the Demon but . . . it . . . disappeared. None of the Demons had done that before.

"Nyx!" Olivia's voice made it through the sound of blood rushing in my ears. "Are you all right?"

I swayed. She caught me by the shoulders as I listed to the side.

"We couldn't get to you." Olivia squeezed my shoulders. "We were surrounded by fucking invisible walls." Her words were rushed, panicked, something I'd never heard from Olivia before—panic.

"Torin did everything he could," she continued, "but we couldn't get past it. All we could do was watch you battle that thing while we tried to get out."

My gaze met T's as my breathing began to steady.

I'm not sure why thoughts started churning through my mind, questioning T.

Had he? Had he done everything he could to try to get to me?

Or not?

CHAPTER 27

My XPhone's muffled ringtone came from inside my purse as I scooted my chair up to my desk. Olivia was already settled in her seat, focused intently on her screen. Must be something important because she hadn't said anything to me since I walked into the office thirty seconds ago.

My body still ached from last night's fight with the gargantuan Demon. The vibrations affected me more than any actual injury.

I dug in my handbag for the XPhone. "Back in Black" was louder when I withdrew it. "Unknown" came up on the caller screen. I pushed the on button and brought the XPhone to my ear. "Nyx Ciar."

"This scene's worse than the other three combined." The tension in Rodán's voice caused my heart to pound faster.

"Where?" I checked my holster to make sure my Kahr was secure.

"Seventy-seventh and Central Park West."

I stopped moving, my hand resting on my Kahr. "*My* territory?"

Rodán gave me the address of an apartment building only thirty blocks from my own apartment. "Had to have happened during your patrol," Rodán said as I slung my purse over my shoulder.

My territory? *My* patrol? The mere thoughts had my ears burning deep inside, and a hot flush made my skin feel as if it might burn off. T, Olivia, and I had been everywhere, and I never once had the feeling something big was going down. Unless it happened during my fight with the Demon?

The Demon. It could have been a deliberate distraction by the major or master Demons.

Olivia already had her Mets sweat jacket on as I headed for the front door. She was right behind me when I pushed the door open against a strong breeze. The cool air didn't lessen the burn of my skin one bit.

"The massacre is contained within the apartment building, so it wasn't discovered until the building supervisor came in for the day," Rodán said as I continued listening to him while hurrying toward the rear garage. "The scene was almost out of control before we had a chance to freeze it."

The word *massacre* echoed in my head, but I didn't have time to ask questions. I had to get hold of Adam.

"Two minutes. We'll be there." I was already in my car and, as soon as I disconnected, I pressed the speed dial number for Adam's cell phone. Olivia climbed in the passenger seat as I pressed the XPhone to my ear.

"Boyd," he answered as I spun my car out of the garage and onto the street.

"This one's supposed to be really bad." My 'Vette's engine revved as I punched the gas and pulled onto Central Park West. As I dodged a taxi, I gave Adam the address.

"I'm close," he said as I neared the street the apartment building was on. "I'll be there in five."

My territory kept pounding in my head. The Demon *must* have been meant as a distraction.

Emergency vehicles, barricades, yellow crime scene tape . . . NYPD officers, SWAT team members, paramedics, and other crime-related personnel had been at work.

Bodies. A dozen or more had been pulled from the building, most being put into body bags. Men, women, children, of all races, were sprawled on the sidewalks. Dead. Definitely dead.

I'd never seen anything so bad in my two years as a PI or a Tracker, and I wanted to throw up. Only the Drow half of me kept the acid from climbing up my throat. The stench of burned sugar and seared flesh almost made me puke anyway.

I didn't realize I'd been standing motionless and staring until the familiar scent of coffee and leather reached me. An arm rested on my shoulder and I looked up to see the concern in Adam Boyd's warm brown eyes as he squeezed me close to him.

"You okay?" Tension radiated from him and was obvious in the tautness of his features.

I nodded. "Lulu must have sensed you're here since you're among the currently warm."

He gave a grim look toward the building. "Let's do it."

From the outside it was obvious why the apartment building hadn't been suspect before the building supervisor made a discovery of nightmares.

T wasn't there—maybe Rodán hadn't gotten hold

of him. I didn't say anything to Lulu, who actually looked like she was going to vomit. Lulu's skin was too pale, her hand clamped over her mouth. I felt bad for her.

Adam, Olivia, and I made it through the front door, and we paused in the middle of what once had been the lobby. The security desk was in front of us, an elevator to the right, a stairwell to the left. The twisted metal staircase was now visible thanks to the door having been ripped off.

Evil clung to broken beams, shattered doors, the destroyed staircase. The smell and feel even seemed to come from the water dripping from crumpled pipes.

Then I saw it.

My stomach clenched even though I didn't know what it was.

Another symbol burned into the floor, in front of the security desk.

Seven circles, with the largest circle on the top and the smallest on the bottom, like an inverted cone.

"Oh, my God," Olivia said from beside me. "All of the symbols we've found are for the Destroyer."

I'd come across that Demon in my research, but hadn't made any connections to him. "How do you know that?"

"When you walked in I was on the Internet." She continued to stare at the symbol. "I was searching with all the info we've accumulated up through the scorpion shell."

"Fill me in," Adam said.

"Abaddon." T was at my other side before I even

knew he was in the building. "The Black Mage, a mighty Great Earl of the human version of Hell. The rutting Demon of the abyss."

When T said the name out loud even the Drow half of me wanted to shudder, and I rubbed my arms with my hands.

"And . . ." Adam said, the tone of his voice telling Olivia and T to get to the point.

"Abaddon has thirty-six legions of Demons at his disposal." T crossed his arms over his chest. "These symbols might be his attempt to create his own fucking Demon Gate. Rodán was right. He hasn't been trying to taunt us—he's been using the symbols to establish points to bring in his army. If he can bring his legions into this world from Hell—"

Olivia said, "It would be like Armageddon."

Rodán closed his eyes and leaned back in his office chair, absorbing the news I'd just given him. His features had become unnaturally taut—unnatural for him—his lips in a firm line. T sat in a chair beside me.

While I waited for Rodán's response, the cool darkness of his office seemed to warm, as if the Demon had already crawled out of the abyss and crowded into the room with us.

"It explains a lot," Rodán finally said as he lowered his head and opened his eyes. "Ancient Elvin texts refer to Apollyon, the Greek name for Abaddon, a lesser God banished to the abyss millennia ago as a Demon."

Rodán's expression was difficult to read, but a feeling of great concern weighted the air as he continued.

"It was prophesied that one day Abaddon would send forth his minions to make way for him, should he find a way to escape the abyss."

I clasped my XPhone and wondered if it was possible to snap it in two if I wasn't careful. "All of this time the Ruhin Demon Gate we've been guarding is the one that leads to the abyss."

"Why didn't you know this already?" T's words were sharp enough to snap my attention to him. Talking to Rodán like that might get him knocked out of the room, maybe into another Otherworld.

"The Ruhin Demon Gate has long been an unknown." Rodán focused on T, and his words were clear, precise, and in the formal phrasing and tone of the Elves. Oh, yeah, he was pissed. "As we discussed earlier this week, knowledge of each Demon Gate is passed from its Gatekeeper to the next Gatekeeper. Over a thousand years ago there was a break in the chain of the Ruhin Gatekeepers and the knowledge was lost."

T grunted. A grunt was the best he could do?

I crossed my legs at my knees and met Rodán's gaze. "Do you think he's already come through the gate, or are his minor and major Demons clearing the path?"

"I believe he's already here," T said. I turned my attention to him. T looked intense, his scars making him appear somehow sinister in the low lighting of Rodán's office, and he didn't look handsome at all. "I think what we discussed earlier is more probable. Abaddon is the being likely to be using the symbols for rituals."

A chill rolled through me as Rodán gave a slow nod. "I'm afraid Torin is probably right."

"What you said back at the scene." I made myself meet Torin's gaze. "You believe these symbols he's leaving are part of a complex pattern that's going to help him open up a door from the abyss to bring his legions here?"

T nodded, while Rodán frowned and looked as if he was deep in thought.

"The question now is what to do next." I didn't give either one of them a chance to speak as I continued. "We need to call all of the Trackers together and distribute this information."

"Do you have a plan?" T asked in a growly-rumbly tone that was filled with doubt.

I straightened in my seat as I curled my fingers around my XPhone. "We call Abaddon out. We fight this battle on our turf and on our terms, not his."

T studied me with the arrogant expression he so often wore. Made me want to punch him. "And how do you think you're going to do that, much less defeat Abaddon?"

I leaned forward, irritation putting a slight growl in my voice. "It's called teamwork. We come up with a plan and execute it when all the pieces are in place."

Rodán gracefully rose from his seat. "I'll call the meeting now."

I got to my feet, too. "Afterward, Olivia and I will use every resource we have to pinpoint the Demon's lair."

CHAPTER 28

My thoughts bounced from one thing to another. Including Adam. After our spectacular afternoon together yesterday, we'd arranged to have lunch today.

I frowned. I hadn't had a chance to tell Olivia yet, with all of the craziness about our time together. I'd only told her about lunch with him today.

"What about satellite images?" Olivia was saying, her words barely seeping through my consciousness. "They might be able to help us locate the Demons in your territory." She rapped her desk with her knuckles. "*Nyx*. Are you in there?"

I frowned as I met her gaze. "Of course."

"I think it could be an excellent shot for us." Olivia leaned farther back in her chair, her feet up on her desk. "James has so many connections he's sure to be able to help us with that kind of thing."

My temples ached and I rubbed them. "What 'kind of thing?' "

Olivia gave me the "Are you stupid?" look.

Satellite. Images. Demons. Territory.

"Oh." I straightened in my chair. "Not sure how that would work."

"Infrared and all that crap," Olivia said.

"Okay, I can see that," I said. "How can we tell Demons from humans?"

"Size, and maybe the fact they have blue blood."

"Can't hurt," I said after I thought about it for a moment. "Good idea."

"Of course." Olivia swung her legs down and moved up to her computer. "Let's see if James is teaching class right now . . ." She pressed a couple of keys on her gel pad as she checked his schedule. "Damn. He's in the middle of one of his applied science lectures."

She grabbed the XPhone off her desk. "I'll type a quick text to him. I'm having a bad hair day so I'll skip sending him a vid message."

"Sure." I looped my finger near my head in a "She's crazy" motion. "You. A bad hair day. As if." Olivia looked gorgeous, as always, with her beautiful dark golden-hued skin, exotic features, and dark hair swept up in a clip.

"There." She tossed her XPhone onto her desk with a thunk after what amounted to a couple of seconds. "Hey, don't you have a lunch date with Adam today?"

I felt a real smile rise up in me for the first time that day. "It's almost time to leave."

Adam and I met at an Italian café a few blocks from my office on Amsterdam. The café smelled of warm garlic bread and marinara when we walked through it to sit at a table outside, in the pleasant sunshiny day.

He took his chair after having helped me into my

own. So he was a gentleman, too. The hostess handed us our menus and then we were alone. The first time since yesterday.

Adam reached across the table and took my hand. Thrills ran through my body, and memories of making love to him sent swirls of desire from my belly to the place between my thighs.

"I keep thinking about yesterday." He stroked my palm with his fingers, and more desire filled me as I looked into his brown eyes. "It was special."

I smiled. "We could skip lunch . . ."

His boyish grin only made me want him more. "Or we could make this a fast lunch."

Imagining being in bed with him had taken care of my appetite, but I nodded. "Works for me."

He released my hand and, after looking at me for another long moment, he studied his menu. I forced myself to look at mine.

"Seems a little surreal when you think about it." Adam set his menu down at the same time I did. He rested his forearms on the table, his bomber jacket stretching across his broad shoulders. "Around us it all looks so normal, when things are really going to hell."

I gave Adam a wry look. "Literally."

A server placed a glass of water on the table for each of us, along with a basket of bread sticks that smelled hot, buttery, and of garlic. I tugged the paper off of my straw. Adam left his on the table. The fresh air blew the short strands of his hair, giving him an adorable, mussed look.

He studied me with his dark brown eyes, and I

felt a link form between us that wouldn't allow me to look away if I wanted to.

"Why has it taken us so long to get together?" His voice was warm, rich. "We should have done this months ago."

"That's because it took some convincing to get you to even believe in the paranormal." I took a bread stick from the basket and put it on my plate, just for something to do with my hands while he looked at me so intently. "I think you were in shock after catching that Metamorph off guard."

Adam's features grew taut. "Seeing that bastard shift to look like Vetri, the cop he'd just murdered—I didn't know what to think." Adam clenched his fist on the tablecloth. "And the Doppler. I'm still amazed it didn't scare the sh—crap out of me to see a malamute transform into a man the size of a professional wrestler."

"You were amazing from what Ice said." I smiled. "You managed to pin a Metamorph to the ground and handcuff him, while keeping your gun on that Doppler."

"Thank God that one of your Soothsayers was able to freeze the crime scene." Adam picked up a bread stick and set it on his plate.

"God" didn't have anything to do with it. Rodán did, but I didn't correct Adam.

He took a bite of his bread stick and chewed for a moment. "I've always wondered, but never had a chance to ask, why you picked me to be a liaison to the paranorm."

"Easy." I wiped my fingers on a napkin. "The way you handled that situation was proof that you were exactly what we were looking for in a liaison."

"You think it's okay to let me take care of business during the day," he said. "Give me a good explanation now why nighttime is another story. Especially since I've already had that one encounter."

I looked down at my plate. It was a relief when the waitress came to take our order. I told her I'd have lasagna with a side salad. Adam ordered the same, but chose minestrone soup instead of salad.

For a moment I glanced over the railing of the café's outside dining area and watched the people walking by on the sidewalk and the traffic in the street.

"Tell me," he said quietly, and I met his gaze. "I should be out there with you at night."

"You sound like Olivia." I pushed my hair over my shoulder and imagined it was blue right now instead of black. But he hadn't cared. He'd told me I was beautiful after the change.

I could see the frustration on his features, hear it in his voice. "But she's been out with you."

"Not on the Demon case." I shook my head. "Last night was her first time out."

"Tonight I'm going out with you," he said in a hard, firm voice.

The waitress delivered my salad and his soup.

Maybe it was avoidance but I ate most of my small side salad before I looked at him. He'd remained silent, and his soup was almost gone.

I was relieved at the change in subject when he spoke. "You said you're Drow. Can you tell me more?"

This didn't seem hard at all now that he knew that part of me. "Like I mentioned yesterday, Dark Elves are also referred to as Drow." I set my fork down on my salad plate. "What are now known as Light Elves banished Dark Elves belowground millennia ago."

Adam had been taking this so calmly, but I wished I knew everything he was thinking. "Why were they banished?"

I didn't really want to say why, but I'd promised to be honest with him. "One reason is that Dark Elves believe females should be subservient to males."

"And you grew up with that?" He shook his head. "Can't believe it. That's not the Nyx I know."

"Fortunately my mother is human," I said, "and she taught me to be strong like her, and never to bow down to any man, regardless of the fact my father is Drow."

"I like your mother already." A busboy cleared away my salad plate and Adam's bowl. "What about your father? Since he's Drow, why didn't he have a problem with your mom's refusal to live that lifestyle?"

"Father would do anything for Mother." Whenever I talked about my parents, only good feelings came to me. "My father is King of the Dark Elves, which makes my mother Queen, of course."

He smiled. "Princess, huh?"

"Yeah, well . . . being Princess has its benefits." I

moved back to let the server place our plates of lasagna in front of each of us before I continued. "My father could let me do anything I wanted, which included becoming a warrior."

"You?" He grinned. "A warrior?"

I raised my brows. "Beneath this Versace suit is a female warrior who has kicked major male warrior butt." That sure hadn't made me very popular.

Adam dug his fork into his lasagna. "I'd sure like to see it."

"The chest straps are kind of uncomfortable, and they chafe," I said with a teasing grin.

He laughed, and fine lines crinkled at the corners of his eyes. "I can't picture you in anything but silk and lace."

"Now I stick with a supple leather outfit when I track. Much more comfortable."

"The subservient thing," Adam said after taking a drink of his ice water. "Was that the only reason why Dark Elves were sent belowground?"

Would he understand this part? "Drow use magic that borders on dark. Not black magic, but not light, either."

He frowned a little. "You use dark magic?"

"Well . . . yes." I gripped my fork, which I'd started to use to cut the lasagna. "I use elemental magic, and sometimes I do things Light Elves wouldn't approve of, no matter my intentions. But nothing I do is ever black."

Adam reached across the table to cover my free hand with his. "I can't imagine you doing anything that is."

Insert another schoolgirl sigh. I could really get used to having this man around.

"Are there other female Drow warriors?" he asked.

I gave him a wry look. "None. Let's say it was a huge shock to everyone when Father let me train with the males."

"That must have been hard in a lot of ways," he said with a thoughtful expression.

It was difficult to admit some things. "In the Drow realm I'm virtually an outcast. I never had any friends other than my human mother. Not only because I'm a Princess, but because I refuse to live the Drow lifestyle." In this Otherworld, women had the freedom of choice—yet they'd had to fight for those choices, too. "Drow women enjoy their submissive role, which I've never quite understood."

Adam studied me. "Are there others here in the city like you—human in the day and Drow at night?"

"I'm the only one of my kind here. Because, well, I'm the only one of my kind," I said, and he looked surprised. "I was born with amethyst skin and vivid, cobalt-blue hair. It was a dead giveaway that I was different."

"I'm not following."

"I'm different from other half-human, half-Drow individuals," I said. "Very, very few Drow males come up at night from belowground and mate with human females. If the human woman conceives, the children are always raised aboveground, because the human half is always dominant." I paused. "Until me. And so far only me."

His sudden smile warmed my insides and settled the anxiety that had started to squeeze my belly. "I always knew you were special."

I couldn't help but return his smile. "Definitely different."

"Special."

I lowered my head, for some strange reason feeling shy and embarrassed, yet pleased.

To my surprise, my plate was empty and, when I looked, so was his. I didn't even remember eating as we talked. He signaled the waitress and she brought the check. Adam insisted on paying. I let him win this round, but told him next time it was my treat.

I sure hoped there would be a next time.

He'd parked not too far from the café, but we walked the few blocks to my office. When we reached it I drew him away from the door, and we stood in the shadowed area between the office door and the stairs to the apartments above.

He took me in his arms and kissed me. Warm, sweet. Goddess, he tasted so good, smelled so good, and being in his arms felt so right.

With our chemistry, the attraction between us, and everything I'd come to know about him, I realized I could easily fall in love with him.

The thought sent a bolt of fear through me that caused me to go still. After Stan . . . No, Adam had already proven he wasn't anything like him.

Adam drew away. "Everything okay?" he said softly as he ran his finger along my moist lower lip.

I nodded and smiled. "Better than okay." I glanced

upstairs, the desire inside me begging to be let out to wrap itself around Adam. "Do you have time to come up . . . for a bit?" I said as I met his gaze again.

A clear look of regret changed his expression. "I wish I could."

Disappointment cooled the desire inside.

"But I'm free this evening if you are."

My emotions bounced from cool disappointment to warm pleasure. "Until nine."

"Is that when you go tracking?" he said.

I hesitated before nodding.

"Then we'll just go straight from your place to get these sonsofbitches," he said with a determined look.

"Okay." What else could I say? Besides, he was just as capable as Olivia, as any of us. I had to stop protecting him.

Adam tugged a lock of my hair. "I need to use the john before I head back to work."

I gestured to the office door. "Don't get lost. We rearranged the piles of folders."

He winked at me and I smiled as I followed him into the office. I stood there for a moment before an eraser hit me in the cheek. "Ow."

I jerked my attention to Olivia, who said, "Jeez, woman. You've got it bad."

A feeling like bliss warmed my chest. "Oh, but it was so good."

"You didn't." Olivia slowly shook her head. "You had sex with Boyd?"

"I was going to tell you." I dropped my purse on her desk. "It happened yesterday, when I got back from Otherworld."

"Don't you think that was a little soon?" Olivia frowned. "You were in bed with Rodán a few nights before that."

I tilted my head. "How did you know I slept with Rodán earlier this week?"

Olivia's eyes widened as she looked past my shoulder and she had an "Oh, shit," look on her face.

The skin on my back prickled and my body burned. Oh, my Goddess. Adam hadn't just overheard us, had he?

I slowly turned and met a gaze that was now hard instead of warm.

"Adam—"

"I need to get back to work." He looked away for a moment as every good feeling drained from me. "Let's talk outside first."

He headed to the door and I followed him. I glanced over my shoulder and saw Olivia's stricken expression. "I'm so sorry," she whispered.

It wasn't her fault. I should have told her already. No, I shouldn't have let it go that far with Adam to begin with. It was *my* fault.

He held the door open for me. When the office door closed behind us he was looking away from me as he dragged his hand over his face.

"I probably shouldn't even ask this." Adam returned his gaze to mine. "Is it true? What I overheard? You're involved with Rodán?"

"It's not like that." How could I explain my relationship with Rodán?

"You just had sex with him a few nights ago."

"Yes, but—"

"Nyx, I can't see a woman who's involved with another man." Adam's features looked tired. "Been there already, and not going there again."

My thoughts were confused, tangled. I didn't know what I was trying to say. "Rodán—"

Adam blew out a harsh, audible breath of air as he pushed his hand through his hair. "I need to go."

"Please, Adam." My heart seemed to jerk out of my chest and stay with him as he moved away. "You don't understand."

Adam paused and looked at me. "Yeah. I do."

He walked away. And he didn't look back.

CHAPTER 29

My heart hurt so much that I held my fists to my chest as Adam disappeared around the corner.

I wanted to run up to my apartment and hide from everything. I wanted to bury my face in a pillow and pretend I had tear ducts and could cry.

Real pain, as well as some anger, had been in Adam's voice when he'd said he wasn't going to go through a relationship like this. *Another* relationship. He'd been hurt, and it must have been awful.

Regardless, I'd screwed up big-time. I'd been wrong in going to bed with Adam yesterday. I should have insisted on waiting.

No excuse. There was no excuse.

My heart ached so badly I couldn't go back into the office. Not yet. Instead, I walked around the side of the building, across Central Park West, and into the cool confines of the park.

It was fairly quiet when I stopped, hidden in the trees. It was well after lunch, when some of the city's residents came here to enjoy a bit of nature as they ate their sandwiches while sitting on a park bench or a blanket on the grass.

A hot dog vendor was not too far down the street. My stomach grew queasy at the smell of food, and I wrapped my arms across my waist. Scents of grass, trees, and earth didn't calm me like they usually did. Instead, everything seemed to make me feel more sensitive, like my skin was raw and exposed.

Lunch with Adam had been so beautiful, but all I could think about now was the tight set of his jaw after he'd overheard Olivia and me. And the combination of hurt and hardness in his expression just before he left.

I leaned against the rough bark of an oak tree and tipped my head back. I stared at the leaves above and watched the light blinking through them and caught glimpses of the gray sky.

Deep and guttural voices came from behind the tree I was leaning against and I started. They sounded like the Demons did when they spoke to each other.

Demons?

Chills crawled along my spine and I glanced out at the sunshine, as if making sure it was really the middle of the day and not night.

A snarl followed a low growl . . . that growl somehow sounded familiar. I'd heard it before. My heart thudded as I faced the tree, then peeked around the trunk.

The thudding of my heart nearly stopped completely. T. It was T and the Chance-Demon that I'd killed. That I thought I'd killed. Both spoke in some guttural language, and their mouths were filled with Demon teeth. Even T's. Sunlight glinted off of T's fully formed Demon claws.

Oh, my Goddess. T was a Demon.

A Demon.

All this time we'd had him in our midst, working as one of us. He'd known everything, been with us every step of the way. He'd played us all along. He'd totally fooled us, even Rodán.

I drew back to make sure I wouldn't be seen and tried to control my breathing. Adrenaline spiked through me, and even the roots of my hair seemed to rise from my scalp.

My gun, daggers—in my purse. Left behind at the office. But I had to take care of T. I had to eliminate him. Along with the Chance-Demon that was supposed to be dead.

No choice. I had to use my elemental powers and I didn't know how they'd work against T. Not after the things I'd seen him do.

The knowledge that T was a Demon was almost too much to process.

Another guttural sound, and then quiet.

I gathered my elemental powers as I stepped around the tree. The Chance-Demon wasn't there anymore. Only T, looking normal again, no claws, no mouthful of jagged teeth. It was as if I had imagined it all.

But I hadn't. I knew it. And, by his expression, so did he.

I drew my elements to me. All of them.

T opened his mouth and said something, but it was only a buzz in the background as I felt the strong white heat flash in my eyes.

The ground trembled and air whipped around T.

A nearby fire hydrant's caps ripped loose, and water shot up into the air and to its sides. I instantly gathered the water, wrapping it around T until he was in the middle of a cyclone of my power. I called up enough static that a lone bolt of lightning cut through the cyclone. T shouted as it struck him, and he dropped to his knees.

Anger at his betrayal—maybe even at our stupidity—drove me like nothing had before. The pain of losing Adam combined with my anger, and my wind element whipped the trees like a gale-force hurricane.

Every emotion, every bit of rage consumed me as T staggered to his feet in the water cyclone.

"You sonofabitch!" I focused every bit of my air power on T and released it.

As if I'd flung a two-ton boulder at T, the concentration of air I'd gathered slammed into his chest.

T shouted again as he was blasted away from me, toward an enormous tree trunk.

Before T's body hit the trunk, a flash of red lightning tore through him.

T vanished in the burst of red light.

He . . . just . . . vanished.

Nothing was registering as I stared at the spot where he'd just disappeared. I dropped to my knees and hit dirt. I kept looking at the place where that bastard, T, had vanished—or disintegrated. A prickling sensation crawled over my scalp and trickled down my body.

Was he dead?

I closed my eyes for a moment and heard the

sounds of a baby crying, a bicycle bell, cars driving nearby, and honking from all the way over on Amsterdam. The sounds rushed at me, overwhelmed me. My sensitive hearing picked up everything and I couldn't block any of it out.

Every smell was an assault. Too many flowers and trees in Central Park, the smell of hot dogs from that vendor a few blocks down, and the sickly sweet scent of ice cream from the ice cream cart. Pollution, dirt, asphalt—I was going to throw up.

I don't know how long it was before I staggered to my feet. The power I'd unleashed, and every emotion that had been churning in my body, had drained me.

Nothing would process. T was a Demon. I had just killed him.

It. T was an *it* after all.

When I walked into the PI office, Olivia came up to me, her face worried, but puzzled, too. She grasped my forearms. "What happened?"

"I—I . . ." How could I explain what had happened when I didn't even know? "I think I just killed T."

Olivia clenched my forearms tighter. "Explain."

I gestured toward Central Park West, just outside our office. "There. I . . . killed him. Disintegrated him."

"You killed Torin?" Olivia didn't relent her hold on me. "You *disintegrated* him?"

"Unless one of his talents involves vanishing." I wondered why I hadn't given that more thought. I'd been too wrapped up in the pain I'd felt from Adam's rejection, and thinking that I'd blown T away. "If he does, that could explain a lot of things. Like appearing when I'm not expecting him. Or beating me to our destination every time."

I told Olivia everything, including what Adam said to me when he left. By the time I finished she had let go of me, had her Sig Sauer out, and was checking the magazine.

"Jesus." Her expression showed more fury than I ever remembered seeing on her face. "That [insert curse words in languages I didn't understand] sonofabitch. If you didn't kill him, I will the next time we see him. A Demon. A fucking Demon."

"I need to call Rodán." My hands shook as I started to come down from the adrenaline rush and jitters took over. I fumbled with the XPhone when I retrieved it from my purse, but I managed to press speed dial for Rodán.

I don't remember the conversation I had with him. It was short and he sounded stunned. The moment I ended the call, Olivia took me by my shoulders.

"Lie down for a little while," she said. "Then get yourself together. You did the right thing." She gave me a hug. "I'm sorry about Adam. I'm so damn sorry."

"It's okay." I swallowed. "I screwed up."

Olivia headed me off to the kitchenette/lounge we had in the back of the office. I collapsed onto the couch and wrapped my arms around myself until the shaking stopped.

"Got a surprise for you." Olivia waved an eight-and-a-half-by-eleven clear sheet as I walked into the office from the lounge an hour later. Still enough daylight to get something done, something to keep me busy.

"Is it good?" I felt like I was dragging my feet through sludge as I walked toward my desk. "I need good."

Olivia sighed and put whatever it was on her desk. "I'm so sorry, Nyx."

"Don't apologize again, or I'm not responsible for my actions." I plopped into my chair and rubbed my temples. "I'm a fast draw with my Kahr."

Olivia picked up one of the erasers from her stash and rolled it with her fingers. She didn't say anything, but her gaze was intense as she looked out one of the windows, toward Central Park.

"Won't be long until we're out of daylight," I said. A change of subject would be good about now. "Show me what you've got."

"Check this out." She set down the eraser. I was glad to hear the normalcy back in her voice. I needed normalcy, and I'm sure she'd realized it. "James called while you were taking a nap, and I told him what we needed." She pushed aside a stack of file folders. "James sent them by courier and they just got here."

"Hold on." My hair kept sliding across my cheeks and into my eyes, and was beginning to drive me crazy. I dug a clasp of Drow platinum out of my desk and fastened my hair away from my face before moving around behind her desk.

On her desk, Olivia had spread several clear sheets with colors and symbols on them.

I examined the sheets but didn't quite get what I was looking at. "Something like infrared?"

"Yeah." Olivia sounded immensely pleased. "Satellite images from before the Demons escaped through that Ruhin Demon Gate, and after."

I braced my hand on her desk and leaned closer. "I see streets, buildings, and blobs. Lots and lots and lots of red, yellow, and green blobs."

"Hold on." Olivia arranged the images side by side. "It's a before and after."

"Ohhh." A little slow on the uptake, Nyx.

We both leaned down and looked at the satellite image of Manhattan from a couple of weeks ago, before the Demons came through the gate. Then, as one, we looked at the sheet with the most recent image.

"The green is a lot thicker now around the Museum of Natural History." I met Olivia's gaze as the air seemed to go cold. "According to this the Demons *are* in my territory, and they're practically on top of the museum."

"Or below it."

"Yeah. That." I hurried to my desk, dug my XPhone out of my purse, and hit the speed dial number for Rodán.

"We know where the Demons are," I said. "They're below the Museum of Natural History."

He said something in Drow that was as harsh as a stake driven into the earth. "By the Goddess," he added, the fury in his voice growing. "How could I not know this? Sense this?"

Rodán didn't ask me if I was certain. He knew

me too well and trusted me too much. I explained Olivia's discovery to him.

"Call the other Trackers and have them meet at the Pit one hour after sundown." His tone was even darker. Angrier. "I may be late, but I want everyone there, waiting."

It was almost an hour yet until sundown, so that gave us nearly two hours. "I'll take care of it immediately."

"I'll see you when I arrive," he said, and disconnected.

"We've talked about the possibility of Abaddon creating another Demon Gate." I set the XPhone down and walked to the file cabinets. "But since the massacre didn't happen until last night, while I was fighting that Demon at Fort Tryon, we didn't have a lot to go on."

"What are you thinking?" Olivia left her seat and followed me to the file cabinet.

"I think the attacks have a pattern." I formed a mental image of each location of a murdered Tracker, a missing liaison, and a symbol. I pulled out the drawer of the file cabinet where we kept all of our maps. "Midtown West, Central Park, and the Upper West Side . . . and something to do with the Museum of Natural History."

Olivia headed over to the large corner table with me. We could have brought up maps on the computer, but there was something about actually spreading one out on a surface and being able to examine it in detail. I handed Olivia an orange marker. Mine was purple. I like purple.

I drew a circle on the map of Manhattan and put the number one inside of it. "Caprice was murdered around Fifty-fifth Street and Avenue of the Americas." I tried to keep my personal emotions under wraps and look at this from a professional angle. I was a PI. That was my job.

And I was oh, so stellar at keeping that emotional distance.

Not.

Olivia drew an orange circle close to my purple one. "The same night, the disappearance of a liaison happened near Fifty-eighth Street and Fifth Avenue."

I made another circle at Frawley Circle on the upper northeast corner of Central Park. "This is where Jon died."

Olivia marked 109th and Madison. "Missing liaison and murdered family here."

"Riverside Park near Seventy-seventh Street is where they almost killed me." I cleared my throat. "Close to where they killed Randy that same night."

"And the third liaison was taken about Seventy-ninth Street, near Riverside Drive." She circled the approximate location.

"The massacre . . ." I drew another purple circle. "Seventy-seventh and Central Park West."

My scalp started to tingle like I was going to go through the transformation. I took a green marker and connected all the orange circles where the liaisons had been kidnapped and the symbols left behind. "An almost perfect triangle." I took a red marker and put a star on the museum.

Olivia dropped her own marker onto the map.

"With the museum and the concentration of Demons practically dead center."

We slowly looked at one another. "Oh, shit," she said.

I nodded. I think that just become my new favorite phrase.

CHAPTER 30

I leaned against the bar and faced the location where almost all of the remaining Trackers had gathered, in our usual corner at the Pit. Everyone was eating dinner and having a drink before Rodán showed up. Probably to fortify themselves for when we would discuss the situation and make our plans to take down this Demon, and every other one that had come through the Ruhin Demon Gate.

A hand on my shoulder, and the scent of fresh air and the woods, brought my attention to Carlos, a Werewolf who had taken over Randy's Central Park territory. "Everything okay, Nyx?" he asked.

Of course not. "Just about to order my martini." I tried to smile but I don't think I did even close to a good job at it. "I could use one. Or a dozen."

Carlos raised his clear bottle of Corona. "I've got a head start on you." He patted my shoulder and moved on to where the rest of the Trackers were sitting.

"When will Rodán get here?" Nancy said as she clenched the stem of her nonalcoholic chocolate martini. (Isn't alcohol the point?) Pixies even smell like milk chocolate.

I remained leaning against the bar, looking toward the other Trackers for a moment. I desperately wanted my martini. Mine would have the good stuff, unlike Nancy's. Mine was *only* good stuff.

"The usual, Streak?" Hector said from behind me, and I turned to face him.

I shook my head. "All I want is a huge piece of chocolate tall-cake and my martini."

Hector raised his eyebrows. "You've got it."

I could really use the cake. Chocolate helped cure all the world's ills, right?

Except Pixies smelled like chocolate, so there went that theory.

Goddess, my head ached. I rubbed my temples and squeezed my eyes shut for a moment. I couldn't stop thinking about Adam, and Torin, and the symbols, and what Olivia and I had come up with. It was all giving me a massive headache.

Hector made my dry martini with three green olives, the olives skewered on a blue sword this time. I like blue. Good thing.

A thought occurred to me and I frowned, even as my friends laughed at a good-natured joke someone was telling about a Doppler and a Shifter.

All Trackers in one place. Trackers being hunted down.

And found.

The Pit would have been a gold mine for any being going after Trackers or other paranorms.

T and Chance. Easy pickings.

With Rodán's protections, no one should have been able to see any of the Trackers leave, much less know the Pit existed or get inside. Anyone unwelcome, or anyone with ill intent—hell, anyone without an invitation—who even came close to the Pit would become disoriented. They wouldn't even know where they were until they were far, far away.

Rodán was too powerful. Or at least I'd thought he was. But he had let T in based on the recommendation of another Proctor. Caprice had probably gotten the Chance-Demon in.

I took in the nightclub, moving my gaze slowly from one end to the other, looking for something, anything unusual tonight. My Drow sight made it easier to see throughout the nightclub.

It made no difference that the room was mostly dark, lit only by flashes of color pulsating with the beat of the music. Bodies were packed on the nightclub floor and patrons crowded around tables.

I tried to sift through the smells of food and alcohol to pick out the signature scent of each being in the room. Nothing seemed out of place, and I didn't smell T's rosewood and musk scent.

"Rodán said he'd be a little late." Kelly, a Doppler, caught my attention. When I looked back at her, she tossed her thick blond hair over her shoulders.

I held back a frown at the image of her naked and in bed with Rodán. The thought made my belly feel like someone was twisting it until I was nauseated.

Jealousy? Me?

I'd seen him with lots of paranorms, but I'd never seen him with another Tracker or Peacekeeper. But why wouldn't he?

The strange feelings of jealousy must be because I'd lost Adam only hours ago. Lost Adam before I even had a chance to develop any kind of real relationship with him.

Rodán strode into the nightclub from the direction of his chambers, and patrons parted for him like he was one of the Gods of old.

Maybe he was.

He wore a long, forest-green, velvet robe and walked with power and purpose, as he always did. He held his head high and his whitish-blond hair glimmered in the light in our corner.

"We don't have a lot of time, and we have much to discuss and plan," Rodán said when he reached us.

He used his magic to erect an invisible wall to block our voices from being heard, and to muffle the loud music.

"Nyx," Rodán said as he looked at me. "Explain your findings to the Trackers."

"We came up with even more since I talked with you last, Rodán." I met his gaze and he gave a slight nod for me to continue.

First I showed them the satellite images that we believed proved that the Demons were beneath the Museum of Natural History. Before anyone had a chance to start questioning that information, I placed down the map with all the circles in a triangular pattern. With a big red star on the museum in the middle of the map.

At first there was silence, before Robert whistled through his teeth.

"Could be a coincidence," Fere said.

Nadia glared at the Werewolf. "Fere, go eat a dog biscuit."

"It's as we feared." Rodán spoke before anyone else had a chance. "Abaddon is creating another, probably much larger, Demon Gate, and the liaisons are meant to be sacrifices. My belief is that he has left his symbols and taken his sacrifices, and now will attempt to open that gate."

"Sacrifices?" Nancy set her unfinished chocolate martini on a table. "Are you talking about the missing liaisons?"

Rodán gave a slow nod.

"Liaisons are just humans." Fere made a scoffing sound. "Why would he choose humans?"

Rodán looked at each of us, the seventeen remaining Trackers. "We've never before made this information public. Each liaison has latent psychic ability. A psychic version of stem cells that can be shaped to meet the Demon's needs."

All of us stared at Rodán, and I'm sure everyone was as shocked as I was. My mind went immediately to Adam. He had latent psychic abilities? That put him even more at risk.

Ice hissed through his teeth. "Shit."

Well said.

"And the Trackers?" Nancy asked. "Is it because of our paranormal powers?"

"Yes." Rodán had taken a sort of military stance. "All of the Trackers taken had strong psychic abilities, also latent."

"You knew about this and didn't tell anyone?" Fere nearly growled the words.

Rodán met his gaze with such a hard, commanding look that it was a wonder Fere maintained his angry expression and didn't shrink away.

Rodán turned back to the rest of us. "With the powers absorbed from the Trackers, and the liaisons soon to be sacrifices, I believe Abaddon has everything he needs to open his gate to the abyss."

"We can't let him do that." Ice stood. "We need to go on the offense and take him at his lair."

"There are only seventeen of us." Meryl rubbed her palms on her fighting suit. "Will the Great Guardian give us reinforcements to go after this master Demon and all of his lesser Demons? And help us keep the gate from opening?"

"I was late because I met with the Guardian." Rodán managed to school his expression, but I could tell he was pissed. "She said she can't help us in this battle."

I clenched my fists at my sides. "That's absolute—"

"Absolutely her choice." Rodán cut me off before I could say something about the GG that I might really regret. Well, maybe I'd regret it. "This leaves us, alone, to conquer Abaddon and keep him from bringing his legions to our world."

"How are we going to do that?" Ice put his hand on the hilt of his sword. "Like Meryl said, there are only seventeen of us."

"Eighteen." Rodán swept his gaze around the

room. "I will join the battle and we *will* send Abaddon back to the stinking abyss."

Everyone seemed to hold their breath. Rodán joining us in battle? But then, we'd never faced anything like this before.

"The Demons don't show until around midnight." I braced my palms on my hips, feeling the comfort of my dagger hilts next to my hands. "If we find where they're hiding below the museum, we can take them before they have a chance to leave."

Rodán nodded, slipped off his robe, and laid the green velvet over the back of a chair.

He had dressed in black this time, a color I'd never seen him in—a black leather tunic and breeches. He filled out his clothing better than any other male could, and all of our males were fine. Rodán looked more powerful, more commanding, and more beautiful than ever.

Strapped to his back he had a carved bow made from Dryad wood, along with a quiver of Elvin arrows—amazing that I hadn't even seen a lump beneath his robe. Elvin magic, no doubt. He also had two elegant swords sheathed at his hips, along with two daggers. Talk about prepared.

"What's the plan?" Hades moved forward and studied the map more closely. "We all converge on the museum before they have a chance to come out at midnight?"

"Our territories." Nancy frowned. "We can't leave them unprotected."

"We have no choice but to use all of our resources to go after Abaddon." Rodán looked at each Tracker gathered around the table. "However, we will have to separate." He pointed to Nancy, Fere, and Ice. "You three will take the building where the liaison was taken and the symbol left in the apartment near Seventy-ninth and Riverside."

He assigned three Trackers to each of the other two points where liaisons had been abducted and symbols burned into the floors.

"This leaves eight, including myself," Rodán said. "We will go to the center of the triangle, where Abaddon will most likely attempt to open a gate."

"Ten." A little flutter brushed my insides. "Two humans as well. My partner, Olivia DeSantos, and Detective Adam Boyd."

Fere scowled at me. "No godsdamn humans. They don't belong."

Rodán held up his hand. "These two humans may join us."

Fere made a sound of disgust. Did I mention I really, really didn't like Fere?

"So three at each corner point, ten at the center." I pursed my lips and didn't say anything else. Talk about bare bones.

Carlos got to his feet. "It's time to rock."

"Indeed," Rodán said. "Let's rock."

CHAPTER 31

I stood alone in the arched hallway leading to Rodán's chambers. The sounds of the nightclub had died away the moment I stepped through the mist. I took the XPhone from its clip on my belt.

My hand shook a little as I pressed the speed dial number, then held the XPhone to my ear. "Hi, Adam," I said when he answered.

A slight pause. "Hi, Nyx." Adam's voice wasn't cold like I was afraid it would be. Instead he sounded resigned, and that hurt more than if he'd been abrupt or terse, or anything else. "What can I do for you?"

I held my free hand in a fist over my heart. I swallowed. Gathered myself so that my voice wouldn't crack like I was afraid it would. "I promised you that I'd let you know when we were going after the Demon responsible for the liaisons' disappearances and all of the human deaths."

"What's the location?"

Professional. Formal. Like I was just someone else he was getting information from.

I clenched my fist tighter against my heart and squeezed my eyes shut before giving him the information, and telling him where to meet us. Me.

"Thanks. I'll be there." He disconnected the call.

My eyes were still closed and I'd shut my senses down, trying to block out everything. Absolutely everything.

When Rodán spoke, he almost startled a shout out of me. "Tell me what has happened, my sweets," he said in Elvin as he came up from behind me.

I looked up at him but couldn't get a word out. Rodán took me in his arms and pressed my head against his chest. His arms felt warm and comforting around me, and I could hear the steady beat of his heart. "Tell me," he said again, his voice low and soothing. His scent of cedar and mountain laurel was as warm and welcome as the sound of his voice.

Rodán listened as I told him about what Adam had overheard and his reaction. What Adam said. How I'd hurt him without meaning to, and how much it hurt me.

Rodán hugged me again and kissed the top of my head.

I perched in a willow tree above the northern end of the lake, where I'd told Adam to meet me. I wanted to see him before he had a chance to see me.

The willow's leaves fluttered against my face in a breeze that carried the scent of the lake and the park's trees. The branch I was on was slender and supple, but it easily held my weight.

It wasn't long before Adam arrived, and this time he wasn't wearing his brown leather bomber jacket. He wore body armor over a black T-shirt, black jeans,

and he was well-armed. His shoulder holster held
two handguns and his Glock was holstered on his
duty belt. He had a sheathed knife along with other
things on his belt, like what looked like a canister of
tear gas. Also attached to the belt were a couple of
items I was pretty sure weren't legal.

He looked so handsome, so real, that it made my
heart hurt more. Especially when I caught his coffee
and leather scent.

His back was to me when I swung down from the
tree to land silently behind him.

The fluttering of many birds seemed to take flight
at the same time in my belly and chest. "Adam."

He wheeled, his hand going immediately to his
Glock at the same time he spun to face me. Then he
relaxed and took the few steps to stand in front of me.

Adam studied my face before he raised his hand,
clasped a handful of my hair, and let it slide through
his fingers. Even in the little light offered where we
stood, my hair looked so blue against his tanned skin.

He cupped the side of my face with one of his
large, callused hands and stroked my cheek with his
thumb as he studied me. "You're beautiful." He kept
running his thumb over my skin. "So beautiful."

His touch made me ache. Had he forgiven me?
His expression was that of a man who cared about
me as he slid his hand from my face into my hair and
stroked the tips of my pointed ears. For a moment I
thought he would kiss me. Goddess, how I wanted
that.

But his expression went almost blank as he stepped

back. He let his hand fall to his side so that he was no longer touching me. "What's the plan?"

I started to say Rodán's name, but after Adam's reaction to finding out about me and Rodán, I couldn't say my mentor and lover's name. I don't know if I should have been ashamed of myself or if I was just trying not to dredge up the memory from what amounted to mere hours ago.

"There are four teams and our Proctor," I said.

"Rodán." That same resignation was in Adam's voice again as my stomach sank. It had been stupid of me to avoid saying Rodán's name, anyway, since Adam would be meeting him in moments.

"You and I will be included in the larger team that's going for Abaddon." No expression from Adam. "Is that okay with you?"

"Of course." He didn't hesitate, but he looked from me toward the museum.

I could be professional, too, and leave personal feelings behind. Hanging onto those kinds of feelings at this moment could get any one of us killed. "Everyone is already in position."

I laid out everything for him. To start with, we had three teams of two stationed around the museum. Rodán, Adam, and I would be going in.

Adam and I moved through the park to our meeting place with Rodán. Because he was human, Adam made more noise than I would have liked—loud for the paranormal world. To humans he would be nearly soundless.

We reached our destination and Rodán stepped

from where he had been invisible in the shadows. If Adam was startled by Rodán's sudden appearance, he didn't show it.

For a brief moment the two stood at the edge of the shadows and appraised each other. They were both about six-two, but with different builds and different coloring. Rodán, with his long blond hair and green eyes, was beautiful, almost ethereal for a man, yet he was all male.

Adam was hard and rugged, his brown hair cropped close to his collar and his brown eyes keen and appraising. He had a cop's wary and controlled expression.

Rodán—it wasn't possible for anyone to surpass him for the level of confidence he carried, yet Adam's confident air seemed just as strong at that moment.

But there was truly no comparison between the two men.

It had been just a couple of seconds, and then they each held hands and gave what was clearly a firm handshake. "You and I," Rodán said as they gripped hands, "shall talk once this is over."

Adam studied Rodán for a moment before he gave a curt nod.

"Let's go." I was impatient to find Abaddon and jam his ass back into the abyss.

Before we made our move, I caught Adam looking at me a couple of times, studying me before he would turn away.

"What about Adam?" I said to Rodán. "The Demons will be able to see him."

Rodán said nothing but stared at Adam who began to . . . vanish.

Almost. I could see vague outlines of Adam, and a slight shimmer beneath the moonlight and streetlights. I saw faint movement as he raised his hands and looked at them—or through them. "Holy sh—crap."

"Are you fine with this?" Rodán asked.

"Yeah, sure." Adam's voice sounded clear despite the fact that he barely had any form. "I always wanted to be the Invisible Man."

With our own glamours, Rodán and I faded into shadows and moonlight, and I knew we were as faint to Adam as he was to us. Rodán must have also done some kind of silencing spell that cushioned every step Adam made, because I couldn't hear a single sound coming from him. Not even his breathing.

We started across Central Park West to the beautiful sprawling stone building of the Museum of Natural History. We passed the statue of President Theodore Roosevelt on horseback, then jogged up the steps to the front doors.

Inside the statue, like all statues, there were Gargoyles, hideous creatures that could turn to stone or metal. These particular Gargoyles protected the museum from night predators. I was surprised the creatures had let anything evil past them, like the Demons.

Abaddon must have found a way to get beneath the museum without being noticed by any being—unless he had killed the Gargoyles and they were dead inside the shell of their statue. I'd never heard of anything like that ever happening, though.

Our three other teams would remain outside until Rodán signaled and gave them instructions. Olivia was somewhere nearby with Nadia, but like the other four Trackers they were completely hidden from view.

Well-secured banners above and to either side of the entrance made barely a sound as the night breeze stirred them.

A feeling of dread and hopelessness grabbed me as we neared the front entrance. Pain, suffering, fear.

Vibrations filled the air. Massive pain seared my spine and my body—my arms, my legs, my face. Everywhere. I choked back a scream with every sting, so powerful that my muscles began to quiver, my body sweat, and my vision blur.

My belly felt like scorpions were stinging my insides.

What was happening to me? Goddess. I couldn't think. My breathing was so shallow I could barely take my next breath.

The moment I reached the top, my knees buckled and hit the landing hard. I had to clench my teeth to bite back every cry that wanted to tear from my throat. I couldn't hold onto my glamour and it dropped. I was completely exposed and crippled by pain.

A glimmer of light let me make out the vague outline of the invisible Adam as he crouched beside me. He put his hand on my upper back and my whole body clenched in an effort not to scream from the pressure of his palm on me.

"Are you okay?" Adam's voice was urgent, concerned. "I can see you. You're totally visible again."

"Goddess." Rodán spoke as he knelt on the other side of me. "It must be Abaddon. I will cloak you with my magic—"

The entryway of the museum exploded.

A powerful sound echoed through the night as if a plane had crashed into the building.

Glass, stone, and metal shards were embedded in my skin as they slammed into me, and I was flung backward.

CHAPTER 32

My head struck something so hard I thought the force of the blow had split my skull.

My mind spun. The world grew light and dark and light again. I opened my eyes and saw that I'd hit the statue and was crumpled on my side at the base of it.

A deep chuckle brought me closer to . . . consciousness? What had I been doing? I had to pull my thoughts together.

Museum.

Pain.

Explosion.

Goddess.

Shouts and cries, snarls and growls, were distant, but rang louder in my ears as I started to come back to myself.

My entire body was nothing but pain. I moved so that I could brace myself with my knees. Acid rose up my throat and I puked beside the statue. I wiped the back of my hand across my mouth and struggled to stand.

I looked up just in time to see an almost invisible beam of power barely miss me. The beam slammed into the statue. Metal and stone exploded, and more shards embedded themselves in my skin.

My battered body screamed with agony. I collapsed. Automatically, I rolled over and over, away from where the statue had been, and this time managed to stagger to my feet.

In time to see three Gargoyles spring out from where they'd been hidden in the statue. The ash-gray Gargoyles looked like hideous bulldogs the size of cargo vans as they raced up the steps.

I raised my eyes and froze.

A flood of green Demons, none like I'd ever seen, came through the destroyed entrance and poured out onto the concrete steps. They moved like apes, powerful hind legs propelling them forward, knuckles scraping stone.

The thirty or more roaring, screeching Demons flowed around T and Chance, who stood on the landing, facing one another.

Oh, my Goddess.

T and Chance.

Then the two males morphed.

My body refused to move, even as the green Demons barreled toward me. I couldn't take my eyes off of T and Chance.

It took only a second or two, but the males' features twisted until each of them looked like depictions of the human version of the Devil. Large, black curved horns, red skin over bulked-up bodies with powerful muscles, and at least eight feet tall. They could have been twins.

Twin Demons.

The first of the three Gargoyles from the statue reached the Chance-Demon. With the back of his hand, the Demon batted the enormous Gargoyle aside as if it were a toy.

With a screaming roar, a Gargoyle flung itself toward the T-Demon, which held up its arm and rammed its fist into the huge being. The T-Demon struck the Gargoyle so hard the creature's body flipped end over end. It sailed over our heads and disappeared somewhere in Central Park.

The Chance-Demon used black/red fire and blasted the other Gargoyle so far down Central Park West I couldn't see where it landed.

Oh, shit.

I didn't have time to think after those first few seconds. The green, snarling, apelike Demons were attacking all of the Trackers, along with Adam and Olivia. Blood already coated one side of Fere's face. Adam was now clearly visible. He and Olivia held their handguns in two-handed grips and fired at oncoming Demons that were so close to them that my heart was beating like crazy in fear for their lives.

The two beings they'd shot shrieked, came to a stop, and shook their massive heads. But then they were going for Olivia and Adam again. Each had already holstered their weapons and unsheathed long knives, and they were in ready battle stances.

One of the Demons was nearly on top of me. Adrenaline rushed through my body and I no longer felt any pain. I only felt the fire of anger and fear for us all.

I unsheathed one of my dragon-claw daggers and

brought it up in a slicing motion just as the Demon flung itself at me.

The Demon wasn't armored like the underlings we'd been fighting and my blade sliced through its neck at just the right place. Bone, tendon, and muscle gave way as my dagger separated the Demon's head from its neck. It was a lucky kill and I knew it.

The headless Demon's body almost plowed into me. I dodged to the side in time but its rough, scaly skin scraped my arm like sandpaper. Its carcass smelled fetid, of rotting meat and spoiled milk, as it slammed into the concrete beside me.

My heart pounded as I gripped my dagger's hilt with both hands and swept my gaze over the completely chaotic scene. Everyone was still alive, thank the Goddess.

Battle cries, gunshots, roars, breaking glass and metal echoed in the night. I glanced behind me and saw that some of the Demons had landed on cars parked at the curb, crushing them. The Demons were surrounding the ten of us. Boxing us in.

A Demon crouched on the concrete, not far from me, no doubt searching for someone to battle. Or searching for someone in particular. It met my gaze and I knew it was looking for me.

I didn't give the Demon a chance to attack. With a Drow warrior's battle cry, I went on the offensive and charged it. If a Demon could look surprised, it did.

I used the advantage of surprise and flung myself forward, gripping my dragon-claw dagger in both hands. Before it had a chance to react, I gave another warrior cry and swung my dagger at the Demon's neck.

It screamed and lunged for me at the same time my Drow blade severed its hideous head from its shoulders. The huge body collapsed on top of me, its scales rasping over my body as it slammed me to the concrete. Air exploded from my lungs and my sight blurred. For a moment I registered every screaming pain that the adrenaline had been masking.

But only a moment. My Drow strength was enough to shove the Demon's body off of me and I lurched to my feet, preparing for another attack, but only two Demons were still alive. Adam and Olivia were handling one, Rodán dispatching the other. I counted ten of us. Everyone was still alive.

At the fringes of the battle humans had come out of their apartments and homes, and were staring or screaming at the sight of the carnage. Several cell phones were out, some humans recording what was happening, others calling 911.

Sirens were already screeching through the night.

Where was a Soothsayer?

The more unusual sirens of the Paranormal Task Force were on their way, too. This scene would need a big cleanup *when* we eliminated all of the Demons.

And we *would* eliminate *all* of the Demons.

My heart thudded at the thought. Ten of us. How many more Demons?

I caught a glimpse of a horrified Lulu. She had her arms stretched out, trying to freeze the scene with her magic. It was obviously too much for her, or Demon magic was overwhelming her powers.

A flash of white light, and then Soothsayers Jeanie and Karen appeared next to Lulu, using their gift of transference to get to her. Lulu gave a tremendous look of relief and said something to the two other Soothsayers. Then the three of them raised their arms. In moments the scene around us froze. The human part of it. The Demons, no such luck.

I whipped my head around to make sure Adam and Olivia weren't frozen, and breathed a sigh of thanks. Lulu must have told Karen and Jeanie not to freeze the pair.

More sirens cut the night in the distance, but I knew the three Soothsayers would take care of them when they arrived. This was not going to be easy to keep under wraps. With this kind of massive attack, we had to worry about news helicopters. I could already hear the *whump, whump* of helicopter blades nearing us.

Lulu, Jeanie, and Karen would probably need the other two Soothsayers. In answer to my thought, there was another flash of light and Nevy and Tara appeared so that the five of them stood shoulder to shoulder.

The roars of the last Demon cut off and I snapped my gaze in its direction to see the body land in a thud at Adam's and Olivia's feet.

The Demons were all down. I looked up at the archway and the destroyed entrance to the museum.

And met the ferocious, burning, red-eyed gazes of the Chance-Demon and the T-Demon.

Fury possessed me as if I, too, were a Demon bent on nothing but destruction and the desire to kill. I gave a tremendous cry and charged up the steps toward both devil-like Demons, using my Drow gift of speed.

My companions didn't hesitate and I heard them charging after me. Rodán passed me in a blur.

A blast of power slammed into me and knocked me back down the concrete stairs. I didn't allow myself to register the pain. I got to my feet and reached the foot of the stairs in time to see the Chance-Demon battling Rodán. The Demon had a smoking black sword, and it clanged every time it met the Elvin blade of Rodán's sword.

Rodán jabbed and made contact with the devil-Demon's belly, his blade sliding into the Demon's flesh. It howled and raised its hand. I could see black/red fire already smoldering in the Demon's palm, ready to blast Rodán.

"No!" I screamed, and charged up the stairs.

My heart screamed, too, as the T-Demon gripped an enormous flaming sword and held it high.

T swung before I could reach them. The fiery blade arced through the air toward Rodán and the Chance-Demon.

Everything seemed to slow down. My scream sounded long and distant.

The blade neared Rodán and the Demon.

The sword passed over Rodán.

T sliced the Chance-Demon's head from its shoulders.

Shock nearly made me stumble. I came to a stop, a step away from the landing. The Chance-Demon's head rolled down the stairs and landed at the foot of the destroyed monument. The Demon head's skin bubbled, sizzled, and hissed, with its wide red eyes staring up at the night sky.

A fraction of a moment, and then the ten of us were charging T. Why he'd just killed the other Demon and saved Rodán, I didn't know. None of us knew. Maybe it was to gain power and position in the Demon ranks.

All I did know was that we had to eliminate T.

A rumbling filled the air, and the steps jerked and shook so powerfully that I fell to my hands and knees. I lost my grip on my dagger and it skidded down the stairs, the metal rattling as the blade hit each concrete step.

Everything kept rocking, and I couldn't find purchase and I slipped down the stairs. Vibrations filled the air again. I twisted and shouted as pain wrenched my body.

I took fast, shallow breaths and started crawling back up the stairs, my muscles straining with each movement. Pain didn't exist. I wouldn't let myself feel it. I focused on the T-Demon that stood on the landing, still holding its flaming sword.

Rodán was in front of T, his footing sure despite the rocking and bucking of the concrete. But Rodán wasn't attacking, and neither was T.

Gritting my teeth, I crawled up the stairs, bracing my forearms on each step as I pulled myself up, barely making headway against the tossing of the stairs.

I reached the landing again, and my blood rushed in my ears.

A figure strode through the wreckage of the front entrance. A tall, powerful being who was dragging a large man's body as if it were dental floss.

Abaddon! It had to be the master Demon, the Destroyer. I knew it as if the being had spoken the truth aloud. The human appearance had to be deceptive, the Demon's powers far more powerful than what he looked like he was capable of.

My skin crawled as I stared at Abaddon.

The master Demon looked as human as the underlings we'd been battling. Abaddon had long black hair that fell around his shoulders and golden eyes. He was handsome. Stunning.

Then I saw who Abaddon was dragging. Officer Jaworski, the second missing liaison. Jaworski looked dazed and didn't seem to register what was going on, much less the fact that he was being dragged by a master Demon.

When Abaddon came to a stop, just ten feet away, he glanced at the T-Demon and then at the decapitated Chance-Demon, but didn't let any feeling cross his expression. He probably didn't have feelings.

Abaddon looked directly at me. He crooked the finger of his free hand and smiled. "Come, Drow Princess. I've been waiting for you."

More shock stung me as his deep, reverberating

voice called to me. He'd been waiting for *me*? For the shortest of moments I didn't know whether to move or stay.

"Don't move, Nyx," Rodán commanded as I got to my feet.

Abaddon looked casually at Rodán. My heart pounded and blood rushed in my ears as Abaddon flicked his fingers at Rodán.

Rodán dropped to his knees as if some great weight forced him down. Sweat beaded on his forehead and trickled down his clenched jaws. He gripped his sword hilt to the point that his knuckles were white. His muscles bulged, straining against whatever power was attacking him.

As I watched in horror, I rocked on my feet, unsteady, as if the stairs were still moving.

The effort it cost him to fight such magic must have been great, but Rodán had the strength to not writhe on the concrete in agony. I wanted to run to him, help him, but I knew the only way to help him was to somehow kill Abaddon.

The T-Demon stood calmly at Abaddon's side, watching Rodán without any expression on his devil's face.

Abaddon cocked his head and looked interested as he stared at Rodán. "I'm surprised, Rodán of the Light Elves. Good show of resistance."

Rodán said nothing as he gritted his teeth, sweat beginning to soak his tunic.

With a glance toward me, Abaddon clearly dismissed Rodán as if he was no threat. "I said come here, Princess."

Adam shouted, "No!"

Abaddon swept his hands toward the six Trackers, as well as Olivia and Adam, and their weapons were jerked from their hands—swords, daggers, handguns. Then their weapons belts and weapons ripped through clothing from other hiding places. My stomach churned as flying metal glittered in the streetlights before the weapons hit the asphalt in the street with thuds and clangs.

Dear Goddess. How were we going to defeat him without weapons?

Strange, but he hadn't taken mine. If I got close enough to Abaddon, I could kill him. I'd lost the dagger I'd been holding, but I still had one sheathed and I had my buckler. Would he have armored skin like his underling Demons?

"Here. Now!" Abaddon roared at me, and I nearly tripped as something that felt like a giant hand slammed into my back and shoved me forward.

Everything seemed impossibly quiet as I stopped when I arrived within ten feet of him.

He smiled. "I've been saving you for last, Drow Princess."

I frowned. But the Chance-Demon had almost killed me. I would have died if T . . .

I glanced at T, and his devil's expression was impassive.

"You didn't receive enough poison to kill you," Abaddon said, and I jerked my attention back to him. "Only to keep you from saving the other Tracker. I needed him to come to your aid so that he'd be in position to enable me to use the power in his body once I killed him. And he had to be in the right location."

Blood felt like it was draining from my body as I tried to register his words.

"What do you think you are going to do with me now?" I asked in a dry rasp.

His smile was dazzling, as if he wasn't a Demon but a gorgeous movie star. "You have the most useful powers to help bring my legions from the abyss." My stomach lurched as he continued. "I have underlings stationed at every point that you've sent your Trackers to. At each point a Tracker and a liaison will be sacrificed simultaneously, as I sacrifice you and this liaison."

"No, goddammit, Nyx!" I heard the strain in Adam's voice, and I realized Abaddon must have put up some kind of elemental barricade to keep him and the Trackers from coming to my aid.

Several things happened in rapid succession.

Rodán broke free of Abaddon's power and charged the Demon, jerking Abaddon's attention from me.

I snatched my buckler and flung it straight for the Demon's throat.

I summoned the element of air to shove the buckler faster toward Abaddon. Only ten feet separated us, and the buckler was buried in the Demon's neck before he registered it.

Abaddon's golden eyes widened.

The buckler cleanly sliced through Abaddon's throat—

Then stuck in his spine.

That remaining thread of Abaddon's neck was enough for the flesh to knit back together almost instantly. The buckler slipped from the Demon's flesh and clanged to the concrete landing.

Rodán shouted dark words in Drow as he reached Abaddon and swung his sword.

The Demon flicked his fingers at Rodán, who stopped hard, as if he'd hit an invisible barrier.

I grabbed every element I could to help throw me the ten feet toward Abaddon.

The power of air. The rush of water storming from the river. The earth buckling at its feet. Flames acting like a rocket accelerator.

It took all my remaining strength, but I raised my dragon-claw dagger as every element took me to him.

I swung the dagger in a two-fisted grip.

Abaddon grabbed my wrists with one hand. The strength of his hold yanked me to a stop and my teeth clamped together. My head jerked back and forth. I lost my hold on my last weapon, and the dragon-claw dagger clanged as it tumbled down the steps. I was so close to him that his burnt-sugar stench made bile crawl up my throat.

A furious expression crossed Abaddon's handsome face. "Idiot! You're no good to me if you drain yourself of your powers."

Good information. Who's the idiot now for letting me know that important fact? I summoned all of my powers again as he held my wrists. A controlled hurricane of earth, fire, water, and air slammed into Abaddon all at once.

He lost his grip on my wrists and his hold on the human. But he remained on his feet.

My body went still as I tried to comprehend what happened next. The T-Demon attacked Abaddon from behind, shearing off the top of the Demon's head with his flaming sword.

Abaddon looked beyond stunned. He had no skull on top of his head, but his brain matter appeared untouched. His skull started to grow back, but slowly.

Goddess! T's attempt wasn't enough.

Abaddon's face grew red and he squeezed his fist. The T-Devil dropped to his knees and reached for unseen hands at his throat.

"You were the traitor." Abaddon's face grew redder and redder. "You were the one helping the Trackers when I thought you were working for me."

"You bet your fucking ass," T rasped as he shifted to his human form, becoming smaller than he had been as a devil-Demon, so that he caught Abaddon off guard again. "No way in all the hells was I going to let you stay out of the abyss where you should be now."

I was just about to fight Abaddon with more of my elemental powers when Adam lunged past me. He was holding the dragon-claw dagger I'd dropped. He raised the dagger high and brought it down in a powerful stroke.

And cleaved the Demon's head.

One half of Abaddon's head slid off and onto the concrete landing. Its remaining eye glazed.

It was dead. Adam had finished it off.

T, in his human form, used his sword to completely separate Abaddon's head from its shoulders.

Abaddon's body started to shift as if it was a one-dimensional figure folding itself into a neat little box. The severed part of the head joined the rest.

Then it was gone. All of it. Abaddon was gone.

I couldn't quite make sense of that, but turned my head and stared at T as the rush of adrenaline continued to pour through me. Everyone was staring at him, unsure of whether to kill him or believe he'd been fighting on our side.

He'd dispatched underling Demons with us, and he'd just murdered the Chance-Demon and finished off Abaddon—after trying to kill Abaddon a first time. And that first time had given Adam the opportunity to cleave Abaddon's head.

T tossed aside his sword. Its blade was now just cool metal. The sword slid across the concrete as T met each of our gazes.

Rodán walked toward T and appraised him. Then Rodán extended his hand, and with no hesitation T clasped hands with him. "Thank you," Rodán said in his strong, clear voice.

T met my gaze, but I had no words to say anything at all.

CHAPTER 33

"Are you okay, Nyx?"

It was like coming out of a nightmare as I looked from Abaddon's remains to Adam when he spoke to me. Instead of saying I was fine, my whole body started shaking and I held my arms tight around myself.

I was crashing after the adrenaline rush, and from draining myself of most of my elemental powers. Every injury on my body throbbed or stung or sent searing pain throughout me.

I looked into Adam's eyes and it came back to me, what else I'd lost—him. I'd never felt so drained and so incomplete in my life.

Adam took me into his arms and held me. I had no strength left to feel surprise. I just sank into his embrace, my head against the body armor covering his chest. I continued to tremble, but his comforting scent filled me and the warmth of his arms made me feel like everything might be okay.

Around us the PTF rushed to rid the scene of any paranormal elements and evidence before the Soothsayers did their thing. Together the five Soothsayers had enough power to do a wide-range memory adjustment of non-paranorms.

Smoke drifted from the Chance-Demon's headless body. The stink of burnt sugar and the stench of rotting meat was everywhere.

Adam kissed the top of my head, and I looked up at his scratched and bruised face. Was everything going to be okay now between us?

"I'm sorry." I winced as each word echoed in my throbbing skull.

He put his fingers against my lips. "Not now."

I nodded and regretted the movement, discovering my neck hurt, too. He studied me for a long moment. The look in his eyes—I wasn't sure what it meant, but it was obvious he still cared for me. Whether or not I had a chance with him again, I didn't know.

"T." I cut my gaze to the place where he'd been standing. "Where is he?"

"Torin vanished," Adam said as I strained to look around us. I met his gaze again. "Sort of melted away."

"Vanished?" I repeated, trying to concentrate and make sense of tonight.

"Let's get you home." Adam held his arm around my shoulders and guided me down the stairs.

"Olivia." I jerked us both to a halt on the sidewalk by the destroyed monument. "Where's Olivia?"

"Right behind you." At the sound of Olivia's voice, relief flooded me.

Adam still kept his arm around my shoulders as I turned to look at her. "Goddess, you're hurt."

"Of course I'm a Goddess." Olivia looked at me

with what would have been a haughty stare if she wasn't a disheveled bloody mess like the rest of us. "And I'm fine." A Healer finished binding Olivia's arm and started sending magic into what had looked like a deep flesh wound. "You, on the other hand," Olivia continued, "look like blue-haired roadkill."

I would have smiled if I hadn't felt like exactly what she'd compared me to.

"Have you heard if Nadia's okay?" I glanced around, looking for Rodán, but didn't see him. "And the others at the points?"

"No news," Olivia said. "Rodán went alone to check the other sites."

Adam stiffened at the mention of Rodán's name, and I closed my eyes for a moment. I'd so screwed up.

After I'd checked to make sure everyone was okay, Adam took me firmly by the shoulders and moved me away from the near-Armageddon. "Let's go."

The museum wasn't far from my apartment, but he took me to a black Jeep Wrangler that was parked just north of all of the destruction. He helped me into the Jeep, then drove the short distance and supported me as we took the stairs to my apartment. My body ached with every step, and I felt dizzy and out of focus. I hadn't stopped trembling. We didn't speak, not even when I managed to use a tiny bit of magic to unlock my door.

Adam scooped me into his arms with power and ease, and carried me the rest of the way to my bedroom where he set me on my feet beside my bed. He didn't let go of me, though. He kept one arm around me as he pulled back the comforter and my sheet with one hand. Then he tucked me into bed, the comforter snug and warm around me.

My blue hair was such a contrast to his tanned skin as he ran a lock through his fingers. "Good night, Nyx."

I tried to push myself up but he pressed my shoulder down with his palm. "Please, don't go. I don't want to be alone." The thought of being by myself right now sent shudders through me.

Indecision played across his features only briefly before he took off his shoulder harness, utility belt, and body armor, and set them on my nightstand and vanity. He kicked off his shoes, then settled on the bed behind me. He wrapped his arm around my waist and held me close. And I slept.

CHAPTER 34

"Are you planning on coming out of that box in your head to play today?" Olivia shut the office door behind her with a jangle of the bells.

"Maybe." I couldn't stop thinking of Adam. He'd been gone when I woke up the morning after the battle with the Demons, a week ago. I knew he'd stayed with me all night because I'd woken up periodically, and fallen back asleep, secure in his strong embrace.

I had gone through the change while I slept, something I'd never remembered doing before. So I must have eventually dropped into a pretty deep sleep to not have sensed Adam leaving or felt the change coming on, much less going through it unaware.

I'd left a message on his cell phone once this past week and he never called me back.

"Come out, come out, wherever you are," Olivia said as she dropped into her seat.

I threw an eraser at her.

It hit her between her melon-boobs. "Ow." She grabbed the eraser and flung it back.

I caught it in my hand. "Heh." Then I pointed to her black T-shirt with its red lettering.

Warning: Does not play well with others.

"Isn't that the truth," I said with a laugh.

"Exactly, so watch it." She took her XPhone out of its clip on her belt and set it on her desk. "So what's the latest from the Great Guardian Goddess Almighty?"

I smirked. "Last night Rodán let us know that more Trackers have been in training, and we'll be getting a few of them in Manhattan. There's supposed to be a male Shadow Shifter—hope we get him."

"Most of the Shadow Shifters I've seen at the Pit are hot." Olivia pushed up the sleeves of her sweat jacket. "But aloof and arrogant. Most of them need to be knocked on their asses a time or two."

Had to agree with that.

"No sign of Torin?" Olivia asked.

I shook my head. "None." I didn't know yet what to think of T and everything that had happened. We'd have to figure it all out if he ever showed up again.

My XPhone burst out with my latest ring tone. "Black" by Metallica.

"Nyx," Rodán said in his warm, smooth voice when I answered, and I smiled just to hear him. "You've been keeping to yourself lately."

I shrugged, even though he couldn't see me. "I've just been a little preoccupied."

"You know I'm here for you."

"Yes," I said, "and I'm here if you ever need me, too."

"How about now?" His words were soft, and the

way he spoke so intimately made me want to be in his arms.

I looked down at my desk and ran my finger over a knot in the polished wood. "I can't. Not in that way." It wouldn't be right. I'd be seeking comfort because of Adam and that wasn't fair to anyone. My voice caught. "I hope Adam will give me another chance."

"If he's an intelligent male, he will," Rodán said.

"Thank you."

"I have a case, and it could be a big one." He sounded completely businesslike now. "The Alpha of one of the New York werewolf packs contacted me because he knows we have the best PIs—you and Olivia," Rodán went on. "Werewolves from several packs are disappearing, and the packs don't know what's happening to them."

"What have you got on this case?" I asked.

"The Alpha will be in Manhattan this evening," Rodán said. "He'll meet you and Olivia at nine a.m. Saturday in your office."

"I'll be here." I glanced at Olivia, who raised her eyebrow and gave me the look as she loaded a rubber band with an eraser. Latent psychic talent—uh-huh. "*We'll* be here," I said.

Olivia set her ammo down. "Damn straight." She returned her attention to her XPhone. "Whatever it is."

When I ended the call with Rodán, I set my own XPhone on my desk. Perfect. A case that didn't involve Demons—just what I needed to get my focus back.

I stared out a window at Central Park and watched branches bending from a strong October wind, and a flicker of leaves already turning burnished gold.

Another change in seasons on its way. I smiled. It was good to be a New Yorker. It was good to be me.

FOR CHEYENNE'S READERS

Be sure to go to http://cheyennemccray.com to sign up for her PRIVATE book announcement list and get FREE EXCLUSIVE Cheyenne Mc-Cray goodies. Please feel free to e-mail her at chey@cheyennemccray.com. She would love to hear from you.

Turn the page for a sneak peek at the next
Lexi Steele Romantic Suspense Novel
by Cheyenne McCray

The Second Betrayal

Coming in August 2009 From St. Martin's Paperbacks

It had been a mistake having totally wild, raunchy sex with Nick Donovan during our first assignment together.

Including the hundred or so times we ended up in bed—or up against a wall, on the kitchen table, on the floor, in my office—when we weren't working on *Operation Cinderella*.

The breath I sucked in burned my throat as I tried to control my lust while I watched Donovan. His jeans tightened against his muscular ass as he bent over the shoulder of Agent Kerrison to look closer at the wide-screen monitor in front of her.

Donovan had become like a drug to me. An addiction. I couldn't get enough of him.

I pushed my hair out of my face in frustration. Lexi Steele had never allowed distractions like Nick Donovan. I had to get a grip.

I'd been telling myself that for a good six months now—since early June, a couple of weeks after we finished our first op together. Here it was, the end of November, and I still couldn't get enough of Donovan.

"Damnit," I said under my breath. This infatuation had to stop. It was like being a freaking teenager.

Another thought crossed my mind as I watched Donovan, a thought that was always there and wouldn't let go of me. The big man held so many secrets tight to his chest and had never let me in far enough to know what any of them were. I had spilled my guts about what had happened when I was in Army Special Forces, and how I'd been forced into being an assassin. Why was Donovan keeping every bit of his past from me?

I shook off the thoughts. This wasn't the time for lust or secrets. It was time to get back to work. I turned my thoughts to the current op and headed toward David Takamoto.

Takamoto stood on the opposite side of the banks of monitors and screens of our Team Center, TC. A blue glow encompassed the whole of the Command Center, the glow given off by walls of screens in the CC where various teams tracked activity on their assignments.

Agents had put up holiday decorations here and there, some for sheer amusement, like a small Santa who dropped his pants every time someone walked by.

There were also some decorations on agents' desks reflecting their own holiday beliefs. A silver and blue depiction of a Jewish menorah with its white candles. A picture of a Kwanzaa kinara with its colorful candles—three red, one black, and three green.

Some wise-ass had put up a Mexican donkey

piñata in a corner of the CC, a picture of Special Agent in Charge Carter on its nose. Our SAC would be entirely oblivious, considering he spent his time in his first floor office playing computer card games as he waited out the last year until his retirement.

Of course our Assistant Special Agent in Charge might not find it amusing. Our ASAC, Karen Oxford, was tough, fair, and had no obvious sense of humor. But then again, the picture was still up and the donkey had been there two weeks before Thanksgiving. Maybe she had a sense of humor after all.

A soft buzz and hum filled the CC as agents spoke into headphones and kept track of their assignments on the large, high-tech screens. I smelled the pine fragrance of a small Christmas tree that overpowered the familiar scent of climate-controlled air as I passed the tree.

"Steele." Takamoto caught sight of me and I tilted my head to meet his brown eyes when I reached him. "I was just about to find you and give you the news. It's about *Wolf*."

A petite five-four, I had to look up at most of the guys at RED. Seemed that Karen Oxford—my ASAC Assistant Agent in Charge—liked to hire male agents six feet and over. Or maybe it was a coincidence.

Ha.

Most of the guys on all RED task forces made me feel like I was in the land of the giants—just like my four older brothers did. Even my twelve-year-old brother towered over me. Little shit. Make that *big* shit.

"I'd give anything for news on Hagstedt." I put

my palms on my hips as I met Takamoto's gaze. "Tell me you have something on that bastard."

Takamoto was excellent at schooling his expressions, and right now I wanted to shake him for looking so calm. He slipped his hands into the pockets of his slacks, causing his shirt to pull against his runner's athletic physique. He pressed his shirts and slacks so stiffly I don't think a wrinkle would dare sneak in. I managed not to look down at my T-shirt and Levis that I'd snatched out of the laundry basket this morning and felt the material almost crawl with wrinkles.

"*Operation Big Bad Wolf* looks like it could be hot in Manhattan just like we expected." Takamoto glanced in the direction of the group of agents on his intel team. "Rublev just reported in after she sent us the coded message. She said the Elite Gentlemen's Club is definitely Hagstedt's. She overheard a conversation that verifies what info Johnny gave us. And if we can crack that coded message she intercepted earlier, that may give us all we need to get in there and get to Hagstedt."

I wanted to pump my fist and jerk my elbow back in a *yes!* motion. We'd known the key men had been involved in kidnapping and prostituting young women in their club, but we hadn't known for sure if that operation was part of Hagstedt's enormous human-trafficking ring. "Thank God. We've been working that club for . . . how long once Rublev was in?"

Takamoto shook his head. "At least two months."

"About friggin' time." I breathed a sigh of relief. *Wolf* had *not* been going so well. Beyond six months of fruitless searching over the summer for Anders Hagstedt grated at me more and more every single day. The so-called mastermind of countless human-trafficking rings in China, Russia, Switzerland, and the U.S. needed to be brought down. *Now*. We doubted Hagstedt was his real last name, but we'd still run all the leads we could on anyone with that surname, with no luck.

Takamoto inclined his head in the direction of the "dungeon," as we liked to call our geek squad's domain. "Now if the geeks can decipher the coded message, we might get some more detailed info. It's been six hours and the geeks are still working on it."

"The new agent, Kerrison, thinks she can crack it," I said. "She's only had it fifteen or twenty minutes, though." My chin-length hair brushed my cheeks as I looked over my shoulder.

I swiveled my gaze back to Takamoto. "I think we're real close to putting *Little Red* into play."

Before Takamoto could respond, I sensed Donovan behind me and caught his musky, spicy scent. My body immediately responded to his presence with an aching desire that made me want to moan in frustration.

Oxford had paired Donovan and me up as team supervisors during *Cinderella* and she'd decided to keep us working together instead of giving Donovan his own team. Karen Oxford was one incredibly savvy, observant woman, but I don't think she knew about my sexual relationship with Donovan, or she would have separated us. Or canned one of our asses. Hell, probably *both* of ours.

His blue eyes didn't show any emotion that might tell me how he felt about the two of us. No, his gaze was entirely professional. Good. That's how it should be—I hoped I looked just as professional.

Donovan looked from me to Takamoto and back. "Kerrison deciphered the communication."

It took some effort, but I managed to keep my jaw from dropping. "She decoded the message in twenty minutes?"

"Fifteen." Donovan's expression bordered on grim as he continued. "Hagstedt's operation isn't relegated to one or even a few clubs. It looks like Hagstedt is doing exactly what we've been able to gather from intel," Donovan said. "He imports girls from Switzerland, China, and Russia, and forces them into prostitution in clubs in all of New York City's boroughs. The club we've been watching on Sixtieth Street is more or less the headquarters for his New York op."

Rick Smithe gave a low whistle behind me and I cut my gaze to my left to see that he and George Perry had joined Takamoto. "What do you know? We finally got something," Smithe said.

Women being lured into the wrong hands with promises of jobs in America, then being prostituted once they arrived in the US, was nothing new—other teams on our task force were working on various ops related to many types of human trafficking.

But to finally locate a ring firmly tied to Hagstedt was like winning a billion-dollar lottery.

A shiver of excitement tickled my skin in anticipation of getting my teeth into the *Wolf* op that was finally going somewhere. Hagstedt was a big fish. Probably the biggest mastermind of human trafficking in the world, judging by the intel we'd gathered.

I filled Donovan in. Adrenaline started rushing through me from the excitement of an oncoming hunt. "What do you have that Kerrison came up with?"

Donovan was holding two pieces of paper and he raised his hand. For a moment I couldn't take my eyes off of his thick wrist and the black hair on his forearm, and I could almost feel myself tracing my fingertips over the back of his hand. I swallowed and met his gaze. Damn.

He handed me the pages and I took them and skimmed the gibberish on the first paper. "The code's so complicated that Taylor and his geek squad couldn't make sense of it in six hours. And Kerrison did it in fifteen minutes?" I repeated more to myself than any of the men standing around me.

Oxford had told me that Kerrison had one of the highest IQs in the world and had also sailed through Quantico's intense physical tests—supposedly she could kick major ass. A Harvard graduate at twenty with an IQ as high as Stephen Hawking or Marilyn vos Savant, Kerrison made an incredible addition to my and Donovan's team. On top of that she was model beautiful, which could work to her advantage in some undercover ops.

My skin prickled as I read the decoded message on the second page. "Hagstedt is supposed to arrive in Manhattan within the next few weeks," I said.

I glanced from the paper to Takamoto, Perry, and Smithe as I continued. "It actually names the Elite

Gentlemen's Club and names the asshole who oversees Hagstedt's entire New York City human-trafficking ring. His name is something we've never been able to get, since he doesn't talk with anyone but a couple of his men and the Madam, as far as Rublev knows. They call him Mr. G."

"Holy shit." Smithe's grin was almost dangerous. "We're going to put that bastard's ass in a grinder."